GET SMOKED OR GO HOME

GET SMOKED OR GO HOME

THE WARRIOR™ BOOK ONE

MARTHA CARR

MICHAEL ANDERLE

DISRUPTIVE IMAGINATION

Copyright © 2021 LMBPN Publishing
Cover by Mihaela Voicu http://www.mihaelavoicu.com/
Cover copyright © LMBPN Publishing
A Michael Anderle Production

LMBPN Publishing
PMB 196, 2540 South Maryland Pkwy
Las Vegas, NV 89109

Version 1.00, December 2021
ebook ISBN: 978-1-68500-641-9
Print ISBN: 978-1-68500-642-6

Thanks to our Beta Readers

Mary Morris, Larry Omans, Kelly O'Donnell, Rachel Beckford, John Ashmore

Thanks to our JIT Readers

Wendy L Bonell
Dave Hicks
Zacc Pelter
Peter. Manis
Dorothy Lloyd
Debi Sateren
Deb Mader
Diane L. Smith
Paul Westman

Editor

SkyHunter Editing Team

CHAPTER ONE

Biting her lower lip in concentration, Idina smeared the charcoal lines of her latest piece for a little extra shading, then redefined the outline on the woman's jaw and a few details of the subject's hair where necessary. Finally, she lowered the sketchpad into her lap for a birds-eye view of the whole thing put together.

"Nope," she muttered, moving the sketchpad into the sunlight flickering through the thick leaves of the giant maple tree's branches stretching out above her. "Something's still off."

With a frustrated *hiss*, she cocked her head and studied the sketch from top to bottom. "It needs more...light? Maybe a little extra..."

Her sketchpad buzzed her hands, and a shimmer of sparkling green light appeared in the corners of her vision. Then as she stared at the drawing, the same green lines curved themselves around her artwork, showing Idina exactly what she'd been missing.

That's it! Of course. It's so obvious.

Her tongue poked out between her lips in concentration, and she hurried to trace the green lines with her charcoal before they disappeared. Her entire hand and the drawing charcoal flashed with the same green light, sending tiny wisps of glittering specks rising from the subject of her focus before they disappeared in the summer breeze.

At least there's one good use for my weird episodes. They make me a better artist.

Idina leaned away from her sketchpad to view her new additions and frowned. "Dang. Or maybe I've completely lost it."

At that exact moment, a shadow much larger and thicker than those of the tree branches loomed over her, casting itself as a long, vaguely human shape from behind.

"Perhaps that's because you're creating masterpieces in the shade."

Idina smirked. "Direct light does funny things to charcoal. At least when *I'm* working with it." *Plus, it makes the green lights kinda hard to see even though I'm the only one who knows they're still there.* Slowly, she turned where she sat cross-legged in the grass and looked over her shoulder at the gray-haired man standing over her with his hands clasped behind his back. "Is that all the advice you have, Reggie?"

The man gave her a small, closed-lipped smile. "I'm afraid my expertise in fine art stops at the necessity for proper lighting."

"Yeah, I didn't think so." She turned back around and studied her piece one more time before lifting the entire sketchpad and holding it high above her head for Reggie to see. "Still. Any idea how to fix this?"

His momentary silence stretched longer than she'd wanted, and she started to think she'd seriously screwed up.

Great. Showing off a work in progress only to be told it's crap. What's the point of having secret skills if they don't help me?

Reggie cleared his throat. "I think it's impeccable."

Idina dropped the sketchpad back into her lap and turned again with a grin. "Really?"

"In my humble opinion, Miss Idina, that piece looks well and truly finished. If I were you, I wouldn't change a thing."

"Ha. If you were me, things would be seriously different around here." Her smile faded when she caught the small frown flickering across his brow. "You didn't come out here to check my sketch progress, though. Did you?"

"That is correct." Reggie drew a deep breath and raised his eyebrows. "She's waiting for you."

"In the parlor?"

"Yes. This time, Miss Idina, I've been asked to escort you there myself."

"Of course you have." The last three times Idina had been *summoned* to the parlor of the ever-important Mrs. Annette Moorfield—which was honestly another office in the estate house—she'd conveniently found enough distractions to keep her from entering the room. Most of them were right out here on the sprawling grounds and impeccable gardens of Moorfield Manor, where she preferred to spend her time. "Reggie?"

"Yes, Miss Idina?"

"I don't suppose you could tell her you couldn't find me."

"Out of the question." He turned toward the massive estate house spanning four stories and stretching across the New Hampshire countryside, nodding in the general direction of Mrs. Moorfield's office. "She spotted you under this tree and asked me personally to fetch you."

Idina huffed out a laugh as she slipped a piece of wax paper between the pages of her sketchbook before gathering up her charcoal and other miscellaneous art supplies. "I'm not a *dog*, Reggie."

"No. If you were, I believe *you* would be the one doing the fetching."

"Well, you're not a dog either."

"I'm merely doing—"

"Your job. I know. Don't shoot the messenger, right?"

Reggie smirked as Idina stood with her sketchpad under one arm and the zippered bag of her supplies clenched tightly in her hand. "A sentiment I must say I appreciate very much."

Giving him a small smile in return despite knowing what was coming for her, she gestured toward the estate house and rolled her eyes. "Lead the way, then."

"You know the way."

"Yeah, but it'd look more like I'm coming back inside with my tail between my legs if you're herding me across the lawn."

He chuckled. "Your references to canine habits are particularly amusing this afternoon."

The man was joking, of course. For a butler—a *manser-*

vant, some people preferred to call him, and Idina had always hated the term—who served one of the oldest and most prestigious families in New England, Reggie Archibald didn't lack in quick-witted sarcasm. Not when he was speaking to Idina, at least. She was the only person on the entire estate not part of the year-round staff who got to see that side of him.

Not part of the staff, and not really part of the family, either. Merely floating here on this massive property while she waited for her eighteenth birthday, only two months away in the second week of September.

Feels like I've been floating here my entire life, no matter what I try to do to change it.

"Very well." Reggie nodded and unclasped his hands from behind his back before gesturing at the estate house. "If you would follow me, Miss Idina."

"Yep. I'm on you like white on rice, Reg."

"What a riveting visual."

She followed the butler across the perfectly manicured lawn, through the gorgeously trimmed rows of the rose garden, and up to the glass French doors on the back patio. That patio was big enough to host tables, chairs, and refreshment tables for a party of two hundred guests at least, which it did at least once a year whenever the Moorfields saw fit to throw one of their extravagant soirees. Now, the dark granite stone was mostly empty, glistening in the sunshine around the thick shadow cast by the retractable awning.

Idina eyed the lounge chairs with perfectly clean, perfectly sun-warmed cushions ten feet from the French doors and wished she could be there instead. Sprawled out in the sunshine, kicked back, without a single worry plaguing her mind. It was summer, after all.

Every other high school graduate was out living it up like they were supposed to—taking trips abroad with friends or putting the final touches on their college acceptance essays. Some were already picking the perfect apartment in the city because their parents could afford to provide them with the ultimate Ivy League experience.

Idina wasn't *that* different from the rest of this year's graduating class from The White Mountain School. Not on the outside, anyway. At least she hadn't stood out at White Mountain like a sore and bloody thumb the way she stood out on Moorfield Manors.

I'm not even eighteen yet. Not a real *adult. Whoever came up with that rule is an idiot.*

Reggie led her through the estate house she knew like the back of her hand. The marble-floored ballroom faced the back patio. The slowly darkening hallways of the main floor led toward the back stairwell on the north wing. They walked past the polished foyer tables stacked with impressively thick books and valuable busts of dead people beneath equally valuable pieces by some of the world's best-known Impressionist artists. Monet, Pissarro, Gauguin.

Looking at those paintings in their immaculate frames—captured forever as part of the Moorfields' extensive collection of all things tasteful yet reeking of wealth—made Idina that much more determined to carve her path. Apparently, it made sense to spend ridiculous sums of money on fine art created by dead people. However, the idea of spending a fraction of that to encourage and nurture Idina's passion was out of the question. No one understood that she was an *artist* above everything else. Except for Reggie, of course.

At least I have the support of the butler. And the gardeners. Maybe even Mrs. Yardly. For all the good that's *worth.*

Finally, they reached the long hall of the second floor's north wing, where the Moorfield family conducted most of their private business. Idina still hadn't managed to wrap her head around the layout of this place or what purpose it served.

The main floor was for hosting events and receiving guests. The second for business, important meetings, poring over numbers and reports at the end of a long day doing the same thing. The third for living, eating, and sleeping, where all the Moorfield apartments had been sectioned off and renovated for each branch of the massive family tree. The fourth for the staff.

They probably haven't even considered switching things up, just because this is the way it's always been. How do they not claw their eyes out from boredom every day?

She stiffened when she saw the open doors of Mrs. Moorfield's *parlor* at this end of the hall.

As astute and observant as ever, Reggie picked up on the girl's hesitation and paused to turn halfway toward her. "I suppose now would be the time to—"

"Ah. There you are." The woman poking her head delicately out of an open doorway was Mrs. Moorfield. Her pearl earrings dangled from her ears as she leaned slightly forward. She wasn't standing in the doorway of the private office she preferred to call by a fancier, more feminine name. "I expected you to be here five minutes ago, but at least you managed to show up this time."

Idina stared at Mrs. Moorfield's dark eyes and grim-set lips emerging from the door to the *study*, then glanced at the parlor doors in front of her and grimaced. "Reggie said—"

"Reggie has his matters to attend to, as do we all. Do be more considerate and stop stalling." With that, Mrs. Moorfield retreated behind the study's open doors.

Idina's heart sank into her gut for a game of Pin the Tail On Her Latest Screwup.

Reggie waited a moment longer, then stepped back toward the wide-eyed girl and lowered his voice. "You'll do fine."

She fixed her grimace on him instead and couldn't quite turn it into the smile she'd intended. "I think you're the only one who believes that."

"Chin up, Miss Idina. It isn't the end of the world."

"For whom?"

The butler lowered his head and muttered, "Good luck."

Then he quickly extricated himself from the second-story hallway to let his employers deal with their much more important matters to which he hadn't once been privy during his fifty-odd years in their employ.

He probably never wanted to know what they all get up to in the first place. Can't blame the guy. I never wanted to know, and now here we are.

Tucking her sketchbook tighter under her arm, Idina steeled herself against the epic tongue-lashing she knew she was about to receive once she stepped through the study's pristinely polished double doors.

This wasn't a private sit-down with the woman of the house anymore. Walking into the study meant Idina would most likely be facing both Mr. *and* Mrs. Moorfield, and she couldn't remember the last time that had worked to her advantage. Because they reserved the study for business meetings only, and Idina was nothing if not entirely unsuited for the Moorfield family business.

CHAPTER TWO

Just tell them you're sorry. Whatever it is, it can't be worse than anything else I've done. I think.

Idina clenched her eyes shut and tried to ward away the flickers of green light reappearing in her vision. Sometimes they were there when she least expected it. Sometimes, they made things easier—showed her what she wanted to know.

At times like this, the shimmering green strands like spider silk were a major distraction. With the Moorfields, distraction might as well have been an eighth deadly sin.

When her vision finally cleared and nothing sparkled, Idina held her breath and stepped through the study doors. She got two feet inside and stopped.

Crap.

It wasn't only a meeting with Mr. and Mrs. Moorfield after all. The conference table taking up the right side of the room sat all the other Moorfields as well. Maxwell and his wife Nadine, Timothy, Bryan, and even Celeste Moorfield and her husband Bruno Cremberloft, though she'd chosen to defy tradition and retain the Moorfield family name after marriage.

Sure. They let Lessie do whatever she wants because she's keeping the damn name. And I'm the one called in for an intervention. I haven't had an episode in over a year since they adjusted my meds, so what is this?

All six of the younger Moorfields—and inherent shareholders of Moorfield & Associates—stared at Idina with stony expressions. Bryan was the only one who offered the barest hint of sympathy when an apologetic frown flickered across his eyebrows. But he recovered immediately as Mr. Moorfield cleared his throat from the back of the study.

"Close the doors behind you, Idina. Then take a seat."

She looked from the conference table to the massive, heavy oak desk at the back of the study where Mr. Moorfield had spoken. Not the Mr. Moorfield married to Mrs. Annette Moorfield for the last thirty-two years. No, this was Harold Moorfield I, CEO of Moorfield & Associates and patriarch to the entire New England clan he seemed only too pleased to have spawned over the last several decades.

Idina swallowed. "What's this about?"

"We'll get to that shortly," Harold Senior muttered, staring at her with dark, slightly narrowed eyes from his chair behind the desk. "After you close the doors and take a seat."

He gestured toward the leather armchair precisely situated dead-center between the desk and the conference table. Ideal for the entire Moorfield family to focus on one target at the same time. And perfect for Idina to take the spotlight in a serious meeting.

About her.

After setting her sketchbook and bag of supplies down on the side table against the wall inside the study, Idina took her time reaching for the polished handles of each double door before pulling them both closed. The latches fell into place with a *click*, then she turned and headed for the single armchair center-stage. Instead of doing exactly as instructed, she stopped beside the chair and set her hand gently down on the incredibly soft black leather. "Now can you tell me what—"

"I said sit, Idina." Harold Senior stared at her as though he believed his gaze would make her burst into flames.

That gaze had burned away the resistance of so many tentative business partners, heavy competitors, and high-maintenance clients over the years. Harold Moorfield I was a man of his word, and he was also a man who got things done.

If he thinks I'm gonna start cowering and blubbering all over this chair, he's gonna be seriously disappointed.

With Mr. and Mrs. Moorfield standing stiffly beside the desk—the essential seat of power at Moorfield Manor and within Moorfield & Associates itself—Idina couldn't justify defying the entire Moorfield family gathered here on her account. Not in this situation. She'd fought them all her life in one way or another, which had only made them tighten their grip on her and every decision she'd made since.

Just suck it up and wait for them to stop yelling. It's not like it can get any worse than that. Unless I start seeing things that aren't there and this does *turn into an intervention.*

Gritting her teeth, Idina took one swift step around the armrest of the chair and plunked herself down onto the thick, stiff cushion. "So *now* will someone tell me what this is about?"

"Harry?" Harold Senior glanced at his oldest son and nodded. "Would you like to take it from here?"

"Yes, sir. Thank you." Harry cleared his throat and settled his fingertips on the edge of the desk to steady himself before fixing his gaze on Idina. It was a calm, collected gesture, but Idina couldn't stop staring at those fingers because it was also a major red flag.

This was bad.

"Idina," he started, his voice low and even and entirely within his control. "Your handling of the Hannaford accounts last week was wholly unacceptable."

"What?" She looked between the three faces beside and behind the desk, all of them scowling at her. "How is that—"

"You had instructions—perfectly detailed instructions, I might add—for exactly how to allocate the incoming funds on precisely which investment opportunities. Despite this, you somehow got it into your head that investing in Valbiol Technologies, of all things, was a viable risk for the Hannafords. In no way whatsoever was that the case."

"Oh, come on." Idina shot a crooked smile at the conference table and the other four Moorfield children plus two spouses. "You guys called a serious business meeting for *that?*"

"No one gave you the authority to redirect the composition of the Hannaford portfolio," Harry added.

"I don't see why you're getting all bent out of shape

about this," she countered, turning a disbelieving smile back onto him.

"You deliberately stepped out of line and purchased shares for a Moorfield & Associates client that did not in any way reflect the contractual obligations this firm holds to its—"

"What are you *talking* about?" Idina started to rise from the chair, but a firm stare and slight tilt of the head from Annette made her sit back down again. "I didn't do anything Mr. Hannaford wasn't aware of and didn't agree to himself, okay? It's an *aggressive portfolio* for crying out loud."

At the conference table, Timothy snorted and muttered, "Not *that* aggressive."

She ignored him. "Listen, I took all the right steps, okay? I saw something that would be lucrative for the Hannafords, I discussed it with him, and he gave the okay. It's not a big deal."

"*You* are not an investment banker," Harry quipped. "Nor are you a financial advisor. You have no official qualifications. You're a paid intern, Idina. Not once since we brought you on with this company have you proven yourself capable of fulfilling the responsibilities of either of those senior positions, and it is *not* up to you to diverge from the instructions you received simply because you *saw something*."

Idina gaped at him and clutched the edge of the chair's cushion with both hands in a grip that immediately made her nailbeds sore and her pulse pound in her fingertips. "You're serious about this."

"Deadly serious."

"Dad, if you don't think I can—"

"Mr. Moorfield!" Harold Senior bellowed as he pounded a wrinkled fist on the desk.

Idina jumped in her chair and thickly swallowed as she turned her gaze onto her grandfather.

"This is a business meeting, Idina. If you cannot address the senior partners of this firm with the proper respect, don't address them at all. Is that understood?"

She glared at him for a moment longer, then stiffly nodded. "Yes, sir."

Harold sat back in his chair, slowly sliding his fist across the desk until it dropped soundlessly back into his lap.

A business meeting? More like a public flogging.

"Idina," Harry continued, his voice softened now after the Moorfield patriarch's fire-and-brimstone outburst.

When she looked back up at her parents again, her mother's lips were tightly pursed in an effort not to speak out of turn, and her father's frown carried a hint of remorse. It wasn't enough to keep him from walking down this road of furious corporate retribution. It never was.

"We've all discussed this at some length," he continued, gesturing briefly toward the conference table with her brothers and sister sitting dutifully at attendance. "The members of this board have reached a decision regarding your careless non-compliance."

"A decision?" Idina wrinkled her nose and almost spread her arms in one more show of defiance but fortunately kept her tight hold on the chair cushion instead.

What are they gonna do? Banish me from the empire?

Harry nodded once. "Starting today, you no longer have a position at Moorfield & Associates."

That caught her out of left field, and she straightened in the chair before looking at her mom for support. There was none. "Wait, you're...*firing* me?"

"I'm sorry, Idina, but you've made it clear for the final time that you're a liability we can't afford."

"A liability." She scoffed. "This was supposed to be my job for the rest of the summer. Working here. I thought that's what everyone wanted me to do."

"We want someone who can do as instructed," her oldest brother Maxwell said from the table. "Which you obviously can't. We're not paying you to screw up some of our most high-profile accounts all summer."

"If you wanted me to work my way up from the bottom," Idina snapped, turning to fix her scowl onto him now, "why did you start me off with a *high-profile account?*"

"It's a sink-or-swim industry," Harold Senior replied drolly. "Unfortunately, some of us sink."

Her father shared a look with her grandfather before nodding. "Maybe if you'd spent more time focusing on admissions to Harvard instead of spending your free time doodling with your head in the clouds—"

"Doodling?"

"—you'd have received your acceptance letter by now. There's still time. If you focus on your future, Idina, you might be able to salvage your position here with the rest of us."

Idina glared at her father, forcing herself to ignore the reappearance of the shimmering green cloud slowly closing in around her vision. *Not now. No. Suck it up and don't let them get to you. They'll use this as an excuse.*

"I'm not going to Harvard," she said flatly.

"That's the only option available to you, young lady," Harold Senior added. "Once you prove you can acquire the level of business acumen required to work in this firm—and Harvard is an excellent school for doing that—the doors in Moorfield & Associates will open to you. Until then, you won't touch a single client account, nor will you have access to company shares. We're family, but we're not running a charity. We don't tow dead weight."

Did my grandfather just call me dead weight?

Idina choked on a bitter laugh, then turned toward the conference table again and her four siblings who'd made Moorfield & Associates the focal point of all their lives because that was what a Moorfield did. Instead of backing down to accept this unanimous decision on behalf of *the board,* she couldn't help but push a little harder one more time. "Did any of you look at the projections for Valbiol? As an investment, I mean."

Celeste raised an eyebrow. Bryan sighed in defeat and shook his head.

Timothy never had anything helpful to say, but Maxwell took the lead like he always did, as the oldest. "There was no point."

"You didn't even look." Idina rolled her eyes. "So you decided that because I'm not a good little slave for the family business, you get to call it a bad decision and boot me out just like that. Way to do your research—"

"This isn't about research, Idina," her father interrupted. "And it's not about any of our personal feelings. None of us are obligated to look into the poor decisions you've made in the name of this firm because none of us have gone against the grain the way *you* have to cause such a stir."

"A stir." She looked back and forth between her parents. "That's what you're calling this? Look, if you don't want to hire me as the youngest junior assistant or whatever, that's fine. But Gra—" She grimaced and gave her grandfather a quick look. "Mr. Moorfield basically disowned me. Because I put Mr. Hannaford's money where he *agreed* it was a good—"

"You have no idea what you're doing," Celeste's husband Bruno cut in. "That's what this is about."

"Easy for you to say. All *you* had to do was marry into this nuthouse."

"Idina!" her mother snapped.

Idina pressed herself slowly back against the cushion of the armchair and met her mother's dark, stern gaze. It softened only a little, and true to form, Annette Moorfield did her best to be both practical and the nurturing mother most people would've expected her to be. The woman was only good at one of those things, and she hadn't exactly won any Mother of the Year Awards.

When her mother glanced down at Idina's hands clamped around the chair cushion, Idina knew what the woman saw there. Shimmering green sparks wafting up from Idina Moorfield's fingers like specks of dandelion fluff.

I can't help it. If they didn't wanna set me off, they should've found a better way to fire their youngest daughter.

Idina shifted in the chair and quickly shoved both her hands under her thighs. For now, that seemed to do the trick with the shimmering green specks. It made her mother comfortable enough to continue.

"This is a business decision." Annette met her gaze. "It affects our reputation. Our entire livelihood. Do you understand?"

"Yeah, you guys have made that impossible to overlook."

"We've said it before, but I'll repeat it now. This isn't a personal attack on you. You're just…you're not *like* the rest of us, sweetheart. For whatever reason, the family talents seem to have skipped one Moorfield in your generation."

Well, that's a major slap in the face. Idina swallowed. "Because the *family* talents are the only ones that matter, right?"

"In this family," Harold Senior replied, "yes."

Idina's eye twitched, and she scanned the table of her siblings for an ounce of empathy she already knew she wouldn't find. Then she studied her parents' crestfallen expressions—disappointment, regret, and an unwavering dedication to putting Moorfield & Associates first. Moorfield & Associates always came first. "Is that it, then?"

Her grandfather looked around the room and briefly shook his head. "Unless anyone else has something they'd like to add, we've reached the end of our agenda for—"

"Great. Thanks for your time." The youngest Moorfield —and the most useless in the eyes of her entire family— launched herself out of the armchair and spun to head for the study doors.

"Idina," her mother called after her. "That's no way to—"

"Let her go," Harry said softly.

Idina felt the eyes of every member of her family on her back as she snatched her sketchpad and art supplies off the entry table. No one moved to stop her when she flung open the double doors and sent them crashing against the wall of the hallway outside. She did, however, hear her grandfather *harrumph* in his grumpy-old-man way, though at the moment, it sounded more like a snigger.

Screw this. She stormed down the hallway toward the far stairwell most often used only by the staff, but at least it went straight down to the closest exit on the estate house's main floor.

If they wanna boot me from the whole company, fine. I'm not like the rest of them, and I sure as hell don't wanna be. But I have talents. If they ever managed to pull their heads out of their stupid bank accounts and quit worshipping the firm, they'd see that. Now I'm stuck here with no job and an entire Board of Directors that hates my guts.

The anger burning through her did what it always did to Idina's odd, unexplained abilities. As she stormed down the stairs and across the main floor, a thin halo of nearly invisible green light pulsed around her body. If the house staff glimpsed her, they'd have to look very hard to see it. Idina had to work equally hard to convince herself she was more than a freak of nature with an inexplicable condition.

Even if I flat-out asked them, they would never admit they stripped me off the board because of a few green lights. That doesn't make me different. It makes them cowards.

CHAPTER THREE

After half an hour of storming around the grounds behind the estate house, Idina still felt like she was about to explode. So she headed for the dojo at the back of the grounds. It had been there since long before Idina herself came into this world so far behind the rest of her siblings.

The place had been designed and built in the late 1800s by some kung fu master with business ties to the Moorfield family. At least that was the unofficial story among the staff and whenever her brothers felt like having a little fun playing around with the history of their oh-so-prestigious bloodline.

Fine. Maybe this *is the only thing I have in common with the rest of them.*

She paused outside the dojo doors covered in thin slats of wood woven together, set her sketchbook and bag of charcoal down on the stone bench, and slipped off her shoes. The doors on their rolling tracks slid open with a whisper, and she didn't bother to close them again behind her. Removing her shoes to show the proper regard for a place she'd learned to respect was as much as she could handle with all the rage and disbelief burning through her.

Her bare feet slapped against the mats as she stalked across the dojo toward the racks of practice weapons along the far wall.

Her grandfather's words wafted through her mind—words she must've heard a hundred times before she was old enough to understand what they were supposed to mean. *"A Moorfield doesn't sit around at a desk all day only to neglect the other half of themselves. A Moorfield is well-rounded. Capable both mentally and physically."*

"That's such bullshit." She reached for one of the bō staffs on the lower rungs, hefted in her hand to test its balance, then hurried to the other side of the dojo where two human-shaped punching bags waited for her to beat them senseless.

Which she did.

The shimmering lines of green light lit up the dummy's midsection with perfect clarity, and she drew the staff back for a swing.

"They don't want any of us to be well-rounded," she hissed, emphasizing her private words with a quick jab to the dummy's midsection. The green light vanished and reappeared at the dummy's neck, so she aimed there. "They want us to be clones." *Whack.* "Good little drones who—" *Thump.* "—don't do any thinking—" *Crack.* "—for themselves."

She spun and delivered a roundhouse kick to the blazing green light in the crook between the dummy's neck and shoulder. The heavy rubber target wobbled dangerously on its sand-filled base, but unlike a living opponent, the thing didn't go down. It stayed there, upright, staring back at her with colorless rubber eyes that were scuffed and a little cracked from so much use.

This is what they want me to be. Idina set the end of the staff firmly on the mat and took a second to catch her breath. *A dummy. A giant walking, talking target with their last name. If that dummy has a few episodes with a couple of flashing lights, they pump it full of pills and tell it to behave. If it doesn't suck it up and do its job, they rip it to shreds.*

With an angry growl, she dove into another series of attacks with her practice weapon, spinning around the dummy and delivering cracking blows of wood against rubber in every major weak spot lighting up in her vision like a Christmas-light display synced to symphony music. At least, they *would* have been weak spots if her opponent were flesh and blood instead of almost a foot of thick plastic.

She didn't hear the soft footsteps behind her, and she certainly hadn't expected anyone to come looking for her here. So it caught her off-guard when an unannounced visitor called to her from across the dojo.

"I can't imagine a scenario in which that practice dummy has done anything to warrant such a vicious attack."

Idina's bō staff glanced off the dummy's wobbling head. The green lights of her target spots no one else could see disappeared, then she spun and immediately drew her arms toward her sides at attention. Bowing slightly at the waist, she blinked at the mat. "Master Rocha."

The martial arts instructor, who was well into his seventies, had worked for the Moorfield family even longer than Reggie. The man had trained *with* Harold Senior before taking on the responsibility of training every subsequent Moorfield in the family line. Now he'd shown up to the dojo already wearing his *gi*.

The traditional uniform in Brazilian jiu-jitsu of loose-fitting pants and a shirt crossed diagonally from shoulder to opposite hip and tied at the waist seemed to be the only outfit Master Benício Rocha wore, day in and day out.

The man had lived in the small, unassuming cottage behind the dojo since the last Moorfield family trainer had grown too old to continue his employment on the estate. Despite that, Idina didn't spend much time with her trainer beyond their early morning sessions four days a week.

She looked up at him with her cheeks flushed from the energy she'd expended on the training dummy and him catching her in the dojo at the wrong time in the wrong clothes. "I didn't think you'd be here."

"I could say the same to you." Benício fixed her with a small smile. "Yet I'm fully aware of your tendency to show up in unexpected places."

Idina scoffed. "In more ways than one. Sorry." She straightened and hefted the bō staff in her hand. "I'll go... blow off steam somewhere else."

"That's a shame. I was about to ask if you'd rather take it out on a worthy opponent instead of a lump of rubber."

She stopped, looked down at her tank top and jean shorts above her bare legs and feet, and grimaced. "I'm not in uniform."

Benício cocked his head and reached for another staff from the shelves of training weapons. "I won't tell anyone if you don't. That is, of course, if you still intend to *blow off steam* somewhere useful."

With a smirk, she took two steps back and squared herself toward her trainer. "Okay. I won't tell."

"Good." He waved her forward. "Then let's begin."

They reached the center of the mats and circled each other. Idina's heart still pounded in her chest. A thin layer of sweat had formed on her forehead, and at her hairline around the ponytail of thick, nearly black curly hair she'd pulled up that morning against the humid summer heat.

I can't believe he's still here, wanting to spar with a seventeen-year-old girl in his dojo when it's not even on the schedule. I'm gonna end up breaking his bones or something.

"Stop thinking," Benício muttered, staring at the center of her chest where her collarbones connected. "Make your move."

Idina looked her trainer up and down, waiting for the green glow of her odd ability to show up and give her the best first move. For some reason, they didn't, and she let out a wry chuckle. "Maybe this was a bad idea."

"Oh? The old man looks too frail, is that it?"

"I mean, it's different when we're—"

"No, it's not. You wanted to spar. Blow off steam. Now's your opportunity."

"Master Rocha, I don't think—"

He lunged toward her, and before she could tell which way he was going to go, the spry older man moved like a lightning bolt and cracked his bō staff against the outside of her leg in a backhanded swing.

"Hey!"

"You have two choices," the man said calmly. "Stop

thinking and let it out, or swallow everything inside you and let it eat you alive. I'll still be here either way."

He wants me to fight him. Like, for real.

"No, that's okay. We can get back to it tomorrow morning when it's time to—"

Whack. His staff came down on her opposite shoulder this time. "I heard there was a family meeting this afternoon."

Idina rubbed her arm and widened her eyes at the old martial arts trainer. "What?"

"Not a very promising one for certain members of the family."

"Who told you—"

"This place is not as airtight as some like to believe." Benício's smile widened. "I imagine that's where your anger comes from."

"*Yeah*, it's where my anger comes from. They basically just—"

Crack. This time, her trainer had struck her in the gut. Not enough to seriously hurt but definitely enough to knock the wind out of her and make her stagger backward. "Stop thinking."

Idina grimaced at him. "Kinda hard when I'm starting to think you're losing your mind."

"My mind is not in question here."

"No, only your—hey!" His weapon came down across the side of her head this time, and she growled. "Stop."

"Or what?" Now the man was grinning, his eyes mere pinpricks from within the heavy wrinkles surrounding them. "You'll show me what's bothering you? You'll let yourself fully embrace who you are and what you can do?

Idina, if I've taught you anything, I would hope it's that you listen to your Master when he tells you to raise your staff and engage."

She looked him up and down, wanting so badly to keep bashing her weapon against anything. Just to get all the pent-up energy out of her body and into something that wouldn't call her a useless disappointment to the family name. Even without the green lights only she could see to show her the way. "Fine."

"Wonderful." Benício stepped back with one bare, age-gnarled foot and nodded. "Begin."

Over the next half-hour, she gave her lifelong instructor everything she had—all the pent-up anger, boiling energy, and bitter resentment at her family for tossing her aside like a rotten piece of fruit because *the family talents had skipped a generation.*

In their place, she'd gotten some other freaky talent nobody could explain or completely cure with a regimen of pills rivaling what any quack doctor would've given her in a mental hospital.

It only took her a minute of sparring before she stopped holding back. If Master Rocha hadn't been going easy on her, it probably wouldn't have taken him even *that* long to take her down.

Instead, he opted to let her flail around, lashing out to strike at his limbs and torso with the bō staff the way he'd taught her. While her trainer parried every blow and deflected all the boiling energy of a seventeen-year-old girl who didn't want to be here, by the end of that half-hour, Idina had enough.

Mostly because he'd swept her off her feet with a final swing and sent her crashing to the mat with a *thump*.

Idina grunted, scrunched up her face, then tapped the mat as a sign that she'd finished.

"That's it?" Benício straightened and tucked his staff under one arm. "You're giving up so soon?"

With a laugh, she gingerly prodded her bottom jaw just below her ear. "Yep. I'm pretty sure you made your point."

The man lowered his head and stared at her until she met his gaze. "Which is what, exactly?"

"That you're older than my grandfather and can still kick my ass."

He threw his head back to let out a deep, baritone laugh that rang through the dojo and startled several birds in the grove of aspen trees outside. Then he stepped toward Idina and offered her a hand up from the mat. She took it, as surprised as ever to find so much strength behind an older man's grip and his ability to haul her to her feet. "Well, that *is* an accurate assessment. But it's not my point."

"So what *was* the point of all this?"

When he reached for her staff, she handed it over and had to stand there waiting for an answer while Benício returned both practice weapons to the shelves.

Don't tell me this is the one time getting beat up by Master Rocha doesn't come with some kinda lesson.

"The point," he finally continued as he turned away from the weapons racks, "is that you couldn't stop *thinking*."

She blinked at him. "No, I did. I think you beat all the brainpower out of me."

"No, you did not." Squinting, he wagged a finger at her and tilted his head. "Anger never made anyone less blind to the solution, Idina. And you are very angry."

Idina heaved a sigh, swiped her sweaty hair away from her forehead, and shrugged. "Of course I am. No matter what I do, it's never good enough. I can't *be* something I'm not. They all expect me to shut off who I am like it's some kinda light switch. It doesn't work like that."

"Is your anger any more likely to provide an alternative?"

She paused, then huffed out another laugh that quickly turned into a grimace when her sore ribs protested. "Okay, I get it."

"Ah."

"Don't take out my anger on a punching bag. Or a martial arts master four times my age. At least."

Benício's warm smile lit up his entire face, even with all the wrinkles. "You haven't answered my question."

"No, Master Rocha. My anger isn't going to make them change their minds. I'll have to do that on my own." The realization wasn't anything new, but it helped the lesson sink in even further when her entire body ached, and the man standing across from her in the dojo didn't have a scratch on him. Idina lowered her arms by her sides and bowed. "Thank you."

"For kicking your ass? You're very welcome." They both laughed, and he wagged another crooked finger at her. "Now get out of here before people start talking about the old man's vicious attack on the young Miss Moorfield outside our scheduled sessions."

Smirking, Idina headed quickly across the dojo, turned to bow one more time—which Benício happily returned—then stepped outside into the warm breeze blowing across the estate and collected her shoes.

He's right. I can't only be pissed about that surprise attack meeting. I can't only be angry that my family's cutting me out because I'm different. I have to do something about it. Make a better plan. Better yet, I have to make them an offer they can't refuse.

Despite her limp and the small bruises on her arms, shoulders, and shins, Idina hurried across the manicured lawn toward the estate house. She'd take a shower and a few ibuprofen, then she'd come up with a plan that would let everyone out of this whole Moorfield & Associates mess with precisely what they wanted.

Idina's family wouldn't have to deal with the disappointment of one Moorfield incapable of what they valued above all else, and Idina could finally get out of here. For good.

CHAPTER FOUR

So far, the only flaw in her plan was that she hadn't yet come up with a reasonable argument for why her parents should invest in the kind of education she *actually* wanted. No, Idina hadn't focused on any of the applications or admissions essays her parents had been waiting for her to submit to Harvard—the Ivy League school attended by every Moorfield since the institution had been founded. Probably.

She didn't want to go to business school. She'd been focusing on all the paperwork—the essays and scholarship applications—for Dartmouth College instead.

That was where she wanted to go, and they'd already accepted her with a scholarship offer that covered a staggering amount of her four-year college education. Her parents had no idea, which was precisely the way she'd wanted it until she could sit down with them both and show them that this was already a viable option, not to mention where her heart was.

The problem was that Harry and Annette Moorfield

didn't particularly give much credit to where someone's *heart* was. A college education was like any other investment in their eyes, and like any investment, they expected to get a positive return on it when everything was said and done.

Being a full-time artist was hard enough. Being a full-time artist who brought in an income remotely comparable to what each of her siblings earned with their obnoxious Business and Finance degrees and all the blood, sweat, and tears they'd each poured into Moorfield & Associates was practically impossible.

That didn't mean Idina had given up trying to change her parents' minds. She had to keep trying.

I'm not giving up on what I want—what I know I'm good at —so I can sell my soul to Moorfield & Associates and keep this stupid tradition in the family. Sure, I'm a Moorfield. That's only because I share a last name with a bunch of people I'll never actually understand.

However, if she could get her *parents* to understand that she'd taken care of all the details to get herself into Dartmouth, and they wouldn't have to lift a finger beyond giving her their blessing…

Maybe they'd be as happy to see her leave as she would be to watch the sprawling grounds of Moorfield Manor fading in the distance behind her.

Okay, fine. They might have to lift one tiny little finger to sign off on me going to Dartmouth in the first place. It's not like I'm asking for a lot of money. What the scholarship doesn't cover, I'll take out in student loans. Once I'm eighteen. I only need their signatures.

She'd taken the rest of the afternoon and evening to

think about how she would approach this with her parents. Popping down to the kitchen for one of Mrs. Yardly's famous barbequed chicken sandwiches for dinner—at least famous around here—added to Idina's confidence. She had the whole thing planned out and ready to go, all the paperwork stacked together in a binder she'd put together for this impromptu meeting with the *board members* of a life she didn't want.

All she had to do was wait until the end of the business day for her family officially to be "out of the office." Unofficially, they never really left, but she was a lot more likely to find them at least willing to listen once the stock exchange closed and they didn't have a reason to be so high-strung. Probably.

So that night, after the rest of the day spent avoiding every single one of her family members and all the other staff at the estate, Idina returned to the second floor of the gigantic house and moved quickly down the hall toward her father's office.

It was rare to find Harry Moorfield anywhere but in his office before 7:00 p.m., finishing up the last reports for the day. The man even took his meals there, sometimes with Idina's mother but mostly on his own. The company expected every family member to finish their work on time, and if that meant burning the candles at both ends in their own home, so be it.

Idina couldn't understand that mindset, but then again, she'd spent the entire day essentially putting together a proposal and a giant speech to go with it. At least she'd inherited the Moorfield work ethic if nothing else.

The fact that she was smiling as she walked down the hallway of the north wing surprised her.

I feel good about this. There's no reason they won't sign off on me leaving this place and going to Dartmouth with almost a full ride. It's not like they'd be losing a valuable employee anyway.

The thought made her snort, which almost made her miss the murmur of low voices coming not from her mother's "parlor" or her father's office but from inside Harold Senior's study. One of the double doors was slightly ajar, and normally, Idina wouldn't have thought twice about a conversation inside her grandfather's study. Those were rare too, but they did happen.

What *did* make her think twice was the brilliant, pulsing flash of green lights strobing up and down the polished wood of the door. Calling to her and summoning her attention.

That was all it took to catch her interest before she heard the timbre of three different voices rising through that small crack in one of the doors—two of them belonging to her parents. She never really expected Harold Senior to sound anything like the crotchety older man he was, but Mr. and Mrs. Moorfield sounded particularly upset.

So Idina stopped before the open door and couldn't help but listen. As she did, the pulses of green light sent a buzzing rush of energy through her limbs and up into her head, making her blink heavily. *Yeah. Guess I forgot to take my afternoon meds. I'll double up tonight.*

"This isn't anyone's *fault*, Dad," Harry said. "It's the way she is."

"It's a disgrace. That's what this is."

"I think *disgrace* is a bit of a strong word," Annette added. "I'd call it more of an...obstacle."

"We can overcome obstacles," Harold Senior grumbled. "This isn't something I see our family overcoming anytime soon. She's too...different. Too wild. We've done all we can to prune that wildness out of her."

Idina sidled closer to the door, waiting for the proof that they were talking about what she thought they were. *It's me. They're having a private meeting in Grandfather's study about* me. *Who else would they talk about like this?*

"It might still be possible." Idina's father lowered his voice. "To get her to come around."

"Oh? What do you suggest?"

"She still doesn't know our entire history, for one. Where we come from. How the Moorfield name has grown into what it is today. It might be time to talk to her about why we've medicated a seventeen-year-old girl as heavily as she is—"

"Harry." Harold Senior clicked his tongue. "Telling her the truth about *our* family will hardly make a difference at this point."

"It couldn't hurt to try," Annette offered.

"It very well could, and you know it. I'm not unsympathetic to the difficulty here and the complexity of this situation, but we've given Idina plenty of chances already." Harold Senior's tone had taken on its business-like note of finality, and even his son wouldn't brook an argument with him after this.

"If we didn't have Dr. Kruchek's help with the inhibitors, she would've already manifested by now. That means our opportunity to prune her skills in the direction the rest of this family has taken is far behind us. We should increase her dose. That's what I say."

Manifested? What the hell does that *mean?* Idina scowled at the door and strained to hear the rest of the conversation.

Harry surprised her with one more attempt to change his father's mind. "Dad, that's a little premature. You can't be sure that's what's happening here."

"I've seen it before, haven't I? We all have."

Annette sucked in a sharp breath. "Are you implying what's happening with my daughter is the same as what happened with Richard?"

"I'm not implying anything, Annette. Of course, it's the same."

"This is a completely different situation, Harold. I'm sorry, but you can't honestly believe Idina is following in *his* footsteps."

"God forbid she ever does." Harold Senior grunted. "That's the last thing this family needs. Richard caused more than enough trouble with his refusal to carry on the Moorfield legacy, and I'm telling you right now, I won't stand for it in another child intent on bringing this family down."

"Dad." Soft footsteps crossed the study. "What happened with Richard was unexpected, yes. We all still recovered. Moorfield & Associates still recovered."

"Hmm. Not quickly enough."

Idina couldn't wrap her head around what she was hearing. Uncle Richard was her father's younger brother. As far as she knew, he was the only Moorfield in living memory who'd estranged himself from the family. He'd taken off from the central hub of this estate in New Hampshire and everything that came with *the Moorfield name.*

The last time she'd seen him was during his brief but highly memorable visit over Christmas when she was nine. That visit had turned into a volatile screaming match between Uncle Richard, Harold Senior, and Harry before Idina's uncle had collected his things and stormed right through the door.

He'd stopped only to chuck a wide-eyed young Idina under the chin and whisper, "Don't let anyone tell you who you are or how to use the power you have. I promise you no one will know the truth of that better than you."

She remembered so vividly seeing his face light up with glittering green specks that danced in his eyes as he stared at her like his final message was the most important thing in the world. A secret she had to guard with her life. Then he was gone.

After that, she hadn't heard a thing about Uncle Richard. He'd disappeared right off the map as far as she knew. Since then, the mere mention of him drove her grandfather into a rage.

Except during this little evening meeting between the three of them, behind the slightly ajar doors of Harold Senior's study and in lowered voices.

Like they don't want anyone to know what they're talking about. Jeez, they could've done a little better with making sure the doors were closed.

"Well," her father stated, then cleared his throat. "Until and unless she gives us reason to believe that's the case, I'm not giving up. We'll do what we have to do to make sure

Idina prepares for her place in this family, and I believe she'll pull through."

"No," Harold Senior whispered. "It's already too late for that. Mark my words, Harry. You'll see it soon enough. I saw it in Richard, and I see it now in your daughter."

"And *your* granddaughter," Annette emphasized.

"Which never ceases to surprise me. She has the same look in her eye. The same...defiance. That hunger you and I and the rest of our family in this day and age have eliminated from the bloodline. Don't think I didn't see her...*glowing* this morning."

"She handled it. Idina still has potential—"

"For what? Tearing down everything this family has built because she was born with obsolete knowledge? No!" Harold pounded a fist onto the desk.

"Whatever potential she might've had only exists because of what *we* have done. We'll *waste* it on Idina just like the family *wasted* it on Richard! If she keeps straying down this overgrown path, Harry, she'll never amount to anything. You know this as much as I do. Don't try to deny it."

"Idina is still a Moorfield, Dad. Through and through."

"No. She's simply not one of us. Not a *true* Moorfield, at any rate. We don't have room for that. Not after the last time."

He's serious about this. Not a true Moorfield? So I have a few episodes. Green lights. An accident now and then. I've done everything they've asked of me, and it's still not good enough. Fine. They can all rot in this soulless place without me.

Tears stung Idina's eyes, but she only noticed they were there when she tried to turn away from the door and found her vision blurred. So of course her next step went farther out than she wanted, and her shoe kicked against the edge of the slightly open door.

"What was that?" Harold Senior barked.

"Calm down, Dad," Harry chided.

Before Idina could sneak away the way she'd wanted, a shadow fell across the light spilling into the hallway. Then the door opened the rest of the way to reveal her mother standing there.

"Idina." Annette tilted her head and opened the door even farther before stepping aside to give her husband and father-in-law a clear view of the youngest Moorfield in the hall.

"What is it?" Harry asked.

Idina looked back and forth between her father and grandfather before finally meeting her mother's dark, calculating gaze. There wasn't a trace of remorse or embarrassment on any of their faces.

They have to know I was standing out here the whole time. How could they not? I gave myself away, and they aren't even sorry they were talking about me like this behind my back. They don't even care...

She forced the tears back and shook her head. "Nothing."

"Well, you must've come down here for *something*," Harold Senior added. "Whatever it is, young woman, speak up."

"No, it's fine. I don't need anything from—"

"What's this?" Annette's eyes widened as she noticed the three-ring binder clenched so tightly in her daughter's hands that the thick cardboard had begun to buckle. Not to mention the swirling lines of green-tinged air like nearly invisible vapor emanating from beneath Idina's fingers.

"I hope it's not another report," Harold snapped.

"Dad," Harry chided. "Let it go."

"Is that what this is?" Annette asked. "Sweetheart, it's too late to change what's happened. The board's already made its decision."

"It's nothing. Seriously." Idina stepped through the open door and lowered the binder in one hand. "Not even worth your time."

She chucked the binder into the empty trash bin inside the door at the foot of Harold Senior's pristinely stocked wet bar, then spun and left. But not before she caught a hint of flashing green around the dented cover of her binder.

No. I don't care how bright the lights get. I'm done.

No one tried to stop her. Her family didn't call after her to ask what she'd wanted or what was in the binder. They didn't inquire why her face must've been as red as it felt now, burning in anger and defeat and as close to pure hatred as Idina could remember feeling.

They don't care. They think I'm some screwup like Uncle Richard, and they're not willing to take a chance on me and what I can do. They only want to keep pumping me with drugs. Fuck that. I've finished taking chances on them too. As soon as I'm eighteen, I'm getting the hell out of here, and I'm never coming back.

CHAPTER FIVE

The next morning when Idina woke in her massive bedroom on the third floor, her head pounded and her eyes were as swollen as if she'd been crying all night. She hadn't shed a tear since her parents had discovered her eavesdropping in the hallway.

That's what I get for doubling up on my missed meds last night.

She rubbed her swollen eyes and let out a heavy sigh.

Master Rocha's right. I can't let my anger overwhelm everything else. What am I supposed to do now? If they think I'm gonna come crawling back into that study and beg for a second chance, they don't know me at all. Not after what I heard.

She took her time showering and getting dressed for the day, then headed down to the kitchens. She'd told Mrs. Yardly at the end of last year that she didn't want the woman going up and down the stairs as many times as she did in the morning to bring Idina breakfast in her room. Every Moorfield on the estate had a perfectly good pair of legs, but apparently, Idina was the only one who felt like using them first thing in the morning.

Mrs. Yardly greeted her with as warm a smile as ever when Idina stepped into the massive kitchen. The place bustled with the head cook's support staff as they prepared meals to be distributed to six separate apartments on the third floor for six different families all living under one roof.

The woman's rosy cheeks dimpled as she hurried around the prep table in the center of the kitchen. "Good morning, Sprout. Go ahead and have a seat, honey. I'll bring you a plate as soon as I make sure the drink cart's fully stocked."

The woman's use of her pet name for Idina since the girl had first started walking usually made Idina smile. Today, she didn't think anything could. "Drink cart for Timothy?"

"Who else?" Mr. Yardly chuckled and inspected the cart that the staff brought up to Timothy Moorfield's apartments every morning—his daily dose of breakfast cocktails that accompanied the half a grapefruit and single hard-boiled egg he ate every morning as a chaser.

Idina shook her head and approached the large spread of prepared breakfast for the staff that they hadn't cleaned up yet after their own much earlier breakfast. "Don't worry about it. I'll grab something."

"Oh no, you don't. Get away from there." Mrs. Yardly tried to shoo the girl away, but Idina playfully leapt out of the way and grabbed a plate anyway.

"It's right here. I'm not gonna make you cook me something from scratch when this already looks amazing."

The head cook huffed and fluttered her hand toward the buffet-style breakfast at the end of the prep table, but she couldn't keep the laughter out of her voice. "You don't want that, dear. It's for the *staff*."

Idina piled fresh orange slices, grapes, sausage links, and two homemade cinnamon rolls onto her plate. "Are you telling me a Moorfield is too good to enjoy a staff breakfast?"

That made Mrs. Yardly stop her distracted rearrangement of Timothy's morning Breakfast of Champions cart, and she straightened fully before turning to fix the girl with a concerned frown. "What happened?"

Idina focused on pouring a glass of orange juice from the pitcher and shrugged. "Nothing all that surprising. The same old thing. I'm not anywhere near as much of a Moorfield as everyone wants me to be."

"Sprout..." The woman clicked her tongue. "They'll come around. You'll see."

After picking up her orange juice, Idina turned to fix the woman with a deadpan stare, then slowly raised an eyebrow.

Mrs. Yardly chuckled. "All right, I can admit that's a bit of wishful thinking on my part." She grabbed a fork and knife from the utensil holder and placed them gently on the girl's plate, followed by a napkin tucked neatly between the plate and Idina's hand.

Then she patted the girl's shoulder and met her gaze with a sympathetic smile. "Whether or not they change doesn't make a lick of difference, you understand? If it were me, I'd focus more on not changing *myself*. Especially when it's not a change that comes from the heart."

Idina smirked. "You're perfect just the way you are, Mrs. Yardly."

"Ha. Well, I've had much longer to practice reaching that perfection, thank you very much. And we're talking about *you*."

"I know. Trust me. I gave up on trying to be whatever I'm *supposed* to be way before they did."

"What do you mean?"

"Nothing. I'm holding you up." Forcing a smile, Idina pulled away from the woman's kind gaze. "Thanks for the amazing breakfast, as always."

"You're quite welcome, dear. If you want more, you know where to find me."

"I know where the buffet is too."

Mrs. Yardly's chortling laughter followed the girl out of the kitchen's swinging doors, then Idina diverged from her usual morning routine and took her breakfast somewhere else. Normally, she ate at the table in the corner of the kitchen, smiling and laughing with Mrs. Yardly's support staff as they went through their daily routine of washing, prepping, cooking, boiling, baking, sautéing, and cleaning. Today, she didn't want to be around anyone.

I'll end up exploding in someone's face and feel worse about hurting the people who work for us than about my family hurting me.

So she took her breakfast out on the sprawling back patio behind the estate house, though the pleasure she'd expected to find in sitting on the sun-warmed lounge cushions beside the French doors didn't have the same ring to it. Nothing did this morning.

After breakfast, Idina gathered her art supplies and headed out to the grounds to find the perfect place with the ideal lighting for the best start to a new sketch. She couldn't find it. Perfection didn't exist today. No matter where she sat or how much she focused on trying to pull up the glittering green threads that always showed her what was missing from her hand-sketched creations, inspiration wouldn't strike. She couldn't get her grandfather's words out of her head.

"She's too...different. Too wild. We've done all we can to prune that wildness out of her."

What does that even mean? I'm not a rose bush they can slash and hack away at to look the way they want. I'm not even the worst Moorfield kid they've had to deal with.

Her second-oldest brother Timothy had a drinking problem everyone ignored. It somehow didn't get between him and his work. Bryan brought a different girl to his apartment on the third floor every week, and no one said a word about that. Because it didn't get between him and his work.

Celeste complained about not getting paid enough despite swarms of personal shoppers unloading van after van of the newest fashion collections and an entire over-haul of the furniture in her and Bruno's apartment at least every six months. *She* still got a pass because she handled the firm's accounting on top of her usual client portfolios.

Maxwell? Well, Maxwell was perfect in everyone's eyes. And an asshole.

I have no idea what kind of wild I am that they aren't.

Because I'm an artist? Because I saw a pattern in the market and impressed Mr. Hannaford with a suggestion? Because I won't roll over and gush about money and money and more money?

Because I have this...ability no one can explain to me, and everyone's terrified?

She roamed the grounds aimlessly, stopping now and then to watch the wild rabbits eating the patches of clover planted specifically to keep them away from the rest of the garden. She sighed beneath the balmy breeze picking up heat as the sun rose in the sky.

Eventually, after a slow meander through the rose garden and between the granite-statue fountains burbling away in the koi ponds, she stumbled upon Edgar Folton and Mason Hardinger. The pair sat at their usual stone table on the other side of the pristine hedges.

Both men were in their early sixties and had been responsible for the overwhelmingly gorgeous upkeep of the Moorfield Manor grounds since they were Idina's age. Maybe even younger. Every day at noon, they stopped their work and met here at this stone table to eat their lunch and keep each other's wits in check over a game of chess.

Idina stopped when she saw them, both men thoroughly engaged in the strategic plays already being put in motion on the board.

There's no way it's already noon. I just came outside with my stuff. She glanced at the zippered bag in her hand and the sketchpad she hadn't drawn in once. *Unless I've been moping around for the last five hours...*

"Don't look now," Edgar muttered, "but I think we have an audience."

Mason frowned in concentration, removed his newsboy cap to swipe a hand over his bald head, then firmly pulled the hat back down in place. "If Miss Idina's an audience, old boy, then I'm a professional athlete."

Neither gardener looked at her, pretending they didn't already know she was there despite not having lowered their voices to avoid detection.

Idina turned to scan the grounds, but of course, there was no one else out there. The rest of her family were holed up in their private offices, pounding away on keyboards and making diligent, split-second phone calls like their lives depended on it. Idina was out here among the flowers and the hedges, completely alone with two older men snickering to themselves and moving chess pieces from square to square.

"It wouldn't surprise me if you *were* a professional athlete," she muttered. "In another life."

"Ha! You hear that, Mason?" Edgar slapped his knee and leaned forward, wheezing with laughter. "*Someone* has a very high opinion of you."

"In another life," Mason muttered before moving his castle.

Idina approached them, glad to be in the company of those who laughed at her comments and didn't seem to mind how little sense they made—that Idina Moorfield wasn't a living machine of rational thinking and number-crunching and orderly steps toward perfect "by the book."

"First game?" She stooped to set her art supplies in the grass before turning her attention to the chessboard.

"First. Last. They're all the same," Mason grumbled.

"Oh, sure. To *you*." Edgar glanced up at Idina and

winked. "I imagine winning every damn day gets insufferably boring after forty years."

"It was boring after year one."

Edgar burst out laughing and rocked backward on the stone bench facing the table.

Idina grinned. "Here you are, still playing him forty years later."

"Still *beating* him. Don't forget that part." Mason shook a finger at her without taking his calculating gaze off the pieces. "I only do it because this old dog has nothing left to keep him going. Every day, he tells himself he'll finally beat me at the masters' game. I couldn't possibly let him win now."

"Why's that?" Idina folded her arms and looked back and forth between a concentrated Mason and Edgar rolling his eyes and shaking his head.

"Well, then he'd have nothing to keep him going. No reason for living."

Edgar let out a low whistle. "You know, that's exactly it. Without this scowling curmudgeon, I'd lose the will to live."

"You're very cute," Mason grumbled, then lifted his queen and moved her two diagonal squares forward. "Checkmate."

The other man's smile disappeared instantly, and he scrutinized the board before spreading his arms. "Oh, for the love of malt liquor, man!"

Idina barked out a laugh and quickly covered it up by clearing her throat.

Shaking his head, Edgar chuckled and tapped the edge of the table. "Looks like I have one more day of getting out of bed in the morning with a good intellectual beating to look forward to."

"*I* look forward to it." Mason stuck his hand out across the table, and they shook good-naturedly. Then he glanced at his watch and narrowed his eyes. "We have another fifteen minutes."

"No, no." Edgar stood. "I'm happy to save another staggering defeat for this time tomorrow."

"Would you play *me?*" Idina asked.

Mason squinted up at her, his wrinkled lips pursing together and wrinkling even further. "I thought you'd never ask."

"Excellent."

Edgar removed himself from the table and gestured for the girl to take a seat. "You're in for it now, my friend. The last time I sat at a chessboard with this young woman, she wiped it clean with my face."

"No, no." Mason waved him off. "If Miss Idina wants to step up against the reigning champion, let her try her hand." As she sat, he leaned forward to bring his grumpy old face closer and pointed at her, lowering his voice. "Don't think for one instant that I'll go easy on you because of who your daddy is."

She scoffed. "I'd be pretty upset if you *did*. So don't worry. I'm not that kind of Moorfield."

"Is that so?" Edgar folded his arms and chuckled. "What kind of Moorfield *are* you, exactly?"

Rubbing her hands together, Idina held Mason's gaze and finally let herself smile the way she thought she wouldn't be able to all day. "The kind who welcomes a challenge."

Mason snorted in amusement, his eyes winking in the sunlight, and Edgar burst out laughing again. "I haven't looked forward to something like this since… Hell. Since Marguerite's lemon meringue pie."

Idina looked up at the man as she and Mason reset the board. "Didn't she make that last week?"

"Trust me, girl. When you get to be our age, it feels quite a bit longer than that."

Mason grumbled something unintelligible, then he neatly set up the pieces and spun the board around on the table. "You take white, Miss Idina. You'll need the extra luck."

She didn't argue with him but nodded. Her pawn instantly lit up with green light that neither gardener would ever see, and she moved it to e4 to set up her opening. "Thank you."

"Whew, boy." Edgar rubbed a hand down his scruffy cheek and gazed at the board with wide eyes. "Different kind of Moorfield is right. Look alive, Mason. If I weren't alone here in the stands, I'd be taking bets right now."

The other gardener ignored him as he scrutinized the board like they were in the middle of a game instead of his first move.

Idina smiled but couldn't help turning that phrase over and over.

A different kind of Moorfield. It feels right to say, but what did he mean? Nobody around here's an idiot. They know I have…issues. But do my lights and weird sparks make me the same as Uncle Richard, or is it something else?

CHAPTER SIX

Once Mason made his first play, Idina immediately moved her knight to f3 for a King's Knight Opening, and the game picked up—the game on the chessboard and the one playing out like a movie in her mind. A green movie with thin strands of light that showed her exactly where the plot was heading and how to counter every surprise twist.

"You know," she started, waiting for Mason to finish deliberating, "I'm pretty sure I have a remedial handle on simple math, but just to make sure... You both were here when Richard still lived at Moorfield Manor, right?"

"If you think starting a conversation is going to throw me off my concentration," Mason grumbled, "you're mistaken."

"Hmm." Edgar stroked his chin as he studied the board. "If *I* were the one trying to derail him, I would've started with an icebreaker like that too."

Idina looked up at the scruffy-cheeked man with tufts of white hair peeking out around his ears despite his being almost as bald as Mason. "It's a real question neither of you has answered."

He glanced at her and raised an eyebrow. "We were around, sure."

Mason moved another chess piece, and Idina only had to study the board for three seconds before countering by removing his pawn and continuing the game. "So you saw what happened the Christmas he stormed out and never came back."

"You remember all that?"

"Girl's mind must be a steel trap," Mason grumbled. "That was a long time ago."

"Only eight years," she replied. "Almost."

"You were a babe."

Idina snorted. "I was nine. Don't tell me neither of you remembers that night."

"The way I *do* remember it," Edgar mused, stroking his chin as he frowned at the board. "We were all having our own Christmas party that night. You know, just the staff."

"Lots of eggnog." Mason grunted and moved another piece into position. "No Moorfields allowed. Only thing I heard was a lot of shouting. Made me glad we stay up there on the top floor, or I'd've thought the whole place was about to come down on top of us all."

"Okay, well, maybe you didn't see what happened exactly that night." She moved another pawn to block Mason's castle and shrugged. "But you have to remember Richard. Right?"

"You said *you* remembered, girl."

"Yeah, the last time I ever saw him. I'm pretty sure I only

saw him twice before that. Both on Christmas. Nobody will talk about him. Unless it's to curse his name and spout off a bunch of angry crap about the fact that he *brought disgrace to the Moorfield name*." She hardly paid attention to Mason's next move before she immediately brought her queen into play, ignoring a confident snort from her gardener opponent.

"You sure you want to make that move?"

"Yeah. Go ahead." Her green lights disappeared from the board, then Idina turned to look up at Edgar again. "I wanna know what you guys remember about my Uncle Richard *before* he left. Not for good the last time but when he was still living here."

A small smile spread across the man's lips. "Where's all this coming from?"

"You know me." She shrugged. "I'm curious."

"So was he." Mason took her castle and smirked.

"See? Those are the kinds of answers I'm looking for."

"All right." Edgar nodded. "When he lived here, young Richard was a...how do I put this?"

"Pain in the ass?" Mason nodded for Idina to play, and she quickly swiped his bishop that had taken her castle after the instant flash of green light illuminating the best play. Then he scowled.

"His words, not mine," Edgar clarified.

Idina frowned at Mason, who was frowning at the board. "Like how? Did he just...run wild around here? Break stuff? Crash parties?"

"Not a pain in *our* asses." Mason reached for his knight, withdrew his hand, then wavered over the other pieces before moving his other bishop. "He was a damn fine marksman. Before your grandfather took down the archery range."

"We had an *archery range* out here?" She laughed in disbelief and swiped a black castle off the board. "Wow. I thought the shooting range for *firearms* was cool. Sounds like I missed out."

Edgar snickered, but a glance from his fellow gardener made him lower his head to hide his amusement. "Might be Mr. Moorfield Senior figured he'd given his boys too much free rein around here. Which boys most certainly need. You know, space to run around and get out all their energy in healthy ways. Especially Richard."

Mason whistled, slowly shaking his head as he studied the battlefield in front of him. "I still remember the month he gave poor Benício a run for his money in that dojo."

"Richard trained with Master Rocha?"

"He and your daddy both," Edgar affirmed. "Harry wasn't much the type to put more into a physical competition than required, but Richard? Whew. That boy could go for *hours*."

"Boy?" The second Mason moved another pawn forward, Idina swiped it with her queen and gently set it aside. The man scoffed and shrank into himself, his eyes darting quickly across the board. "You two are only...what? Five years older than my father?"

"Oh, sure. But when Richard was old enough and big enough to start using his skill with a bō staff, Mason and I were nearing our mid-twenties."

"How old was he then?"

"Twelve." Mason clicked his tongue and ran a hand over his mouth. "Maybe thirteen."

"He gave Master Rocha a hard time when he was *thirteen?*" Idina tipped her head back and studied the cloudless blue sky before gazing across the lawn toward the dojo. "That'd be even harder to do than it is now."

Edgar chuckled again, shuffled his feet, and lowered his head to stare at the soft grass beneath him while he went down his version of memory lane. "There were a lot of things your Uncle Richard could do back then that only seemed to get harder as time went on."

"Harder for everyone else." Mason finally made his next move and folded his arms. "I figure that's what made it so hard for him to stick around much longer after he turned eighteen."

"He left when he turned eighteen." Idina's eyes widened. "I didn't know that."

"Like you said, Miss Idina." Edgar nodded. "Nobody talks about him much. He's still alive and kicking, as far as any of us can tell. Sends a postcard now and then. But I don't think he'd come back here even if the family wrote it all off as water under the bridge and welcomed him home with open arms."

The thought of her parents or grandfather opening their arms for anyone but some high-society hotshot coming in from the Hamptons for a long weekend made her laugh. "I get that."

She moved her next illuminated chess piece across the board but didn't give it more than a moment's glance. Mason shrank farther and farther into himself, his shoulders hunching and making him look quite a bit older than his sixty-something years.

"What else did he like? Richard, I mean."

"Little bit of everything, I suppose." Edgar looked off across the lawn the same way Idina had, and his smile flickered back and forth across his thin lips. "He was *good* at everything he set his mind to. Except for when it came time for him to play his part within the family. Harry was always the dependable one. Richard, though..."

"Bit of a loose cannon," Mason growled, still glaring at the chessboard as his fingers twitched and drummed against the edge of the table.

"There, now. That's closer to the truth than *pain in the ass*. It *is* interesting to think of now."

"Ha! There we go." Mason furtively brought his queen forward over the remaining lines of his pieces and sat back in satisfaction. "Go on now. Let's see what you have for *that*."

Idina didn't bother to look at the play he'd made but stared up at Edgar's musing profile. "What's interesting?"

The tall, thin gardener—quite the opposite of his shorter, rounder, more cantankerous counterpart—turned his warm, sun-weathered smile onto the girl and nodded. "Truth be told, Miss Idina, if there's anyone in the Moorfield family you take after most, I'd say it's your Uncle Richard."

"Even *he* wouldn't keep me waiting for the next play in the game," Mason added.

Idina ignored him. "Are you telling me you think I'm a pain in the ass and a loose cannon, Edgar?"

He laughed. "Not in any way. But I imagine both Mr. Moorfields might not quite see it that way."

"Did Richard have any other major hobbies? Like... I

don't know. Something that made him that much more *different?*"

"Hobbies like art? No, ma'am. At least not as far as I saw. Mason, you ever see Richard with a notebook out like Miss Idina?"

She didn't bother to correct him and say it was a *sketchpad*. Because now she was interested in this. She only had to wait for the part where she told them she wasn't talking about a sketchpad or the kinds of "normal hobbies" most people in the world developed to fill their time.

I spent so much time trying to figure out who Richard was and where he went. Should've asked the gardeners a lot sooner. When I still felt like I was missing something.

"Nope. Can't remember Richard with a paintbrush." Mason folded his arms, unfolded them, then tapped the table with a finger. "Never saw him take so damn long to play a game of chess, either."

"No drawing, then." Edgar shrugged, looking thoroughly amused by his friend's frustration.

"What about weird...abilities?" she asked softly. "You know, like the supernatural kind. Lights. Sparks. Knowing things he shouldn't have been able to know..."

Mason's gaze darted up from the board to latch onto Idina's.

Yeah. Now they know I'm onto something.

Edgar cleared his throat. "Are you...having trouble with all that again, Miss Idina?"

"What? No. Dr. Kruchek took care of all that after last time. I'm good. You said I take after Uncle Richard, so I thought maybe that had something to do with it." She glanced at the two glowing green squares of her next chess move but ignored them to look back up at Edgar. "Does it?"

The man sniffed, rubbed under his nose, and shared another look with Mason. "That, Miss Idina, is a question I'm not sure either of these two old gardeners can answer."

"Because you don't know," she prodded.

"Not nearly enough to tell you what you want to hear. Or even what you don't. But if the doc's helping you out the way he said he would, that's all right." Edgar wouldn't say anything else after that, and Idina had to change her strategy.

I can't say he's completely lying. But they both know some-thing, and they don't wanna say. Can't blame them. If there is another secret here, keeping it is probably a life-or-death respon-sibility for them. Literally. Especially with Harold Moorfield as their employer.

Idina huffed out a quick sigh. "Okay. What about every-thing that happened the Christmas he left? Obviously, it was some kind of falling out with the rest of the family, but it had to be something really big, right?"

"Could've been big. Could've been his time to branch out and follow his path." Edgar tilted his head from side to side. "No telling after this long."

"Oh, come on." Idina shot him a coy grin. "You had to have heard *something*. I mean, it's nine years later, and the entire family still uses him as a scapegoat for everything. 'Don't screw up like Richard.' 'Don't ruin the family name like Richard.' 'Don't be so wild like Richard.' What did he *do*?"

"Sorry, Miss Idina." Edgar gestured between himself and a borderline furious Mason. "We're only the gardeners.

Unless someone has a heated argument out by the apple trees, and nobody ever does, we're not privy to that kind of sensitive information."

"Reggie would know," Mason added. "Reggie hears everything. Makes the good and bad of being head of the staff. So if you need to know so badly, ask him. After you *make your move* so we can finish this game!"

"Better humor him, girl." Edgar tried again to hide more laughter as he checked his watch. "And we'd better get back to work. Those bleeding hearts aren't going to water themselves."

"Right." Idina nodded and turned back around to face the board. "Sorry, Mason. Guess I just had my head too far up in the clouds."

"Don't be sorry. Just play the game."

She scanned the board one more time, which lit up like a green-only fireworks display to show her all the possible moves she could take that would either end the game or keep it going a little longer. Idina shrugged, then took out Mason's knight with one of her pawns. "Checkmate."

"What?" Mason leaned forward over the table. "No, no. See here? I'll just… I'll…"

When Edgar burst out laughing again, the disgruntled gardener sitting across from Idina blew out a huge sigh through loose lips, making him sound like an old horse more than an older man. Then he flicked the crown of his black king and knocked it over on the board. "Well, I'll be damned."

"What did I say, huh?" Grinning, Edgar thrust his finger at the board. "I told you that you were in for it. Shouldn't have played her."

Mason squinted at the girl and tilted his head. "You weren't even paying attention."

"Oh, I was." Idina fixed him with a winning smile. "I'm good at multi-tasking."

"Uh-huh." After another sweeping glance of the finished game, he picked up the pieces to put them back in the foldable board that latched into a carrying case. "I'll tell you what. You're a hell of a better chess player than Richard Moorfield."

"That counts for something, right?"

Mason scoffed and waved her away. "Get out of here, girl. We got work to do, and I'm this close to asking for best two out of three."

"Good game, though." She extended her hand over the table, and Mason finally laughed as he took her hand in a firm grip.

"Yeah. Multi-tasking. Pah."

"Well, I'll let you guys get back to it, then." Idina stood, smoothed down the front of her t-shirt, and nodded.

As the gardeners wished her a good afternoon and collected their tools from the pile of them at the base of the stone table, Idina grabbed her unused art supplies and headed down the rows of hedges until she came to the bleeding hearts. The leaves fluttered in the breeze, streaked with the flickering green light that came from Idina's mind. She followed the thread patterns moving through the air and around the garden until she knew what was wrong.

The small potted plants looked incredibly sad, their leaves slightly yellow and the usually heart-shaped blossoms held tight together this late into the summer without being able to bloom fully. *No wonder they're having a hard time.*

"Are these the bleeding hearts you were talking about?" she asked.

"Hmm? Oh, sure. That's them." Edgar dropped his gear into a wheelbarrow and hoisted it onto its single wheel. "Mrs. Moorfield wanted a bit more color on this side of the fountains. Can't figure out why those things don't seem to want to cooperate, though."

"Yeah." Idina scanned the five potted plants, which would've added that burst of color to this part of the grounds if they weren't so sickly. "You should try moving them next to the end of the hedges. And take them out of the pots. They need a lot more sun than this, and they won't ever bloom if they feel stifled."

"Say what now?" Mason straightened and leaned backward to eye the pots beside her. "You trying to take our jobs, Miss Idina?"

She laughed. "No. Only a suggestion."

"Huh." Edgar stroked his chin, looked back and forth from the bleeding heart pots to the edge of the hedges, and huffed out a laugh. "Didn't even occur to me, but you know what? I think that might just be what they need."

"Good. Hope it works out. They're still beautiful."

"Edgar, did you hear me tell her to get a move on?"

Edgar shook his head at his old friend, and they got back to work as Idina strolled across the grounds again.

She wasn't thinking about sick plants or easily won chess games. At this point, she honestly wasn't even thinking about the ridiculous family meeting yesterday or the conversation she'd overheard between her grandfather and parents last night.

At least I'm not the only one around here who's different. If I do take after Richard the way Edgar and Mason said I do, maybe my uncle's the key to getting out of this whole mess. I only have to convince Reggie to spill the beans on a nine-year-old family secret. Piece of cake, right?

CHAPTER SEVEN

Fortunately, cake was what Mrs. Yardly had whipped up after dinner that night. A delicate angel food cake with strawberries baked inside and homemade whipped cream slathered all over the top.

After hearing that Reggie was holed up in his suite on the fourth floor to go over the staff payroll reports—unrelated to Moorfield & Associates' financial matters and therefore the head of staff's responsibility—Idina snatched up two plates and forks from the kitchen and headed out again.

"You're taking that to Reggie?" Mrs. Yardly looked entirely unconvinced.

"Well, I wouldn't grab two forks if I planned on eating both of these." The girl flashed a devious smile.

"Honey, that man never touches my cake."

"He does when I bring it to him. Looks delicious." With that, Idina left the kitchen and headed for the back stairwell. The three flights of stairs didn't do a thing to dampen her spirits or make her rethink her latest plan.

Reggie can keep a secret. He's been keeping them for over fifty years, hasn't he? No one will ever know I went to him for this little talk.

When she reached the fourth floor, it was easy to find Reggie's apartment—much smaller than any on the third floor inhabited by the Moorfields, of course. It was the only open door at 6:24 p.m., and the light from his room spilled out into the hall that remained empty between the hours of 4:00 a.m. and 9:00 p.m. At least when the staff wasn't preparing for one more epic party hosted at Moorfield Manor.

Idina stopped in front of the open door and found the butler sitting in a room that looked very much like a miniature version of Harold Senior's study—dark paneling, dark walls, wooden furniture in dark fabric, an old grandfather clock along the wall. Unlike the study, however, Reggie's retiring room lacked the massive conference table and the imposing oakwood desk centered in the back. There was a set of double doors there instead, which Idina assumed opened into the butler's bedroom.

A thin stream of smoke snaked into the air from the red and black pipe Reggie held in one hand. He puffed on it while diligently typing into a laptop with only the index finger of his other hand.

I'll be standing here all night like this.

Idina cleared her throat, and the butler practically jumped out of his armchair. "Miss Idina." He instantly withdrew the pipestem from his mouth and moved to tamp it out. "What are you—"

"Is that the tobacco I got you?" She leaned against the doorframe with a grin.

"I... Yes, as a matter of fact." Reggie chuckled and let out a demure little cough of surprise. "It's quite good."

"Well, don't waste it. I don't mind if you smoke a pipe around me. I'm pretty sure my lungs are developed by now."

"Ah. Old habits, I suppose. There won't be any little Moorfields running around here for quite some time."

"Not unless Celeste suddenly decides she wants to..." Idina glanced at the ceiling. "Incubate a tiny parasite."

"That *is* what she called it, isn't it?" They both laughed, and Reggie sat back in his armchair again, once more at ease. "So then. To what do I owe the honor of this..."

His smile faded and his eyes widened when he saw two plated slices of Mrs. Yardly's angel-food cake in her hands. "What did you do this time?"

"What, I can't bring a piece of cake upstairs to eat with a friend?" She waltzed into the room and plopped down in the only other chair opposite the coffee table where he worked.

"I'm a seventy-two-year-old butler, Miss Idina. Surely you have more appropriate friends."

"Not tonight." She set down both plates and slid one of them toward him, *clinking* the fork down gently beside it. "Thought you might want some."

"Yes, I can see that. What, may I ask, would give you cause to believe tonight is a night for sharing cake with a friend?"

They'd played this game so many times before, Idina didn't have to say anything at this point. Reggie retired every night to his private quarters the second the kitchen staff finished serving dinner to their employers to avoid the dessert. The man had a weakness for such treats, especially Mrs. Yardly's. Idina was thirteen when she discovered an alliance offering like this could get her almost anything she wanted from the man. Within reason.

Cake better be enough for this. Or I'm out of ideas.

Reggie slowly closed his laptop, set it gently down on the side table beside the standing lamp hanging over his armchair, then removed his reading glasses. "You're not going to tell me what this is about, are you?"

"There's nothing to tell, Reg." She cut off a small bite of cake and shoved it quickly into her mouth before stabbing her fork toward the dessert. "Except for how delicious this is."

"I see." He watched her for a moment, then sighed heavily and finally relented. The pipe settled gently down on the coffee table before he raised the dessert plate delicately into his lap and got to work.

Idina watched him intently.

For how much he loves this, he still looks like I put a gun to his head and told him to get back to work.

That made her chuckle, and Reggie looked up at her with wide eyes. He swallowed before speaking. "What's so amusing?"

"Don't look like you enjoy it or anything."

"Hmm. No, I enjoy it very much." He brought another bite to his lips and sat back in the armchair, briefly closing his eyes. "Too much, perhaps."

Idina didn't say anything for a few more minutes as the butler savored his rare dessert. She'd stopped touching hers altogether, but when he opened his eyes, she went right back to eating as though she'd never stopped.

Now I got him.

"You know what I've been thinking about today?"

He chuckled. "I couldn't possibly begin to guess."

"I've been thinking about Uncle Richard."

Reggie paused with another bite raised halfway to his mouth, then slowly lowered it back to the plate. "I see."

"You know, about the last time he was here for a visit. That one Christmas, remember?" She took another bite to show him they were still enjoying dessert together.

"How could I forget?" he said dully.

He's onto me. Crap. The cake wasn't enough.

She had to dive in quickly, or the door would shut right in her face. "Reggie, what happened that night?"

With a grimace, he set the cake offering back down on the coffee table and pulled a handkerchief from his breast pocket to dab at the corner of his mouth. "That was a long time ago."

"Not that long ago. Come on. You remember everything. You're like a machine keeping this place running."

"Miss Idina, I understand your frustrations with the way certain events took place yesterday—"

"I'm not talking about yesterday, Reg. Already forgotten about." She scooted toward the edge of the armchair cushion and leaned forward. "I'm talking about Richard. I hope you'll talk about him with me. Because I have questions."

"That doesn't surprise me in the least." He fixed her with a concerned frown and took on that highly condescending tone of pity used around the very young and old. Or the very outcast like her. "Miss Idina, are you feeling well?"

"What?"

"I can't help but notice a bit of odd behavior from you lately. Would you like me to get in touch with Dr. Kruchek?"

Idina pressed her lips together and tilted her head. "There's nothing wrong with my medication, Reggie. I wish people would stop asking me that."

"We're all invested in your wellbeing. Even those of us who can't claim you as a blood relation."

Why is everything about my stupid meds and who I'm related to? Fine. I'll play.

"I bet my Uncle Richard appreciated you being invested in *his* wellbeing too, right?"

"I beg your pardon."

Okay, well, at least I've got him begging now.

She leaned forward a little more and nodded. "Was he on the same medication? Dr. Kruchek's...up there in years. He could've already had his practice when Richard was my age, right? Before he left Moorfield Manor."

Reggie lowered his head and shook it very slowly. "I believe that would breach a certain level of doctor-patient confidentiality, don't you think?"

"Ha. You're not Richard's doctor."

"True. I don't have the kind of information you're looking for, Miss Idina. If I did, it's simply not my place to say. You're already well aware the topic of Mr. Moorfield's youngest son is highly frowned upon in this house."

"I am." Idina sighed. *Worth a shot, I guess.* "I still can't get rid of this feeling that something about what happened with Uncle Richard is important for me to understand, you know? Specifically why the whole family practically blew up when he stormed out that Christmas. It *was* a falling out, right?"

Reggie raised his eyebrows and scanned the surface of the coffee table. "There was an exchange of words, yes. Beyond that, there's really nothing more I can tell you."

"What about what happened afterward? Where did he go?"

"Hmm. I believe he left New England to branch out on his own. I imagine he went in search of something that fully utilized his unique skillsets, whatever those turned out to be."

"Just not the *family talents*, right?"

Reggie's eyes widened, then he blinked quickly and cleared his throat. "Something of the sort."

"What about talents like mine?" Idina quickly fluttered her hand through the air in front of her. "Maybe you don't know if Richard had to take the same meds, but you must remember whether or not he had episodes like mine."

The man studied her for a long moment, tapping his right thumb and index finger together like he did when he was trying hard to keep his composure.

Come on, Reg. If anyone's gonna tell me about Richard, it's you. Who'll know?

Finally, he flashed her a weak smile and nodded. "I'm sure you could find one Richard Moorfield in a directory somewhere. Online, perhaps. Right now, Miss Idina, I really must be getting back to the rest of my work for the evening."

Damn. I almost had him.

"Yeah. I understand." Snatching up her plate and fork,

Idina stood and took the rest of her dessert with her. "Thanks anyway."

The man hummed in enjoyment, and when she turned, she found the other plate back in his lap and the butler lifting his fork toward her in farewell. "Thank you for the cake."

"Anytime."

"I certainly hope not."

Idina smirked and headed down the hall toward the back staircase used only by the staff, and the one Moorfield who didn't feel like a trip to the fourth floor was beneath her.

The cake worked, all right. He's way too calculating. And looking out for himself. Can't blame him for that. Grandfather would lose it if anyone found out the butler's reviving old stories nobody wants to think about anymore. Then they'd all know I was the one who asked about Richard, and that's not gonna get me anywhere. Maybe I should try to look him up online.

She snorted.

Right. Like the outcast Moorfield has a bunch of social media accounts pointing right to where he is, what he's doing, and all the family secrets he knows. If he went off the grid enough for our family to leave him alone, I wouldn't be able to find him. Unless our family doesn't care about where he went or what he's up to these days. How is that even possible?

CHAPTER EIGHT

When she reached the third-floor landing, the loud pounding of some godawful music blasted down the hall from Bryan's room. As the two youngest Moorfields, he and Idina hadn't received their "full-on apartments" yet, mostly because those didn't exist. Bryan hadn't been working with the firm for more than two years. He might not have asked for an upgrade to his room, which rivaled any large suite at a five-star hotel anyway.

He'll probably never move out of there. Not if he stays here to keep working for the family. They'll never let him move anywhere else in the house because all his noise is as far away from everyone else's rooms as possible. Except mine.

Her brother's noisiness never really bothered her. It wasn't as bad as when Timothy went over the top on a weekend bender and strutted up and down the halls in the south wing of the third floor, reciting obtuse poetry and begging anyone who got too close to listen to the whole thing while he poured himself another gin.

Idina hardly ever saw her sister Celeste and their oldest

brother Maxwell outside normal working hours. They were both married. They shared a fully functional apartment with their spouse. Why would they be walking around the manor at night when they had their private lives contained inside it?

The music coming from Bryan's room turned down a notch, then his voice carried above it down the hall. "No, Baxter. I don't *want* the next best thing. This isn't about the pricing, dammit! It's about you giving your word and me expecting you to keep it!"

He let out a frustrated growl, and at the same moment, a blaze of green light flared across Idina's vision, streaking from her brother's open bedroom door and across the hall right in front of her. The buzzing jolt of warning she'd had at least ten years to recognize flooded through her and made her stop.

A fraction of a second later, Bryan's glistening cell phone flew out the open door and crashed against the far wall of the hallway before falling to the floor in a dozen pieces.

Okay... I knew something *was coming. Just didn't expect it to be* that.

She stared at the phone pieces and tried to muffle a snort.

This whole family's insane.

"Shit," Bryan grumbled. "One job. How hard is that?"

Idina peered around his open door and found her brother sprawled out on the couch with his arms slung over the back. His head dropped back before he let out a heavy sigh of frustration, and with that sigh came a massive cloud of pungent white smoke.

"That's the third one this month, isn't it?"

Bryan jumped and twisted over the back of the couch to see her standing there in the doorway. "Shit. Shit. Idina, what..." He scooted forward and leaned over the coffee table to frantically snuff out the joint he'd just lit. "What are you doing here?"

"I live here."

He snorted. "You know what I mean."

"Besides almost getting my head taken off by a flying cell phone? Not much. Just walking around. And eating cake." She lifted the plate as proof, and her brother glanced behind her into the hallway.

"Cool. Hey, shut the door, will ya?"

"Because I'm *not* the only one who walks down this end of the south wing?"

Bryan rolled his eyes and pointed at the door. "Just do it. Last time Dad found me with this, he... I mean, he lost it."

"Must've been awful for you." Her sarcasm wasn't lost on either of them, but she closed the door and joined him on the suede couch in front of his seventy-two-inch flatscreen.

"You don't know what it's like, man." He ran a hand through his disheveled brown hair and gazed at the ceiling again. "Always having him on your back like he is."

"Really?" Idina set her cake plate down beside the snuffed-out joint still smoking a little on one end. "*I* don't know what it's like?"

Her brother turned toward her and blinked as if he'd only now realized his little sister was in his room and talking to him. "Shit. Of course, you know. I know you know. Hey, about yesterday—"

"I didn't expect you to stick your neck out for me." She shrugged. "So don't worry about it."

"They said unanimous decision, Dee, but it wasn't. Not really. Hell, if Dad and Mr. Senior didn't give *me* a second chance—and a third—I wouldn't have made it this far in the company either. Hang in there."

"That's the thing, though." Idina crossed her legs beneath her on the cushions and stared at the end of his joint. "I don't want to hang in there. I want out."

"Really." He rolled his eyes toward her, then noticed she wasn't kidding around. "Wait, for real?"

"Yeah. Hey, can I ask you something?"

Bryan leaned against the armrest and shrugged. "I mean, even if I say no, you're still gonna ask."

She let that little jab slide and focused instead on the best way to frame her question. Out of all her siblings, Bryan was the only one she felt remotely close to, and it was only on a surface level. He was twenty-four—seven years older than Idina and only two years younger than Celeste. The first four Moorfield children had all been born two years apart. Perfectly planned. Perfectly groomed to take on their roles within the family and Moorfield & Associates.

It wasn't like she and Bryan were best friends by any means. At least she could see him smoking a joint in his room, he could listen to whatever she had to say, and neither one of them would make a big deal out of it.

"Well?" He snickered. "Am I finally wrong about you, or do you have a question?"

"Bryan, do you *like* what you do?"

He wrinkled his nose, then burst out laughing. "Damn, Dee. You're cutting right through all the bullshit, huh?"

I have no idea what that means, and he's stoned. Which probably makes this the perfect time to ask.

"I'm serious. Do you like it? Working for the firm and being a part of that whole...thing."

"Yeah, I'm good at it. They never would've brought me on if I wasn't."

Idina shook her head. "That's not what I asked."

Her brother stopped laughing and cocked his head like a bird of prey wondering where all the mice scurried off to. "Are you screwing with me?"

"Nope. Do you like what you do? Like, does it make you happy?"

"Huh." Scratching his head, Bryan looked her up and down. "Yeah, I guess it does. I mean, that's what we *do*, Dee. We're Moorfields. It's in our blood."

She grimaced and looked away from him. *That's what I didn't wanna hear.*

"Why? You have some other big plans for your future?" He'd obviously meant it as a joke, and whatever her face looked like now, he quickly picked up on his having hit the nail right on the head. "Oh, shit. Wait, *that's* what this is about?"

"I hate it. I know I only worked on those accounts for... what? Six weeks? It sucks. What we *do* makes me wanna gouge my eyes out with a letter opener."

"Here I was thinking you'd gone off your meds or something."

Idina opened her eyes as wide as they would go and

fixed her brother with a deadpan stare. "You're kidding, right? Tell me you're kidding."

"Aw, man. Come on." Now he looked worried. "Don't tell me you're considering something like that."

"Gouging my eyes out? Or going off my meds?" She let out a bitter laugh. "'Cause I kinda need my eyes."

Bryan looked her up and down, squinting and leaning slightly closer as if he were looking for clues on her clothes. "What about…"

"No. I didn't go off my meds."

Did the whole family and staff get together for a manor meeting about keeping Idina's little supernatural episodes at bay or what?

"Yeah, okay. Good." Bryan nodded and bared his teeth in discomfort. "'Cause that… That'd be pretty messed up."

I don't think all the pot is gonna make him any better at his job than he is right now. He sounds like he's lost all his brain cells already.

They sat quietly on the couch with the pumping bass from his state-of-the-art stereo system softly filling his room. Then Bryan turned toward her again and drew a sharp breath. "Okay, but what do you mean, 'Does it make me happy?' 'Cause it sounds like you've got something else in mind that makes you feel that way."

Finally.

"I do." Idina sat back against the couch cushions and rolled her head toward him. "Art."

"Art."

"Yeah."

"Like, pretty much the complete *opposite* of what we do. Like, the total other half of the brain. That kinda art?"

"I didn't know there was another kind."

He barked out a laugh.

"Why is that so funny to everyone, huh? I'm good."

"Hell, I know you're good. I thought it was a hobby or something, okay? Something to kill time. Chill out." Bryan surged forward to snatch up the joint and a lighter, lit the end, then puffed a few times before offering his little sister the joint while holding his breath.

Idina looked him up and down. "Nope."

"Suit yourself." He exhaled deeply, then dangled the smoking joint over the armrest of the couch. "So that's what you meant yesterday when you said you weren't going to Harvard. Because of art."

"Wow. You're *not* as dumb as you look."

"Hey, the weed's only at night. You know, for my nerves."

She huffed out a laugh and gazed around his tasteful-yet-scattered bachelor pad of a room. "I wonder where *those* came from."

He ignored her and took another drag. "Lemme get this straight. You don't wanna go to Harvard, for whatever reason. Fine. What the hell are you gonna *do* with your life after that?"

"Oh, man... You know what?" She batted her eyelashes at him in mock surprise. "I never even *thought* about it."

Hissing out a laugh and another cloud of smoke, Bryan shook his head. "Smartass."

"Pothead."

"No, really. You asked your question. Now I'm asking mine."

Idina drew a deep breath, stared at the cloud of smoke

hovering above them, and shrugged. "I want to go to college. Just not Harvard."

"Okay, like where?"

"Dartmouth—"

Her brother's violent laugh quickly turned into hacking coughs as he choked on the smoke and opted to snub out the joint again. Then he grinned at her and blew more smoke away from both their faces. "Are you fucking serious?"

"Yeah." She stared at him. "I am."

"Shit. Hold on." He grabbed a universal remote for all the weird gadgets in his room and clicked it a few times before finally turning on the air purifier mounted to the ceiling. "Dartmouth. Jesus. Do Mom and Dad know?"

"Not yet." Idina thought of the entire binder with her full *proposal* probably still resting in the trashcan in Harold Senior's study. That hadn't been her only copy, of course. She wasn't *that* naïve. But it still hurt to think about the binder. "After yesterday, I'm pretty sure it'll take hell freezing over for them to even listen to what I want."

"That's what you want?" Bryan slung his arm over the armrest again and licked his lips. "Like, for real? You wanna go to art school and be an artist, get a degree in all that, and…what? Draw for a living?"

"There's a little more to it than that, but yeah. Basically."

He puffed out his cheeks. "That's a lot of student loans."

"It's not. I got a massive scholarship."

"You…" Squinting and trying to figure out if she was still screwing with him, Bryan jerked back against the couch. "You already got in?"

"Yeah. Filled out all the paperwork. Got accepted. Got a

scholarship. All I need is their signatures. This isn't a pipedream, okay? I'm not running around looking for 'anything but Harvard.'"

"Ha. Okay. That's fair. I mean, the board's gonna have a stroke when you tell them…"

"The *board* isn't a living entity. Which everyone seems to have forgotten."

"Damn, you really do hate it, don't you?"

Idina swallowed. "That's what I said."

"And you're in love with art."

"If that's how you wanna look at it, sure." She rolled her eyes and studied his collection of DVDs on the entertainment center despite DVDs mostly going out of use when she was still a kid. "Yeah. I'm in love with it."

"All right, how about this?" Bryan pressed a fist to his lips and cleared his throat. "If this is what you want, and you're not making shit up about getting in and having a scholarship just to impress me—"

Idina snorted and folded her arms.

"No, wait. Hear me out. If all that's true, Dee, and you wanna go to art school, I'll put in a good word for you with Dad and Senior."

The bottom of her whole world fell out for a second, and the only thing that brought her back was her brother's low chuckle.

"You still there?"

"Seriously?" She grinned. "You'd do that? Even after the whole *unanimous decision* to—"

"Screw unanimous decisions, okay? Listen, I don't understand what the whole point of art is beyond hanging it on the wall. Let alone making the stuff. Goes right over my head."

"Understandable."

"Ha. But yeah. Really. I'll talk to them for you. Let them know you already have everything squared away. Hell, it's not like *I* have anything to lose. You wanting to go to *any* college is a lot better than you refusing to go anywhere. Right?"

"Yeah." Idina huffed out a laugh. "That's what I think. I hope they'll see it that way."

"I mean, I'm not making any promises, and I have no idea how much it'll help. You know Grandfather. He's… stuck, sometimes. Like, tunnel vision, you know? And yeah, they run the firm like it's the only thing in life that matters and won't admit to all the lovey-dovey shit, but we're family. Even if you're not in the *family business.*"

"Thanks. Really, that's—"

"Don't. It's no big deal. You going to *any* college is better than you staying here and screwing up client accounts all summer, right?"

"Ha. Right."

"Call it an early birthday present. When you're all famous and doing art tours with all your groupies following you, I get a big-brother discount. Just saying."

Idina thought she might explode trying to hold in a laugh. "I think you might have being an artist confused with being a rockstar."

"Oh, yeah? See, that's what I mean. Just goes right over my head." Her brother playfully smacked her knee with the back of a hand, then pointed the universal remote at the giant TV to turn it on before scrolling through the available channels—which were all of them.

Subscriptions to every single TV network must be his smallest bill. Especially when he keeps breaking his cell phones like that.

It felt like a strange thought to have, and she quickly shook it out of her head. Money wasn't an issue for the Moorfields, obviously, and neither were bills. Now that she was one step closer to the *possibility* of going to Dartmouth to pursue what she loved, the idea of having to take responsibility for her finances felt a lot closer to reality than she'd expected.

If they let me go this year. Even if they do, *there's no way they'll keep paying for everything I need while I'm gone. Not when they see it as me defying the whole family.*

"Oh, wait. Check this out." Bryan selected something on AMC, and the gigantic screen filled with the dark, gritty, bloody scene of some war movie playing out. The actors were almost life-sized on the TV as they belly-crawled through the mud between waves of bullets throwing huge clods of dirt into the air all around them.

"Man." He snorted and shook his head. "Look at that, Dee."

"You have a problem with explosions or something?"

"What? No. It's a movie."

Idina pressed her lips together. *Yeah, he's still stoned.*

"Shit like this happened, you know? It *still* happens. War. I don't get how people still join the military without a draft. Like, they *choose* it. Who the hell would do that?"

She glanced sidelong at her brother. "You ever think about joining the military?"

"Hell no. Are you kidding? Senior would've lost his shit. Probably have an aneurysm or something."

"Probably because he can't get his hands on military spending."

They both laughed, and Bryan cocked his head as he studied the gruesome scene playing out in front of them. "Probably. Whatever his reason is, he's *not* a fan of the military. Dad isn't either."

"What did he say about it?"

"Huh? Oh, nothing much. I mean, I think you were still wearing diapers the last time I heard either of them talk about it as a major issue. But I remember. Always have. They think the military's only for people who can't use their heads well enough to stay above water. So they resort to their fists and blindly following someone else's command, no matter what it is."

"They said all that?"

He leaned toward her without looking away from the TV. "I'm probably paraphrasing."

Okay, so his brain is still in there somewhere. I guess if Mr. and Mrs. Moorfield had to have a pothead for a youngest son, at least he's not an idiot.

"Listen, Dee." With his red-rimmed, glassy eyes still glued to the screen, Bryan shook a finger at the movie. "If your only choices were between going to art school and…I know, joining the Army or something, Dad would jump on art school for sure."

"You think so?"

"In a fucking heartbeat." A bomb went off in the movie, and Bryan cringed away before laughing and reaching for the joint again. "You sure you don't want any of this? It's good stuff, I promise."

"Still sure. Good talk, though." Idina stood. "You're not gonna forget about talking to them for me, right? About Dartmouth?"

"What? No way. I won't forget." He lit up for another hit, held his breath, then blew it back out again straight up at the air purifier humming on the ceiling. "Can't get my damn weed guy to keep his word, but I sure as shit do."

Her brother didn't take his eyes off the screen once, absorbed by the action and whatever weird thoughts were swimming around in his half-baked brain.

"I'm holding you to it, Bryan." Idina set her hand down on his shoulder and shook him.

He hissed out a laugh and playfully slapped her hand away. "I'm not hugging you."

"Good." For another minute, she stood behind his couch and watched the wartime scene playing out on the TV. The more she thought about this great new idea her brother had given her, the more lifelike the uniformed soldiers on the screen seemed. Idina leaned farther forward, imagining it all in perfect detail until she realized a second too late she'd gone too far.

A low hum rose from the TV, followed by a sharp zap and a crackle of green sparks rippling across the screen.

"What the—" Bryan jumped halfway to his feet, then slumped back onto the couch again and groaned. "Are you kidding me?"

Shit.

"Enjoy the movie." Idina spun and headed toward his bedroom door.

"Was this you?" he called after her. "Dee, I'm serious. Why are you trying to break all my shit?"

She didn't have an answer for that, so she carefully opened his door enough to slip out quickly and avoid any more rank smoke spilling out.

"Take your fucking meds, Dee! Or you owe me a new flatscreen!"

Stifling a laugh, she shut his bedroom door, blinked, then hurried down the hall. Only when she reached her bedroom door in the same wing did she realize she'd left her half-eaten cake on his coffee table.

He won't even notice. Or he'll eat the cake when he gets the munchies and forget all about it. And the fact that I might've done something to his TV even I can't explain. And that's just because I'm focused.

As she entered her bedroom and closed the door behind her, Idina's mind worked all on its own to put the pieces together. She hadn't gotten anything particularly useful from questioning the staff about her Uncle Richard, but she also hadn't expected Bryan to be so weirdly helpful.

Anything but the military, huh? That's a hell of a card to keep in my back pocket. Even if Bryan does talk to them for me, we both know he couldn't promise anything.

She dropped onto the edge of her bed and scanned the furry gray rug beneath her feet. A slow smile of realization and renewed determination spread across her lips.

I'll have to play the game like Dad does. Better than Dad, even. He'll never see it coming.

CHAPTER NINE

With no "paid internship" to keep her busy during the day and none of her family bothering to ask what the youngest Moorfield child was doing with herself and all her newly released free time, Idina got to work.

She researched, made appointments, made a few preliminary calls, and scheduled two critical meetings. The first didn't require that much talking, but she was fine with it. The second, though—*that* was the meeting that would count. She had to put her best foot forward to make it go exactly the way she wanted.

Her work ethic and dedication to this little side project alone were one of the very few positive effects of being born into a family like hers. Still, the more she prepared for her upcoming meeting that Friday, the more she realized how overqualified she was. Even at seventeen.

It's not like this is plan number one. I have to impress the right people. Then I'll have everything I need.

When Friday rolled around, Idina raced through the

first floor of the manor and nearly ran into Reggie on her way out.

"Oh...my." The man spun and shot her a surprised smile. "Feeling better, I see."

She skidded to a stop beside the front door and spun with a grin. "Definitely. One might even say I'm...*excited*."

"About what, may I ask?"

"Just a little meeting I put together. Hey, if anyone asks, I took the Buick into Manchester for the day. I should be back by dinner."

"Shall I inform the Moorfields of the most appropriate method for contacting you?"

She snickered. "Really?"

"Should there be a need, of course."

Idina patted her back pocket with one hand and turned the doorknob with the other. "If they even have my cell number, they can call me. I doubt they'll notice I'm gone."

"I hope it goes well."

"Thanks, Reg. See ya." With that, she sped across the grounds toward the long garage that held all fifteen of the Moorfield family vehicles.

Two of them were town cars her grandfather still preferred to be driven around in whenever circumstances required his physical presence outside the manor. Her dad had a Mercedes and two Audi convertibles, her mom only drove the Lexus—and that was rare—and Maxwell and Celeste each had three luxury sedans between them and their spouses.

The other three were *supposed* to be shared between the three youngest Moorfield children, but Bryan and Timothy hadn't touched the Buick in years. Which, by default, made it Idina's.

She slid behind the wheel with a grin, waited for the garage door at the end to finish opening with agonizing slowness, and she was off. Not wanting to draw any attention, she drove slowly down the long drive leading from the front gates of the estate to Moorfield Manor.

Once she was through those gates, it was nothing but Idina and her car and the open road to Manchester, New Hampshire in front of her. Plus a few errant glints of green light in the corners of her vision and several possible sparkling bursts the other drivers on the road *might* have seen. If they were paying attention.

Idina was too excited to care what anyone else in the world saw or thought of the strange things she could do.

This is gonna work. It's actually gonna work. I'll get what I want, and they'll all think it was their idea.

The laugh that burst out of her didn't sound anything like herself, which was a little startling.

Focus. Drive. This is the first day of you taking charge of your life, Idina. Exactly the way you want.

Two and a half hours later, she sat in a small cubby with only a table and two chairs, her hands clasped patiently in her lap as she studied the woman on the other side of the table.

Idina glanced at the woman's nametag. *Staff Sergeant Johansen. I'll have to remember that, just in case.*

"Well, Idina. I have to say everything looks great on paper."

"Thank you."

"Looks like you've had fairly extensive martial arts training over the last ten years."

"Yes." Idina tried to peer over the top of the documents the woman held but sat back immediately when Staff Sergeant Johansen briefly looked up. "Brazilian jiujitsu, mostly. Also a few years of Taekwondo. And boxing."

"Definitely comes in handy." The woman flipped another page in her folder. "You said you're seventeen?"

"Yes, ma'am."

"You've already received an Associates in Business Administration from Southern New Hampshire University? Completed this past May right before you graduated from White Mountain with a four-point-two GPA."

"Correct. The GPA comes from honors classes. My parents wanted me to take those business courses, so I went along with it. It was easier that way."

Staff Sergeant Johansen raised her eyebrows, and the hint of a smile flickered across her lips. "Easier to complete a degree during your junior and senior year of high school."

Idina shrugged. "I mean, it was all entry-level stuff."

"Okay." The woman flipped through a few more pages, scanning the information Idina had already either sent over or had gotten various other parties involved to send directly to the woman's email once she'd made this appointment. "You seem pretty eager to get a move on with this."

Plastering on her most sincere smile, Idina nodded. "I am. This is what I want."

"I can see that. You know, everything else aside, you really wouldn't have to go through the traditional route from the bottom up."

Staff Sergeant Johansen tapped the papers in the folder with the tip of her pen. "The best path for you at this point might be to go to college for a few more years. There are excellent ROTC programs at the University of New Hampshire and Plymouth State. With your associates, you'd only have to spend another two years in school before you'd be able to come on as an officer. Most likely an O1 second lieutenant at that—"

"No!" Her knees bumped against the underside of the table when she jumped, but fortunately, the furniture blocked the burst of shimmering green light floating up from her hands. Staff Sergeant Johansen frowned and leaned sideways to check beneath the table, and Idina cleared her throat to distract them both. "Sorry. That was a little intense. I'm not interested in *more* school, you know? If I'm gonna do this, I want to do it now."

The woman chuckled and dismissed the incident. "I understand. There's one question I'm sure you've already answered, but I haven't heard personally yet, so bear with me, huh?"

"Sure." Sitting back in her chair, the girl looked straight ahead into the woman's gaze and nodded.

Whatever it is, I have an answer. She's easy enough to read. As long as I keep my emotions in check, and I've been doing that my whole life. Mostly.

"Why do *you*, Idina Moorfield, with all these opportunities at your fingertips, want to join the United States Army?"

That wasn't the kind of question she'd been expecting. For a moment, Idina's mind went completely blank. Then she dropped her gaze to the table and started talking without any real idea what she was going to say.

"I want to do this because where I am right now doesn't fit, you know? Those might look like pretty great opportunities on paper, but in reality, things feel...empty. I want a sense of purpose, Staff Sergeant Johansen, and I think the Army's where I'm gonna find that."

Wow. I have no idea where that came from, but at least I didn't have to make up a bunch of crap about being a diehard patriot or anything.

The woman's lips quirked again, and she set down the stack of papers in the folder before folding her hands on the surface of the table. "Well, I've heard less convincing answers."

"So that's it?" The girl sat a little straighter in her chair. "I'm in?"

"If this is the way you want to go, yes. You have one foot in the door. The first door of many. Right now, you still have a few options."

"Perfect."

Staff Sergeant Johansen chuckled. "First, if you go this route, you'll take the ASVAB. That's the qualifying exam to get your other foot through the door. If you have no problem passing that, the exam held at MEPS should be no problem for you either. Assuming you pass those and the physicals, you'll head out to basic training. The Army holds multiple cycles a year for enlisted recruits. Which, again, you wouldn't necessarily have to pass through if you decided you'd rather go the academic route with ROTC and become an officer."

Idina shook her head. "I'm sure that's a good option for some people, but I don't want to wait."

"Fair enough. Assuming you graduate basic, did you have an occupational specialty in mind?"

Idina shrugged. "The Corps of Engineers, I think. Unless you have a better suggestion."

The woman shook her head with a knowing smile. "I think that would be a great fit for you.

"Before you get that far, as a minor, you need your parents' permission to take the ASVAB exams. Until you turn eighteen, you're still in your parents' care. Getting them to sign off on emancipation to enter the military is *the* next step. Without that, you can't move forward until you're eighteen and would then start the next available cycle of basic."

"Right. And...if for whatever reason I *can't* get my parents' signatures?"

"Well, I always like to offer potential recruits the opportunity to bring their families in to discuss what those first three months would look like during basic. Especially families of bright young people like you who require those signatures to start right away. If that doesn't work, I'd then suggest you wait until you *are* eighteen and sign up for the next cycle. At that point, there would be nothing to stop you."

"I don't suppose you can waive the parent signatures since my birthday's so close?"

Staff Sergeant Johansen pursed her lips and shook her

head. "Nice try. Waiting an extra few months isn't all that long in the scheme of things. If you're that dead-set on joining right away, I'd work on getting your parents to sign off on it."

She pulled the necessary forms from the folder and slid them across the table. "When they do, you can send these right here to the office, and we'll get you on your way. If you'd like to take a general knowledge practice test today, I can get that set up for you now."

"Great." Idina grabbed the papers and didn't want to read over the forms her parents would never sign.

Not in a million years. Dad won't sign me into the Army, and if he somehow did, Grandfather might have that aneurysm Bryan was so sure about. Or a heart attack. That's the whole point.

It didn't take her long at all to complete the practice exam—even if she *hadn't* taken the time to read over every multiple-choice question and all the answers carefully, she would've known the correct answers based on which one glowed green in the computer.

The lights have never let me down with anything else. Taking a practice test for the Army isn't any different.

When she finished, she returned to Johansen's table to go over the results with the recruiter. The woman softly chuckled as she flipped from page to printed page. "You'll have no problem with the ASVAB, Idina. This is great. So, you have those forms for your parents and the next steps ahead of you. Are there any other questions I can answer for you now while we're sitting here face-to-face?"

"No, Staff Sergeant. Thank you so much for your time." Idina stood and stuck out her hand.

The recruiter for the U.S. Army looked her in the eye and nodded, though she hesitated a little before taking the girl's hand. But her smile widened as they shook. "Then I hope to hear from you soon."

"Absolutely." With the necessary paperwork in hand, Idina spun and headed through the recruiting office's front door.

This is what I needed. Now I have to set it all up, and I'll be packing for Dartmouth before the end of the month.

CHAPTER TEN

That next step, as it turned out, was scheduling a meeting with the three heads of Moorfield & Associates for that evening. Idina still had access to the online company calendar. For whatever reason, *the board* hadn't found it necessary to remove her from the database yet.

She went right in and picked the perfect time for tomorrow—6:15 p.m.

During the week, most of the family didn't stop working until it was almost time to hit the sack for the mandatory six hours of sleep before getting up to do it all over again the next day. Idina understood her parents well enough by now—if not her grandfather entirely—to know they'd be intrigued by a meeting their daughter had scheduled at the appropriate hour. It wouldn't cut into the most important hours of their work, and they'd have something to look forward to at the end of the day.

Once she hit the submit button on the calendar from her laptop in her room, Idina snorted.

Sure. They're looking forward to seeing what kind of crazy scheme I'm pulling out of thin air this time. They probably think I'm trying to redeem myself. I guess I can give them the same chance.

She went to bed that night without speaking to a single person in her family, and it felt amazing. No one asked where she'd been or tried to corner her into a confession. The thought of finally getting to make her move tomorrow pushed her down into a deep, fully satisfied sleep.

The next day was an exercise in patience if nothing else. Idina checked her emails obsessively as she meandered around the manor grounds. The calendar system would show her everything she needed to know about the process. First that both her parents *and* her grandfather had viewed the meeting request last night. They sure did keep her in suspense all day by neither confirming nor denying her request.

The meeting wasn't set.

They're trying to screw with you. Don't let them. You'll get the email. Then you're in.

It did occur to her how odd it was that she had to schedule a meeting with her family—outside of business hours—to sit and talk to them about something important to her. That was the way the Moorfields operated, and she'd learned a long time ago that trying to circumnavigate the system wouldn't get her anywhere.

It certainly hadn't gotten her anywhere when she'd wanted a souped-up bicycle for her eighth birthday. Once she'd drawn up a complete proposal for why she wanted that *specific* bike and how it would improve her childhood to receive it on that *particular* birthday, the doors opened right up. She'd learned how to play the corporate game within her family. Now she was using it.

That didn't exactly make it easier to wait around for a response from the top three executives of Moorfield & Associates.

Idina tried to take her mind off things by starting a new sketch, but the light was wrong, the wind picked up too heavily, and when it died again, the swarms of gnats wouldn't leave her alone. Beyond that, the pressures of waiting for this damned meeting wouldn't let her focus on working with her artistic green threads only she could see. Or maybe that was her meds deciding to work today.

She abandoned her attempts to take at least ten meandering strolls through the entire property, appreciating the blooming flowers and the apple trees starting to bud and the maples growing full and lush. By the time she considered trying to occupy her mind with another game of chess against either of the gardeners, Edgar and Mason had returned to work.

She didn't realize she'd skipped dinner altogether until she checked her email one more time and saw that her parents and Harold Senior had, in fact, accepted her request. At 5:55 p.m.

"Yes! Crap, it's almost six."

Idina shoved her phone back into her pocket and raced into the manor, her feet pounding across the marble floors and up the grand, sweeping staircase off the foyer only because it was closer.

If she'd been paying attention to the time, she

would've grabbed the Army intake forms sooner and given herself enough time to get back down to the study on the second floor without cutting it this close. The time crunch hardly mattered. Her heavy breathing and sore legs from so many stairs and her heart pounding in anticipation hardly mattered either when she hit the second-floor hallway in the north wing and finally slowed down.

This is it. They want me to take responsibility for my future? Great. There's no way they'll let me go into the Army just because they don't wanna send a Moorfield to art school.

She stopped, brushed her black curly hair away from her face, and drew a deep breath to steel herself. A final glance at her phone showed she still had one minute to spare. *Right on time.*

Her brisk knock on the door sounded like the call of her future. The one she wanted instead of what her family had written in stone for her because she'd been born into their bloodline—a family she sometimes didn't believe was hers.

"Come in," Harold Senior called from across the study.

Wiping the grin from her face, Idina turned the handle of one French door and swiftly opened it to step inside. Her parents stood beside her grandfather's imposing desk, behind which Harold Senior sat, of course, his hands folded on the oiled surface in front of him and his eyes slightly widened with intrigue.

Idina nodded at them all, pulled the door shut behind her, then walked calmly across the study to begin her meeting. The backup manilla folder of Army enlistment forms jutted crisply from one hand, bolstering her confidence and her dedication to get this done, one way or the other. "First, thank you for the opportunity to…"

She stopped when her father removed his hands from behind his back. Because in one of them was the white three-ring binder in which she'd put together her entire proposal for attending Dartmouth. The one she'd thrown in the trash after hearing how much like Uncle Richard she'd turned out to be and how much her family couldn't stand it.

Okay, so they probably know what this meeting is about. At least the terms will still hit them out of left field.

"You were saying?" her grandfather prompted.

"For the opportunity to speak with all of you about this," she finished, nodding at her grandfather. "I won't take up too much of your time."

"I'm assuming this is what you wanted to discuss tonight." Harry lifted the binder in his hand and tapped the outside with a finger. "Correct?"

"Yes." Idina stared at the slightly dented cover where she'd almost broken it with her bare hands the weekend before. "When I left that here, I wasn't…exactly in the right frame of mind to go into the details."

Her mother let out a soft, humming chuckle through her nose as she exchanged a knowing glance with her husband.

"I hope you have a backup copy," Harry added, his lips twitching into a small smile.

Wow. They're taking this a lot better than I expected.

Idina watched her parents looking more amused than frustrated and couldn't help but return the same small smile—one she didn't dare let grow much bigger than an acknowledgment of the circumstances. "Of course I have copies."

"That's good to hear."

After looking back and forth between his son and granddaughter for several seconds, Harold Senior cleared his throat. "Well, what is it?"

Idina looked at her scowling grandfather in surprise. *They didn't tell him. I didn't think anyone was even capable of keeping secrets from the head honcho. Holy crap, they're actually on my side.*

"Idina," Harold barked.

"Right." She nodded and clasped her hands behind her back. "It's—"

"Quite an impressive portfolio." Harry opened the binder and flipped through the pages, his eyes roaming back and forth and taking in the information she'd gathered at nearly inhuman speeds. Inhuman, at least, for anyone who wasn't a Moorfield, trained to take in any kind of information and absorb it completely at first glance.

"Financial statements included and organized efficiently. Projections for the next four years. Workable allocation of the provided funds among all the necessary—"

"I asked what it is, Harry," Harold snapped. "Not what I'd find in a portfolio. I already know how those work."

Idina's father looked up at her with a raised eyebrow, then bent over the desk and set the binder down before sliding it toward his father. "It's a proposal for college. A traditional four-year program to add on top of the associates Idina already received at the end of her last semester."

Harold Senior let out a surprised-sounding grunt and

met Idina's gaze without looking at the binder. "So you've finally decided to come around. Well, I can't say I'm not pleased with the idea. Every Moorfield for the last five generations has received their degrees from Harvard."

"Dartmouth," she corrected.

"Pardon?"

Idina glanced at her parents and received a subtle though entirely unexpected nod of approval from her mother. "It's not a proposal for Harvard, Grandfather. It's for Dartmouth. In Hanover."

Harold narrowed his eyes at her, then barked out a laugh and turned toward his son. "Dartmouth. Did you hear that? Why the devil would she hand in a proposal for some wishy-washy institution parading itself as an accredited university?"

"I imagine part of it has to do with Dartmouth having been an accredited university for quite some time," Harry muttered. Annette didn't smile, though her hand lifted delicately to her lips clearly showed she was on the verge of it.

Harold Senior had nothing more to say on the matter, but he surprised everyone by sliding the binder closer to inspect it the way Idina hadn't dared hope he would. The pages flickered back and forth under his wizened fingers, and when Idina looked at her parents again, she caught her father's slight tilt of the head toward the CEO of Moorfield & Associates sitting behind the desk.

He wants me to keep going with this. Because he supports what I want to do, or because he's trying to teach me a lesson? This is the weirdest meeting I've had with them, and that's saying something.

Idina cleared her throat. "I received my acceptance letter last month. The admissions essay I submitted is right there after the financial statements and cost projections for each semester. Page thirteen. Plus photocopies of the sample pieces requested as part of the application."

Her grandfather grunted again and kept flipping through the pages.

Jeez, now I do sound like a Moorfield. I can't even say how excited I am about this. I have to stand here like some dry, boring number-cruncher at a quarterly assessment.

She couldn't stop now, in case something she said caught her grandfather's attention and got him to listen.

"They've offered a sizeable scholarship as well," she added, unable now to look away from her grandfather diligently skimming everything in the binder. Any second now, he'd get to the personal portfolio of her work. "Merit-based, of course. But it's almost a full-ride."

"Almost a full-ride is not a full-ride, Idina." He didn't look up at her once.

"I understand. If you look at the projections, you'll see that the way I've allocated the offered funds across eight total semesters brings the out-of-pocket costs down to only five thousand a semester."

"Hmm. I suppose you expect *us* to provide forty thousand dollars out-of-pocket to this *accredited university* during those four years."

Idina swallowed thickly. "I don't expect anything, sir. I *do* believe this proposal shows the merit of my plan to attend Dartmouth and the benefits of such an investment toward—"

"Benefits? For whom?" Her grandfather finally looked

up at her, then turned his head toward his son standing right there beside the desk. "Harry, do you expect an appreciable return on an investment like *this*?"

"Perhaps not fiscally," Harry replied slowly. "But not all returns are."

"Nonsense."

"Idina has already sold a number of her pieces," Annette added. "Two at the charity gala last fall, I believe. Another at the silent auction during the annual—"

"Revenue and charity are two very different things."

"Her work *does* sell," Harry added.

"Not enough." Harold Senior sat back in his chair and tilted his head at his granddaughter. "Where are the projections for that?"

Idina pressed her lips together, determined not to show her frustration during the meeting she'd called herself. *I set myself up for this. Now I have to see it through.* "The pieces purchased at the charity gala last year each went for a little over five thousand dollars."

"And?"

"And the Admissions department at Dartmouth was impressed. If you turn to page seventeen, the first two photos are of those same pieces." She pointed at the binder. "Take a look."

Harold sat there with his hands folded on the desk again and blinked at her.

It's not like he can tell Van Gogh from Andy Warhol, but he should at least look at the artwork.

"I can make a career out of this, Grandfather. I know I can. Dartmouth thinks I can, and they've offered the scholarship because of it. This is what I want to do."

"What you *want*." He scoffed. "What you want has very little to do with it. What you *need,* on the other hand, is an impeccable education and something to show for it in the end."

"Yes, sir." She nodded and finally risked one more glance at her parents.

"Her admissions essay was particularly enlightening," her father added. "No doubt some would even call it moving. Her portfolio of past works has a certain *je ne sais pas* about it."

"Harry, you know how I feel about the French language."

Her father tilted his head but gave no indication of caring all that much about his father's eccentric reprimanding. "I think there's an opportunity for all of us here."

Idina's heart stopped, and the next time it pounded in her head, it sounded like all the other doors around her closing so the only one she wanted could finally open. *He called this an opportunity. This is happening!*

Harold Senior said nothing.

"We can all agree that Idina pursuing further education at any university will be beneficial to her," Harry continued, "no matter what path she chooses to pursue. Since it's come to our attention that securing a position with Moorfield & Associates may not be a stop on that path, I'm willing to take another look at additional options."

"Additional options." Harold pressed his lips together so tightly, they all but disappeared. "She doesn't have a job, Harry. No income. No assets of her own, at least for another few months. Who's going to fund the rest of that education?"

"We will," Annette said. "Provided, of course, that certain agreements are in place."

"Moorfield & Associates has invested in the higher education of young Moorfields for generations." Harry lifted his chin and looked at his daughter, fixing her with that stern gaze of his that, for her entire life, forewarned of his next statement being something he knew Idina wouldn't want to hear. "As long as Idina can agree to—"

"No."

Harry blinked quickly, then turned toward his father. "No *what*, Dad?"

Harold Senior sucked on his teeth, slid one hand beneath the cover of Idina's white binder, and slapped it shut before pushing it across the desk with a flick of his fingers. "Absolutely not."

Her parents had surprised her with their support for this—in *any* decision that came from her and wasn't someone else's idea first—but Idina had fully expected her grandfather to react this way. The patriarch was rigid in his beliefs. He'd inherited an empire from his father, and he'd grown that empire to staggering heights since.

What she didn't expect was to react forcefully to the way he'd denied her request.

"We most certainly will not fund Idina's attendance at Dartmouth," her grandfather continued. "All your other children, *my* grandchildren, have attended Harvard. You received your degree there, Harry, as did I. My father and his brothers. *Their* fathers."

Idina stared at the white binder.

He flicked it away like a crust of bread...

"This is the way Moorfields in *this* country, in *this*

century, better themselves to join the family." Harold stabbed a finger on the desk. "Idina is not an exception."

Harry cleared his throat. "Dad, I don't think—"

The Moorfield patriarch slammed a gnarled hand down on the desk. "I will *not* sanction the investment of Moorfield & Associates funds into *this* type of so-called collegiate education so Idina can sit around this estate all day with her...*doodles*! That's final."

It might've been final for Harold Moorfield Senior, but it also happened to be the last straw that broke Idina's self-restraint.

CHAPTER ELEVEN

"Doodles?" She hadn't meant to shout, but what she'd intended hardly mattered now anyway.

Her grandfather scoffed and lifted his hand for a flippant wave in her direction. "Or whatever you want to call it."

A blaze of electric heat and prickles of icy cold surged up and down Idina's spine, across her shoulders, and down her arms to her fingers. "I'm not *doodling*."

"Please. This isn't up for debate, Idina."

"I didn't earn this scholarship with doodles."

"Young lady, my decision is—"

"I earned it with my talent, *Harold!*" Idina's shout startled her parents more than anyone else. What surprised all of them more than they expected was the burst of shimmering green light like fading mist streaking away from every part of her body when she spat out Harold's name. Her grandfather and parents immediately dropped the argument they hadn't had the chance to begin. They all turned to stare at her.

The light and the inexplicable fog faded instantly, which gave the other three Moorfields in the room plenty of time to recover from the shock to focus on the real slight.

Idina had called him by his first name. Not "sir." Not "Mr. Moorfield." Not even "Grandfather."

Now she was on a roll, and there would be no stopping her.

"I have a chance to do something with my life that aligns with what *I* want." She took a small, furious step toward his desk. "I don't expect you to understand what that's like, since the only thing the rest of this family ever wants is to work for Moorfield & Associates, build the company, trade, grow a client base, and bring in more profit quarter after quarter.

"This is what I want to do. I made it this far, and I don't understand why you can't—"

"You are correct, young lady," Harold replied firmly, his eyes narrowing again in his wrinkled face. He didn't move a muscle as she stepped closer again. "I certainly *don't* understand."

Idina huffed out a wry laugh. "Fine. I *did* think you'd at least respect my decision and all the work I put into bringing this to you. To all three of you."

"*You* are not entitled to my respect," he barked. "Until you've earned it, I have no obligation to entertain such a frivolous daydream completely lacking in substance!"

"Dad," Harry cut in quickly. "Maybe we should take some time to think it over. Reconvene later to discuss more thoroughly—"

"There's nothing to discuss!" Harold Senior leapt from

his chair and slammed both hands down on his desk this time. "I was never this soft at your age, Harry. I do expect you to recognize your mistake in thinking this is a viable option for anyone, especially her."

"It's getting late," Annette said softly. "I think it's best if—"

"Don't coddle me like some old fool with half of his wits! As long as I draw breath, *I* am the head of this household, and *I* make the decisions." Harold pointed at Idina. "The only university you'll attend is Harvard."

She glared at her grandfather, vaguely aware of how tightly she clenched the manila folder in her hand, which had now dropped to her side. She kept her voice low and even in the face of his righteous indignation. "I'm not going to business school."

"Idina, you are a *Moorfield*!" A thin spray of spittle flew from his lips as he violently enunciated the last syllable.

The study fell incredibly quiet. Neither Harry nor Annette dared to intervene further on their own daughter's behalf, no matter how willing they'd been to find a middle ground with their youngest child. No one wanted to push Idina or Harold Senior any further than they already had. The Moorfield patriarch had a temper like a raging bull and Idina?

Idina was even more unpredictable. Even when she took her medication.

The only thing she could think of was how vehemently her grandfather had insisted she *wasn't* a true Moorfield when he thought no one was listening.

I guess true Moorfields are hypocrites too.

"You don't believe that," she muttered.

111

Harold blinked at her and cocked his head, his chest rising and falling much faster than usual as he tried to collect himself. "What are you talking about?"

"You don't believe I'm a Moorfield." Another surge of energy prickled along her flesh, but this time, she managed to keep the source of her weird green light show down to another slowly rising flutter of glittering specks. They floated into the air all around her before winking out again in seconds.

It was still enough to make Harold bluster all over again. "What I *believe* is none of your—"

"I know that's how you feel," Idina interrupted again, feeling her parents' stares on her and the telltale signs of another *episode* in the making. She didn't care. "It might help not to talk about your family behind their back. You know, in case you want them to believe you the next time you give your 'we're Moorfields' spiel."

Her father stepped forward toward her. "Idina, now is not the time."

"I think it is." She marched forward, whipped the manila folder up from her side, and slammed it down on her grandfather's desk. More green mist spewed from beneath the folder, and her grandfather shoved himself away from the desk as though she'd dropped a bomb on it instead.

With another brisk flick of her hand, she had the file open and quickly spread out all the necessary forms for everyone to see. "So I'll repeat it. I am *not* going to Harvard or any other business school. If you won't sign off on Dartmouth, there's always a third option."

Idina stepped back, folded her arms, and glanced from a

scowling Harold Senior to a wide-eyed Harry and finally to Annette, who'd lifted a hand to her mouth again, this time in dread.

"What's all this?" Harold growled, trying to skim the forms upside down and still refusing to look at her.

"Enlistment forms."

"*What?*" Her grandfather snatched up the first piece of paper he could get his gnarled hands on and almost scattered the rest of them right off the desk.

"For the Army."

"Idina." The concerned disbelief in her mother's voice was entirely new. The young woman held her ground as her parents shared a horrified look.

The sound of fluttering paper in Harold's hand made her look at him again, and she found her grandfather trembling from head to toe, his face reddening deeply. "How *dare* you try to threaten me with such...such—"

"It's not a threat, Grandfather. I met with an Army recruiter yesterday."

"Why in God's name would you even consider such a thing?" Harry croaked.

"Because I want to get out. I can't go anywhere without your permission and your signatures either way. Not until I'm eighteen."

Her mother stared at the forms scattered across the desk and slowly shook her head. "Sweetheart, this isn't a game."

"Oh, I know. The next cycle of basic training starts September first. Either I go to Dartmouth with the same blessing you gave everyone else to pursue their passion, or you can sign these papers right now, and I'll be out of your hair."

Harry shook his head. "This isn't what you want."

"Well, at least I'm giving *you* a choice." She gestured at the forms. "Dartmouth isn't going to hold that scholarship forever. So if you don't choose anything, I'll miss both deadlines. Once I turn eighteen, *then* I'll sign up for the next cycle of basic in December all on my own. Bottom line is I'm not staying in this house for the rest of my life, and I'm *not* going to business school."

"This—" Harold Senior cut himself off with a thick choking sound, and the form he'd clenched in his shaking hand fluttered to the desk. Then he pounded his fist on the heavy wood and let out the kind of enraged roar Idina had only heard in movies.

"This is the *same* insolence Richard brought into this household. Only he had the decency not to blackmail the entire family into doing what he wanted."

"I'm not blackmailing anyone," Idina shot back. "I'm giving you guys options, which is way more than anyone's ever been willing to give *me*—"

"Richard left on his own! Cut ties swiftly and decisively without drawing everyone else into his petty daydreams. He had *integrity*, dammit. You want to follow in his footsteps by bringing goddamn *enlistment* papers into *my* house!"

He swept an arm across the desk and sent most of the forms fluttering to the area rug in front of him. "Is this what you want, Idina? To cast aside your legacy and end up like *my son*?"

Idina slowly dropped her gaze to the paper that had halfway landed on top of her shoe.

Guess I pushed his buttons. Bryan wasn't kidding about hatred for the military. Of course, no one's gonna bring up my meds or another little fireworks episode at a time like this. That would only prove they're afraid of me. But there's no other way for me to get out of this.

"Idina Moorfield," Harold roared, "I asked you a question!"

"That's enough, Dad," Harry barked. His father turned a scathing glare on him, still trembling with rage, then slowly lowered himself into his office chair.

When no one else moved or looked like they were about to speak, Idina crouched to collect the scattered forms, carefully rearranged them, and set them on the desk one more time. "Dartmouth needs an answer from me in the next two weeks. I hope that's long enough for the board to reach a *unanimous decision.*"

That extra bit of sarcastic disdain on her part made her father whip his head toward her, his eyes wide and his lips pressed firmly together. "This meeting is over, Idina. You may leave."

She nodded and briefly met his gaze before glancing at her grandfather again. Harold fumed in his chair, looking so much older after his outburst—as if the furious loss of his composure had sucked ten years off the end of his life.

"Thank you for your time," she muttered, then spun and quickly crossed the study. Before she could shut the doors behind her and block out all sound from the study on the other side of the thick wooden panels, she caught her father's final admonishment to the head of the Moorfield bloodline.

"No one's impressed by the way you handled that, Dad."

Harold grunted.

"We can discuss how to move forward with this once you've had a chance to calm down."

The doors *clicked* softly shut behind Idina, and she froze in the hall for a few seconds to take it all in.

Holy crap, I did it. I played hardball with Harold Moorfield I, and I might be the first person to break him down. Weirds lights or no weird lights. A huge grin split her lips as she thought of how well she'd handled herself and her grandfather's raging outburst against the defiance of Moorfield tradition.

Mom and Dad want me to go. They see how great Dartmouth will be for me. They know I can handle it. If I started a chain reaction of the family finally thinking for themselves, I'm gonna get out of here exactly the way I wanted. I can't believe it.

When a small bubble of laughter burst from her lips, she clapped a hand over her mouth and breathed deeply through her nose. Then one of the study door handles turned, and Idina raced down the hall to head up to her bedroom before whoever opened that door had a chance to see her standing there. She could celebrate alone in her room.

She'd given her entire family an ultimatum. The way the Moorfields operated, they would choose the path of least resistance—meaning she'd be packing up her things two weeks from now to start her first semester at Dartmouth.

Whatever she'd done in that meeting to trigger her

grandfather's anger the way her Uncle Richard had, there was no possible way her family would sign her up for basic training as a minor. Whatever Richard had done nine years ago, Idina didn't think it was anywhere near as bad as threatening to join the Army.

———

Those next two weeks of waiting for a decision from her parents, however, were more excruciating than waiting for them to accept her request for a meeting. Idina managed to create a few new sketches during that time, and she poured all her energy and focus into her morning training session with Master Rocha. Even that wasn't quite enough of an outlet for all her pent-up excitement.

They'll eventually cave. It's a matter of time, and the clock's ticking for all three of them like it is for me. There's only one good decision here. I'm going to art school.

None of her family tried to approach her about the incident with her grandfather or what the fallout would be when they agreed that they'd have to break the family tradition of a four-year education at Harvard on Idina's account. Her mother was strangely cordial whenever they passed each other in the halls. Her father readily met her gaze and nodded, muttering a soft, "Good morning, Idina," or, "Good night, Idina. Sleep well."

Beyond that, she avoided her family as much as possible, including Bryan. She had no idea if he'd spoken to their parents about Dartmouth the way he'd promised he would, but at this point, she was sure it didn't matter.

She'd already proven her point in that meeting, and none of them could go back now.

Two days before the extended deadline the Dartmouth admissions office had given her to make her decision, Idina sat in the rose garden, studying the flowering blossoms all around her for some new still-life sketches. In one of them, she'd even captured a round, fuzzy bumblebee and was particularly proud of the attempt. The warm New Hampshire breeze fluttered through the bushes, rustling the leaves and rose petals and filling the air with the strong fragrance of so many perfect blossoms.

Idina closed her eyes and drew a deep breath, letting herself enjoy the moment on a beautiful summer day where everything finally felt like it was happening *for* her instead of *to* her.

This is everything I want. Either today or tomorrow, they'll say yes. They're waiting until the last minute because they want me to squirm.

As she was packing up her sketch supplies to head into the manor for lunch, her cell phone buzzed in her back pocket. She whipped it out and found an unknown number there that solicitor screening hadn't caught.

"Huh." Idina stood with her supplies tucked under her arm and answered the call. "This is Idina Moorfield."

"Hi, Idina." The woman on the other line sounded happy and upbeat. "Is now a good time to talk?"

The butterflies in Idina's belly buffeted around with

renewed excitement. *Maybe they already called the school to accept the scholarship for me...*

"Definitely. May I ask who's calling?"

"Oh, sorry. I thought I'd given you my number. This is Staff Sergeant Johansen with the Army recruiting office in Manchester."

Idina swallowed thickly, and the butterflies instantly dropped into the pit of her stomach. "Oh. Hi, Staff Sergeant. Listen, I know it's getting close to the cut-off date for sending in the forms, but I—"

"No, no. You're fine. I wanted to let you know that we received them here at the office, and everything's squared away. You were incredibly proactive, so we have everything else we need here on our end. You're good to go."

"Wait, what? When did that happen?"

The woman chuckled. "It looks like your parents faxed in the signed release for minors yesterday afternoon. There are still a few more steps to take between now and starting the first phase of basic.

"If you pass the ASVAB, you'll make it in time to start the next cycle at Fort Leonard Wood in Missouri on September first. The next available date to take those exams is August twenty-second at the MEPS in Manchester. Get to that, pass your exams, and the rest is a piece of a cake."

"I..." For the first time since she was a young child, Idina couldn't think of anything to say. "August twenty-second?"

"That gives you a few days to decide. Things can get a little crazy if you wait 'til the last minute. I've emailed you all the information you'll need before you come in, so take some time to look that over. Call me if you have any questions. Now you have my number."

"Right. Um...thanks."

"Don't mention it. It was great meeting you. Good luck." Staff Sergeant Johansen ended the call before Idina had a chance to say anything else.

She stood there for at least a full minute, staring blankly at the home screen of her cell phone and seeing nothing but shimmering green light. Only now, it had crept in farther than the corners of her vision to glaze everything with a glittering film. Then thoughts finally trickled in.

They signed the Army *papers? Seriously? How is that possible?*

Blinking furiously, Idina scanned the manor grounds around her, looking for a familiar face or any sign of this being a practical joke—some way for her family to get back at her for daring to use their game against them. She would have welcomed a sign from her lights—a green thread in places here or there to show her where to go or which right move to make next.

There was nothing.

"No, no, no, no. This..." Her mouth suddenly ran dry.

This has to be a mistake. There's no way I was this *wrong about how they'd react. But they signed the wrong papers and sent them to the* Army. *Why? Just to make a point?*

She slid her phone back into the pocket of her khaki shorts and barely heard her startled, disbelieving laugh.

Wow. That's what this is. Either they want me to know I can't manipulate them the way I thought, or they want to get rid of me. Because they believe I'm as useless in this family as Uncle

Richard. Useless for what they want me to be, anyway. Maybe I pushed too hard and scared them.

She didn't know how long she stood there in the rose garden, stunned and working over all the possibilities in her mind. She'd thought she knew her parents, at the very least. That she understood them and how they operated within the world. Some part of her had believed they would be proud of the way she'd presented her proposal for Dartmouth and had stood her ground in support of what she wanted.

That was the Moorfield way.

Of course, she could always still bow out of taking the ASVAB. She hadn't been processed through any of that yet.

Turning in a slow circle, Idina gazed up at the large bay windows of the manor's first floor and smaller but no-less-impressive windows lining the offices and the bedrooms of the upper stories.

You know what? I don't care why they did it. Even if they signed those papers to get me to cave. Fuck them.

Another bitter laugh escaped her, and she sat right back down on the grass in the middle of the rose garden. Because now she had a whole new perspective.

They don't want me around. They don't want to swallow their pride to help me fulfill my dreams. Fine. If they're so willing to toss me aside like this, I will join the Army.

Somehow, that decision lifted a massive weight off her shoulders. She wasn't getting her first choice, obviously, but she'd gotten *something*. Her parents had released her. The entire family had released her. Idina Moorfield had nothing left to lose.

Now there's nothing they can do to stop me. I'm already in.

CHAPTER TWELVE

No one said a word about Idina's impending departure from Moorfield Manor to take her Army entrance exams in Manchester in the next few days. Her parents didn't act any differently toward her. Her grandfather hadn't said a single word to her since his explosion during their meeting.

He was willing to hold a grudge, though. Harold Senior avoided his granddaughter like the plague. On the few occasions she stepped into the kitchen or the family living rooms on the second floor and he was there, Harold either left the room immediately or closed the door in her face.

So much for Moorfield respectability.

None of it changed her decision. She'd made up her mind, and there was no going back for any of them.

That only thickened the tension filling every hallway and room of Moorfield Manor. Of course, they didn't summon her to any of the family meetings, where she was sure her parents and all her siblings allotted at least ten minutes on the agenda to vent about what they thought was her terrible decision. Or maybe they expected her to give in at the last second and refuse to follow through on her promise.

Bryan kept his door closed whenever she walked down the third-floor hallway to reach her bedroom. Idina barely saw the rest of her siblings anyway, so it wasn't that much of a loss. The day before she was supposed to leave—assuming she passed the exams, she wouldn't come home again—the palpable apprehension spread through the manor staff, and Idina started to wish someone would say *something*.

Mrs. Yardly gave her sympathetic smiles but stopped being her usual chipper self. Edgar and Mason smiled and waved at her whenever they saw her out on the grounds. She returned the waves, but they didn't invite her to join them for another chess game or an amusing conversation over lunch.

Master Rocha didn't seem all that affected either way, though he'd surely heard about Idina joining the Army by now. He didn't mention it once during their sparring sessions, nor did he ask when their last session would be.

It's like my whole family thinks the epic cold shoulder will make me back down, and none of the staff want to talk about it. They're all terrified of what Grandfather will do if he overhears. This is what it felt like after the Christmas Uncle Richard left. I guess I do take after him.

Finally, someone *did* approach her.

Idina sat at one of the staff tables in the corner of the massive kitchen, finishing up the last of a cranberry- and poppyseed-dressed summer salad while reading over the instructions and prep details Staff Sergeant Johansen had emailed her. Among them was a brief, incredibly bland breakdown of what the ASVAB entailed, followed by a list of things to pack with her and items not approved to take into either MEPS or basic training.

That included any current medication.

Interesting. I guess I'll have to talk to the Army docs about the inhibitors when I get there.

The kitchen had cleared out half an hour before while the kitchen staff took their midday. It was quiet, almost peaceful, and she was so immersed in reading her prep material that she didn't hear Reggie approach until he stopped in front of the table and cleared his throat.

She looked up at him and smiled. "Hi, Reggie."

"Miss Idina." He inhaled deeply, his hands clasped behind his back, and nodded. "May I have a moment of your time?"

"Sure." She set her phone face-down beside her plate and gestured toward one of the empty chairs. "Have a seat."

The man managed to look both stern and severely uncomfortable before he finally joined her at the table and folded his hands on top of it. Then he stared at her intently, and Idina almost laughed.

"What's going on?"

"Beyond the obvious contention filling this estate to the brim?"

"Ha. Well, I'm sure everyone has plenty more important things to focus on than what I do and don't decide to pursue. Right?"

Reggie raised an eyebrow and leaned slightly forward. The concern in his eyes was more than she'd received from her parents in an entire lifetime, and it hit her harder than she'd expected.

This is why I have to leave. My parents won't talk to me about any of this, but I'm about to get a genuine lecture of concern from the butler.

"Pardon my frankness, Miss Idina, but I do believe you're playing this game rather close to the heart."

She shook her head and held his gaze. "It's not a game. I'm not playing. Apparently, neither are they."

"Your parents, I assume?"

Wrinkling her nose, she spread her arms and shrugged. "Everyone, Reggie. The whole family. We're all doing what we have to do, right?"

"Hmm." He studied the table for a moment, then patted it with both hands like he was trying to soothe a crying baby.

He probably did *do that to all of us when we were babies. Or maybe only me. Seeing as there's a serious lack of the soothing type in this family.*

"I'd like to share a bit of...complicated history with you, if I may. About your family."

"Okay." *Awesome. More family secrets. From someone who's not even* in *the family.*

"I've spent the majority of my long and content life living and working with the Moorfields. A certain trust has developed between us as part of it. Of course, my relationship with your grandfather and your parents is altogether different. Still, over nearly six decades, this family has entrusted very specific details about where you come from and how the Moorfield name has developed into what it is today."

Idina folded her arms and sat back in her chair. "We came from Scotland. In...what? The late 1700s? I know all this, Reggie."

"Those are irrefutable facts, yes."

"So why the history lesson?"

Reggie frowned, clearly picking his words carefully. "Because *some* truths of history, Miss Idina, only exist within oral retellings. And within the blood."

She couldn't help but grin at him. "Sounds mysterious."

"Hmm. Well, then allow me to explain it to you like this. Yes, the Moorfields hail from the Scottish Highlands. Yes, your ancestors were successful enough and possessed the necessary resources to journey from their homeland across the sea to America.

"Of course, it had only recently *become* America then. They viewed the birth of a new nation as a unique opportunity to explore and put down roots in a world that hadn't yet fully formed."

Idina wrinkled her nose and gave him a playful frown. "You lost me there, Reg. What are you trying to say?"

He patted the table again. "I'm merely trying to share an understanding with you that your family hasn't always been...like this. The Moorfield legacy hasn't always been what you've known your entire life. I believe your ancestors had an entirely different purpose in mind when they settled in New England and built this estate."

"What kind of purpose?"

"As far as I understand it, Miss Idina, the Moorfield *clan* were warriors."

She snorted. "Uh-huh. Scottish warriors."

He inclined his head in concession. "If your grandfather

were willing to speak to you about it any more than that, I might have a sufficient answer for you.

"Nevertheless, you come from a long line of powerful, dedicated, diligent, incredibly skilled people who have dedicated their lives to pave the way for future generations. To uphold the responsibilities granted to your ancestors centuries ago and across the ocean. Somewhere along the way, as the United States of America blossomed into what it is, your family changed with the times."

Idina frowned and glanced around the kitchen, but they were alone. *Why is he bringing this up now? How's any of this supposed to change a thing?*

"Okay. So you're saying my family used to be...what? Leaders of a Scottish fighting clan, and now they've evolved into investment bankers?"

"*Evolved* might not be the right word. But they have changed. Most of them, at any rate. The old ways of who your ancestors were when they were truly at the peak of their prosperity are far different than the unspoken laws your family upholds today.

"Industrialization and the dawn of the technological age, while convenient, have taken their toll on many things. Including, perhaps, the heart of what it first truly meant to be part of your family."

Kinda puts all my green-spark freak-outs around technology into perspective.

"You know," she added with a tiny smile, "you're kinda making it sound like we were Scottish royalty or something."

Reggie chuckled. "Nothing quite so extravagant, I'm afraid. Powerful and respected, yes. Particularly...efficient.

That part of your heritage hasn't changed, Miss Idina. It seems most especially prevalent still in *you*. As it was very much in your Uncle Richard."

"Wait, you think *that's* why they're so upset? Why they don't want me around?" Idina huffed out a laugh. "Because I haven't changed with the times like the rest of them?"

"I imagine your family, your grandfather in particular, have developed a strong aversion to any reminder of what this family once was. Perhaps even to the parts of what made a Moorfield a Moorfield that were lost.

"I'm not saying the way things are now is any better or worse than in the past. They're very different. The entire world is very different. Who the Moorfields are now has transformed by necessity, you understand? There came a need to grow with a rapidly changing society, so they merely turned their abilities and unique skills toward... other things."

Idina sighed. "Reggie, I appreciate you trying to explain all this. I just don't know why. Nobody ever talks about this stuff. If you're trying to make me feel sorry for them, if that was possible, I don't think this is the way to do it."

Not to mention that I have no idea what he's talking about. It's not a heart-to-heart if it's all mystery read-between-the-lines.

He nodded. "I understand. Someday, perhaps you will too. I simply wanted to offer a broader view of what's happening here. Something bigger than any one person or a board of directors or a family-run company.

"There's a lot more to who you are than you think, Miss Idina. The same goes for every other Moorfield as well.

Their unique skills happen to have diverged from their original intentions."

"Unique skills?" She couldn't keep back a smile despite the bitterness creeping into it. "What unique skills? They're investment brokers."

"It's...quite a bit more than that."

A suddenly cold weight settled in her stomach, and she leaned forward over the table before lowering her voice. "Are you... Are you trying to tell me the rest of my family has these weird episodes too? Like, it's a genetic thing or something?"

That didn't make sense. She'd never seen anyone in her family exhibit anything more than constrained emotion and hard logic.

Reggie let out a thoughtful hum, then swallowed thickly. "That may very well be the case, Idina. I do know for a fact that *you* are not the only one who has...struggled with this particular condition. After decades of keeping my peace around the issue, I'd like to note to you personally that I find the use of the word *condition* to explain your unique situation highly distasteful."

"Wow." A small chuckle of surprise escaped her. "That's new."

"I must admit it's quite freeing to say out loud."

"Good. I'm glad you got it out of your system. Are you about to admit to me too that Uncle Richard has the same thing? The episodes?"

Reggie stared at her and pursed his lips. "Your uncle had his failures and successes, Idina. If I were you, I'd focus on yours. There may come a time when the rest of your family opens their eyes to how important you are, even when everyone else around you has changed so much since—"

"Okay, let me stop you right there." Idina held up a hand and gave him an apologetic smile. "No offense, Reg, but sitting down to talk about how much the family has changed and why they...I don't know, *resent* me for not changing with them doesn't really help me. No amount of business school will make me suddenly sprout these *unique talents* of theirs. There's nothing for me here that's going to change me *that* much or help me fit in."

Reggie blinked and leaned quickly away from her, tilting his head. "You believe the Army *will?*"

Here we go. That's *what this whole talk is about. Trying to change my mind again.*

"I don't know," Idina said firmly. "Maybe it will. Maybe it won't. If I have any unique talents beyond my art, like the kind you're talking about that are somehow connected to the episodes I take daily medication for, they're useless here. Unappreciated. That's the whole point of this. *I'm* unappreciated. Who knows? Maybe the Army will change that."

"You're about to enter a very different world. *If* this is the path you choose." The older man's bushy gray eyebrows drew together in remorse, and he took a long moment of silence to choose his next words carefully. "A military career is also complicated. You must know there's still a possibility to back out of this decision if you truly understood—"

"No. There isn't."

"Have you spoken to your parents?"

"Reggie, you know they won't listen to me. They had

their chance, and it's over. I get it. Everyone's surprised. Nobody likes the choice I made. I'm not backing out of this now." She smoothed her hair away from her face with both hands, then shrugged. "Besides, that's the first lesson Dad taught me, right? Never back down. Never give up."

"Idina—"

"Look, I might not be like everyone else in this family, and that's the way it is. If there's *one* thing that makes me a Moorfield, I guess it's that. I'm not backing down."

With a heavy sigh, Reggie nodded and returned his gaze to the table. "That most certainly does sound like a Moorfield's unwavering dedication. As long as this is something you want to do."

"It is *now.*" They sat together in silence for a moment, his eyes closed as he contemplated their conversation or his regret in not being able to change her mind.

Jeez. I'm going into the Army, not my grave. Why is everyone acting like this is the end of the world?

Finally, Reggie pushed himself to his feet and nodded. "Very well. I'll leave you to your…work." He nodded at her overturned cell phone and clasped his hands together. "I do truly hope you're making this decision of your own accord and for no other reason."

"Yeah, I think I'm finally starting to figure out how important that is."

With a weak and flickering smile, the butler nodded and turned to head out of the kitchen.

"Reggie, hold on."

"Yes?"

"Did my parents send you to find me? You know, soften

me up a little with some secret family history and a lot of vague allusions to who we *used* to be?"

He lowered his head again, his eyes glinting beneath the bright kitchen lights. "No, Miss Idina. I came to you on my own."

"Because you think me joining the Army is a terrible idea."

"Because I don't want to see this family fractured again the way it was when Richard left."

"Oh." Idina swallowed, affected more by the loving concern in the eyes of a man who wasn't blood-related but had become family all the same. *Of course. Here I am, following in Richard's footsteps as everyone says. And they won't tell me why.*

"I understand my attempts to illuminate a complex history in ten minutes might not have been nearly as successful as I'd imagined. But I was motivated to try." Reggie's smile flickered in and out again. "They're not bad people. They just don't know how to handle what they can't see with their eyes."

"Well, they *can* see it. Sometimes." She lifted both hands and glanced pointedly at them, and they both knew she was referring to her green lights and the odd displays no one could explain. "Even if they couldn't, that doesn't mean it's okay for them to condemn it."

"Certainly not. You're the only one who can truly judge the merit of your decisions. It seems you're prepared to do so, come hell or high water."

Not knowing what to say, Idina exaggerated a tight-lipped smile and gave her family's butler two thumbs-up.

Reggie playfully rolled his eyes and turned. "I *will* miss your scintillating sense of humor."

"Wish me luck, then, huh?"

"You won't need it." Then he disappeared through the swinging door of the kitchen, and left Idina alone to contemplate his last remark.

That's a weird thing to say to somebody who pissed off the entire family. I haven't had any *luck being who they thought I'd be. I guess I don't need any for this either.*

CHAPTER THIRTEEN

August twenty-first arrived—the day Staff Sergeant Johansen had told her to come down to Manchester to be ushered to MEPS the next morning. The day Idina would leave her life at Moorfield Manor behind and set out to become someone else with the United States Army. Who that person was, she didn't know.

She was certainly starting with the right foundation beneath her—stepping away from the family mold that hadn't been made for her, starting over fresh, and sticking with her conviction.

After all, she'd given her parents and grandfather her word that if they didn't support her college education at Dartmouth, she'd join the Army anyway. They'd only hastened her departure. Maybe that was best for all of them.

When all the arrangements were complete and the day finally came, the Moorfields' driver Todd pulled one of the town cars up to the manor's grand entrance. Idina stepped outside with a small duffel bag slung over her shoulder and something of an adventure ahead of her.

The staff had planned an estate-wide break from their daily schedules to see her off. There were plenty of hugs and well-wishes, a few jokes about how the Army wouldn't be less strict than the hierarchy of Moorfield & Associates, and pleas for Idina to send word of how they could get in touch with her once she'd settled into her new life as an enlisted trainee.

Reggie seemed to have gotten over his heavy remorse regarding the situation, and he surprised her by wrapping her up in a tight, warm, entirely un-Reggie-like hug. "Take care of yourself, Miss Idina. That's quite important."

"I'll be fine, Reg. Thanks for the advice." Before she could step away from the gathered staff—most of whom she'd known all her life—the front door of the manor abruptly opened. Idina's family had one more surprise in store for her too.

Bryan was the first one through the door. He walked calmly but swiftly toward her, practically jumping down the large stone stairs from the front stoop, wearing a massive grin and his eyes wide. "You didn't seriously think we'd let you ship off to boot camp without saying goodbye, did you?"

She laughed. "Did you look that up so you could sound like you know what you're talking about?"

Her brother barked out a laugh and yanked her in for a tight hug that crushed her arms at her sides and made it impossible for her to hug him back. Then he whispered in her ear, "That's what it's called, right?"

"Yeah, but I think most people call it basic training now."

"Cool." He quickly released her and stepped back. "It's still really fucking weird that you're joining the Army."

"Uh...thanks."

Timothy stood back by a good ten feet and folded his arms. "Don't do anything stupid and get yourself kicked out."

"Sage advice, Tim."

He shrugged. "Just saying."

"You know, as long as they don't ask me to handle any investment accounts, I think I'll be fine."

Bryan snorted and quickly tried to cover it up when Timothy scowled and glared.

"Well. This is a first, isn't it? The *Army*." Maxwell adjusted his tie—which every Mr. Moorfield in the family insisted on wearing day in and day out in their home—and cleared his throat. "I still don't get it."

His wife Nadine shook her head. "Some things just don't, honey."

"Right." He stepped forward and stuck his hand out toward Idina with a stern frown. "Well, I suppose it's better than nothing."

"Wow." She took his hand and grinned. "It's great to get so much support around here. Thanks."

"Just don't screw it up." Maxwell backed up with his wife on his arm, looking around uncomfortably despite no one paying any attention to him.

"Even if you get your ass kicked," Timothy added. "That's basically what you signed up for."

Idina laughed. "Well, at least I have experience in *that*."

"Don't worry, Dee," Bryan added. "We'll still take you back if you fail out of boot camp."

"I won't fail. But nice try."

Nobody knows how to handle this. At least they're taking me seriously. I just had to do something this big to convince them I can do anything.

"Hey." Her sister Celeste set a cool, manicured hand on Idina's shoulder and leaned in, her gray eyes glistening in the sunlight. "Be careful."

"It's basic training, Lessie. Not—"

"I know what it is. I've…heard a few things."

"Oh, yeah? Like what?"

Celeste pursed her lips and lifted her chin. "It doesn't bear repeating, but I had to say it."

"Okay. I'll be—whoa." Being swept into a hug by her only sister was a brand-new experience too, and Idina couldn't help but laugh as she patted Celeste's back a few times. "Is it just me, or is it getting super huggy out here?"

Bryan thrust a fist in the air. "You're taking it like a champ, Dee."

Timothy grabbed his younger brother's arm and jerked it back down, shaking his head.

Idina and her sister released each other, then she pointed at Bryan. "Yeah, I'll make sure to say that to *you* the next time everyone comes out to throw *you* a giant goodbye party."

He scoffed. "Never gonna happen."

"Idina." All five Moorfield children turned and parted to let their parents through. Harry walked tall and straight, his jaw firmly set and his eyebrows raised as he approached his youngest daughter flying the coop before all her older siblings.

Annette looked as poised and well-put-together as always. Her eyes were a little red, but if she'd been crying, she'd pulled herself back together to make an appearance.

Idina gave her mother a small, sympathetic smile. *I've never seen her cry before. Or as close to crying as she can get.*

Her father reached her first and swallowed thickly, his Adam's apple bobbing beneath his consistently clean-shaven chin. "I can't say I'm particularly proud of this decision."

She raised her eyebrows and nodded. "You still signed the papers."

"I did."

They stared at each other, and it seemed like Harry didn't have anything else to say to his youngest child who couldn't for the life of her follow in his footsteps.

He didn't say he wasn't proud of my *decision. Maybe he's talking about his. Either way, it doesn't matter. He's not backing down, and I definitely won't.*

Then her father gently cleared his throat. "For what it's worth, I'm sure you'll have no difficulty accomplishing what you've set your mind to. So there's that."

"Yeah. There's that."

Harry nodded, then Annette stepped forward to give her daughter a weak, fluttering embrace that lasted all of two seconds. Then she quickly released Idina and inhaled deeply through her nose to collect herself one more time. It was clearly too hard for her to say anything at all, so she kept her silence and stood elegantly at her husband's side on the gravel drive in front of the manor.

Idina shrugged. "Thanks for seeing me off, at least."

"It's important to say our goodbyes when we can," her father replied dully.

They're intent on this whole cold-and-distant act, aren't they?

"Right." Idina glanced around the front of the house, where a few straggling staff members had stayed behind to see her off. Most of them, though, had left to return to work the second Mr. and Mrs. Moorfield had stepped through the front doors. Out of the dozens of faces she knew and most of them she loved, she hadn't seen one in particular. "I'm guessing Grandfather doesn't feel the same way."

Her parents shared one of their silent, stoic glances that could've meant anything at this point.

"He's feeling unwell," Annette replied before her husband could say anything else. "We thought it best he stay inside this morning."

Idina looked back and forth between her parents and bit down on her bottom lip.

Harold Senior's feeling unwell. That man doesn't get so much as a cold. And they know I know that.

"Well." She drew a deep breath. "I hope he recovers quickly."

Neither of her parents gave much of a response beyond the polite nods proper etiquette dictated.

"Miss Idina," Todd called as he opened the rear passenger-side door of the town car. "I believe they're expecting you to arrive on time."

It was an incredibly polite euphemism for 'hurry up, already' disguised as a gentle reminder.

Idina nodded and looked at each of her family members in turn. "Thank you, Todd." She gave her siblings a small wave and caught Bryan's gaze long enough to flash him a quick grin before rearranging the strap of her duffel bag over her shoulder.

Part of her hoped her parents would say something else —anything else that would at least indicate they were sorry to see her go. Even her mom's red-rimmed eyes didn't exactly mean Annette had been crying over the idea of *missing* her youngest daughter. Or even that she was worried for Idina.

They could've been tears of disappointment, for all I know. They've already dealt with one Moorfield breaking away from the dynasty. Maybe she had to get all the mourning out of her system before she could handle watching me leave.

That seemed a lot more possible by the second as her parents stared stonily back at her.

Idina didn't know what to say after that, so she turned and headed across the gravel. Todd immediately grabbed the duffel bag from her, then held the door open while she climbed into the back seat. The door closed, the driver stuck her bag in the trunk, and Idina studied the odd array of expressions on her family's faces. Amusement, disbelief, confusion, hesitation, and absolutely nothing from her parents.

That's how they get things done, isn't it? They turn off their emotions, and everything's okay again. Would've been nice to get something *on my last day home. I'll officially be an adult the next time I see them, and I don't know when that'll be.*

As Todd climbed into the driver's seat, Idina found Reggie standing on the top of the front stoop with his hands clasped behind his back. In a surprising show of silent solidarity, the usually stoic man subtly lifted one hand and gave her a thumbs-up. Idina smirked and nodded. Then the purring town car pulled away from the front of Moorfield Manor.

The wide turn around the circular drive seemed to last forever. But it was long enough for Idina to take what felt like a long, final glance at her home and everything that came with it.

Most of this place I won't miss at all. But a few things... I guess home will always be home in some way, even if it's not the kind I can't wait to come back to.

Her gaze automatically lifted toward the third story of the manor, where she easily found the large bay windows of her grandfather's private apartments. Movement in another window on the second floor caught her attention instead, and time seemed to freeze when she recognized the figure standing there.

Harold Moorfield I stood perfectly erect at the window of his study, where the thick curtains had been drawn aside and tied up for the first time that she could recall.

She had a perfect view of the man, and if he'd been standing there looking *out* at her and the town car rolling away, it would've given Idina at least a little hope that he still felt anything for his youngest grandchild.

He wasn't looking out. Her grandfather faced the interior of his office with his hands clasped behind his back. He didn't turn once, nor did he move naturally as if he happened to decide the curtains should be drawn aside today before going about his daily routine, with no idea Idina was leaving.

He knows I'm out here. He knows I can see him.

The town car finally rounded the circular drive, and they picked up speed to head across the sprawling grounds toward the massive front gates marking the entrance to Moorfield Manor. Idina could've turned to watch her grandfather through the rear window, to glimpse him maybe finally giving in to see her off.

She didn't.

Instead, she clenched both fists in her lap and stared straight ahead through the windshield. Small clouds of glittering green specks rose from her hands to fill the car. If Todd noticed, he didn't give any indication.

If that's how Grandfather wants to treat his flesh and blood, that's on him. He can think I'm a disgrace all he wants. I'm finally free.

CHAPTER FOURTEEN

Todd dropped her off at the recruiting office, where she'd driven herself a week before to take the practice test for the qualifying ASVAB exams to enter the U.S. Army. Only this time, once she sat with Staff Sergeant Johansen, she'd be signing on the dotted line somewhere with her parents' signatures. Then the real testing would begin. Based on her practice test scores, Idina was sure she wouldn't have a problem with any of it.

She had to wait a while to see Johansen again. The recruiting office was a lot fuller than the last time she'd stopped by. When the staff sergeant finally called her up to the desk, she couldn't help but grin.

"Good to see you again," Johansen said as she extended a hand over the table.

"You too, Staff Sergeant. Thank you."

They shook, sat, and the recruiter pulled out another folder with Idina's name on it. "As I said, we have the release forms signed by your parents. The next step before anything else is to get you to sign these papers too.

"I want to make sure you understand that once all the I's are dotted and the T's crossed, in the eyes of the U.S. Army, these forms are essentially your emancipation papers. Your parents can't do anything at this point, and once *you* sign, you're acting as a fully competent adult. Make sense?"

I've been a fully competent adult for a while. Now it's on paper.

"My birthday's not that far off."

Johansen nodded. "Then it sounds like we're on the same page."

Idina smirked. "So where do I sign?"

Once everything was squared away with the paperwork, she got a surprisingly overwhelming rundown of what would happen next.

"You came down at the perfect time. Like I've mentioned, the ASVAB exam is the next step. If you pass, we'll shuttle you down to Springfield for the night. Then you'll head to the MEPS there in the morning. The rest of it depends on your results there, but I don't think you'll have any trouble with those. Good luck."

Idina had already researched as much of the process as possible once she received the call that her parents had dumped her life into her hands a few months sooner than expected. Apparently, she'd be on her way to the Military Entrance Processing Station in Springfield, Massachusetts.

Just another adventure, I guess. One of many, right?

She'd thought the process would move a lot faster once she'd gotten back down to Manchester to sign her future into the Army. It didn't. The recruiting office put her aboard a shuttle with other young people ready to head to the Springfield MEPS the next morning as well, and they got to the hotel in Springfield around 7:30 p.m.

Idina and a few other potential recruits received their room keys and a full meal to eat alone at their leisure. It was brought to her by the same civilian contractors who'd shuttled her to the hotel, and she thanked them before sitting at the tiny table in the single-bed hotel room.

When she opened the delivered to-go box, she didn't expect to see a steak dinner with braised asparagus, mashed potatoes, gravy, and still-warm slices of bread with butter. *Last meal, huh? I mean, it's not Mrs. Yardly's steak dinner, but I guess most recruits didn't have a Mrs. Yardly at home.*

After dinner, Idina took a shower so she wouldn't have to in the morning, then settled into bed and ended up pulling out her cell phone to check her emails. It was a force of habit at this point—making sure she stayed on top of any messages she might've received from anyone in her family that required her immediate attention.

Her inbox was empty.

With a sigh, she set her alarm for 3:30 a.m.—which would get her up in plenty of time to catch the bus that would take her to MEPS—set her phone on the nightstand, and crawled under the covers.

Of course, no one's sent me anything. I left this morning. What would they say, anyway? "We screwed up, Idina. Come home?" "Glad you're gone?"

She turned off the bedside lamp and stared at the ceiling in the darkness.

I don't expect anything from them. They let me out, and now I'm on my own.

Then she thought of her Uncle Richard and wherever he'd gone nine years ago when he'd stormed out of Moorfield Manor that Christmas and never came back. What had *he* wanted that didn't align with who the Moorfields had become? Where had he gone? What was he doing now? If she took after her uncle so much, what would he think of another Moorfield going against the grain to live her life *in the Army*?

Her last real memory of the man rushed back to her—when he'd stopped that night to look his niece in the eye and give her his final piece of advice.

"Don't let anyone tell you who you are or how to use the power you have. I promise you no one will know the truth of that better than you."

The power she had.

Idina fell asleep staring at her hands and wondering why she'd ever let her parents try to hide who she was.

The next morning felt like a dream, even when she somehow managed to wake up fully bright-eyed and incredibly curious. The other potential recruits shuffled along with her out of the hotel and into the bus, most of them still half-asleep.

One man who looked more like he was in his late twenties grumbled about the lack of coffee.

"You'll have to get used to that." The driver chuckled, and they were off.

By the time they reached MEPS, the place was packed. Hundreds of people who'd passed the Army entrance exams filtered into the building. Most of them were Idina's age, and some looked like the Army was a last resort. Without any real understanding of exactly what would happen from here on out, though, the entire gathering sat quietly with bleary eyes and waited for the next step.

This is the part where they figure out who's able to handle basic. It looks like herding a bunch of lost sheep.

In her mind, Idina went over the ASVAB questions and her answers again.

They weren't yes-or-no questions anyway. It was about picking the best answer out of what wasn't immediately obvious. If I learned anything about getting my parents to sign me up for the Army and not Dartmouth, it's that nothing's a done deal. Except for me keeping my word.

When another NCO finally called her name, she was led to the next open testing room and asked to hand over every personal belonging she had on her.

She handed over her duffel.

"No phone? No papers in your pockets?"

"No. Everything's in there."

The NCO nodded. "Then have a seat. The computer will prompt you for everything. When you finish, come down to the reception desk, and you'll get your results."

"Okay. Thanks."

The man closed the door, and she was pretty sure she heard it lock behind her.

Of course, they don't want anyone sneaking out in the middle of a military entrance exam. I bet plenty of people still try it.

She wanted to test the door so badly, to confirm the sound hadn't been that of a heavy lock keeping her in this room until someone decided it was time for her to come out. She didn't.

The whole thing felt like she'd entered some top-secret facility where only the people stationed here regularly were supposed to know what was going on. As Idina walked toward the table and the computer set up on it, she scanned the room and tried to hide a smile.

Two security cameras stuck out from the walls. A large mirror rested perpendicular to the table, facing her from the side as she sat.

Big Brother's always watching, huh? I wonder how many people they have behind that mirror looking in?

If it was supposed to be intimidating, it wasn't. Idina sat, typed her personal information into the computer, and began the test.

Piece of cake. If I can handle growing up as a Moorfield, I can handle this no problem.

Halfway through reading the ninth question, though, she reached for the mouse and prepared to select the correct multiple-choice answer. It was one of those complicated questions meant to judge a potential soldier's character and how far they'd go to put a mission or their fellow soldiers first. Idina didn't have to think that hard about what the best answer was, but when her hand settled on the computer mouse, a static *crackle* and *snap* rose beneath her fingers.

A green line of electric energy raced from her hand, up the mouse cord, and into the old, clunky computer monitor. Jagged green lines slashed across the screen's thick glass. Sparks flew.

Idina shoved herself away from the table with a *hiss* and instantly raised both hands in front of her.

What the hell?

A buzzing awareness on the back of her neck reminded her of the two security cameras in the corners and the two-way mirror beside her.

There's no way they won't have questions about that. Shit. Keep going. Keep acting natural. You're too good for them to pass up, and there's no way anyone's gonna connect that little spark-show to you, Idina. They don't know about it.

She forced herself to scoot back toward the table and continue taking the test. Fortunately, she hadn't broken the computer. No one stormed into the test room to interrogate her about a strange power with green lights and an apparent grudge against technology.

She must've finished the test more quickly than the other young people trying to get their spot in the Army because the reception area was far emptier when she returned than when she'd arrived. She reached the desk, and the woman sitting behind it glanced up at her with bored blankness. "Name?"

"Moorfield."

The printer *whirred* and *rattled* behind the woman, who snatched up all the papers, folded them crisply to stuff them into an envelope, and handed that envelope to Idina. "Someone will be with you to go over your results."

"Thanks." With nowhere else to wait but the chairs lining the hall, Idina sat and quickly whipped out her test results to scan them before anyone else had a chance to tell her what they meant.

Huh. No surprise there.

Glancing around the lobby as a few other test-takers finished early, Idina pursed her lips in an attempt to hide a smile.

Time to see how far a test with no wrong answers gets me. Nobody's calling my name to ask about a little episode with—

"Moorfield." A sergeant stopped by the reception desk and looked over the tired, bewildered, nervous faces.

"Here." She stood.

"Come with me, and we'll take a look."

Idina hurried after the NCO and sat across from him at a cramped table surrounded by other cramped tables that quickly filled with test-takers and NCOs sitting to go over results, options, and next steps.

The man across from her reached for her envelope, and she instantly handed it over. He didn't say anything as he studied her results, his eyes roaming briefly over each page before he flipped it over to turn to the next. His face remained entirely expressionless as he read, and Idina watched him intently.

He's working the 'don't give anything away' face. Trying to keep me waiting here in suspense, but I already know how I did. It's all good, as long as we don't start talking about green sparks and computer problems.

"Okay." The NCO returned her papers and nodded. "These look pretty good. If your recruiter didn't tell you before sending you here, your overall ASVAB score was ninety-three. So you have a couple of options."

"Like what?"

"Well, you're eligible for a wider range of jobs. So now we'll pick your MOS. What do you want to do?"

"You mean besides join the Army?"

He snorted and raised his eyebrows. "You're choosing your military occupational specialty."

"Right." Idina scanned the table and swallowed. *I prepared for everything but making it in and choosing my* job. "I think I'll be good with anything. Whatever's available as soon as possible."

"All right. Well, with your test scores and wanting an available opening..." The NCO scanned another sheet of paper on top of a folder and tilted his head back and forth. "You said you're interested in the Army Corps of Engineers, right? That'd be a good fit for you. How do you feel about combat?"

"I..." Idina huffed out a laugh. "I can handle combat."

"Uh-huh." His smile flickered, and he opened the folder to flip a few pages back and forth before grabbing a pen and scribbling something down. "So we'll set your MOS as Bravo Twelve. Combat Engineer."

She wasn't exactly sure how to respond, so she went with the first thing that popped into her head. "That'll get me to basic training right away?"

The man looked up at her with wide eyes, and his smile widened. "Yeah. You won't have to wait long at all. Take these and go sit in the lobby."

Idina accepted the folder—which only had a few papers—and stood from the table.

Combat Engineer. Something tells me that doesn't have the same definition as a normal engineer. Whatever it is, at least I'm in. There's no going back at this point.

CHAPTER FIFTEEN

Passing the test and choosing her Army job was a lot more anticlimactic than she'd expected. Until another NCO called her up with a group of four other recruits, Idina had to sit and wait in the reception area, wondering how much more there was until she could hit basic training and this would all feel real.

However, when someone called them by name and told them to follow an NCO upstairs for the next steps, she couldn't help but think that *this* was the next big thing. Whatever it was, she could end the nonstop waiting and finally *do* something.

She wasn't here to go over her options, pick her job, or pretend she would go through with this so her family would concede to let her live her dream.

This *was* the dream now.

She was wrong again.

The next room they entered was large and held only plain tables and chairs. Two other NCOs stood at the far end, watching the recruits cluelessly roll in.

"Sit," the NCO told them. "Grab a questionnaire. Read every question and answer *honestly*. The Army takes a lot of people in, but we don't have room for liars."

The recruits filtered out around the room to sit silently at the various tables. Only one questionnaire and one pen rested on each desk, so all five of them sat alone at the tables. Idina looked up to see two more NCOs enter the room, all of them silent and stoic and scanning the recruits' faces.

Idina sat and pulled the questionnaire closer to begin filling out more paperwork. After reading a few of the opening yes-or-no questions, she wrinkled her nose. *Medical history. Criminal background. Recreational activity. These are the same questions I answered when I started. I guess they wanna double-check everything, right?*

So she picked up a pen and got to work, reading each question as thoroughly as she read anything set in front of her and circling the appropriate answer. It was impossible to get anything wrong when the green lights kept flaring around the best possible response, but that didn't mean she trusted her weird ability without making sure it was still working.

After all, she was going on twenty hours without her medication.

After a few minutes, a redhead kid who looked younger than Idina sat up straight and raised his hand.

"What is it?" the closest NCO asked.

"I have a question."

The NCO walked swiftly toward the kid's table and peered down at the questionnaire. "What part of this confuses you?"

"I, um… This question. 'Have you smoked marijuana?'"

"What about it?"

The kid shrugged. "I mean, I don't know what I should—"

"The truth. That's what you write down."

"So I circle yes?"

"What's your name?"

"Ian Brock."

"Have you smoked marijuana, Brock?"

The kid's eyes widened. "I mean, yeah. Sometimes, when I—"

"So you haven't smoked marijuana." The NCO nodded slowly and widened his eyes. "Pretty simple answer."

"Okay…" The kid looked around the room in utter confusion.

"Don't look at them," the sergeant snapped. "They're not answering your questions. Fill it out."

Brock—whatever his first name was—slowly lowered his head and kept circling the yes-or-no answers. The room fell silent again except for the scribble of pens, a few coughs, and the echoing footsteps of the NCOs circling the room and watching them.

Idina glanced at Brock one more time, then immediately went back to her form. *They don't have room for liars, and an NCO told him to lie. Okay, so this is all still a test. Pretty much par for the course with what I already read about how all this is supposed to go. They want to make sure we want to be here.*

Luckily for her, there weren't any questions about whether or not she had *family members* who smoked marijuana.

Throughout the rest of their repetitive test-taking, the NCOs circled the room and answered whatever occasional questions arose with the same kind of confusing starkness.

"It's not a hard question, Abernathe. Do you have asthma? No. You don't."

"You broke your arm ten years ago? Then there's no record of it, Dinley. Move on."

"No, you sleep like a baby. Doesn't matter."

Idina kept her head down and filled everything out as indicated. *They're not hard questions. I guess it's easier for me to get them right.*

When everyone finished, the NCOs collected the questionnaires and led them into another room that looked like it had been pulled right out of an urgent care clinic and dropped into the MEPS building. The recruits waited in the very short line of only five of them for the one doctor to pull them into a semi-private room in the back and examine them on the spot. He drew blood, took their vitals, asked more of the same questions about their medical history, and handed out plastic cups to collect urine samples.

Idina stood at the back of the line, waiting for the tiresome process to finish so they could get going and land at Fort Leonard Wood. *We'll get out of here soon. I have nothing to hide. Mostly. Nobody's asking about fireworks and smoke coming out of people's hands. Might've been easier for them to weed out those of us who can't handle basic if they did all this before we signed our contracts.*

A simple exam with a doctor who probably wasn't Army personnel shouldn't have taken as long as it did. It felt like hours, but there was no way to tell how long they'd been here. The room didn't have a clock.

When it was her turn to speak to the doctor, she couldn't help but ask about prescription medications that would be available to her once she reached Fort Leonard Wood.

The man didn't look up from the gauge of the blood pressure cuff. "That's something you'll have to talk to the doctors on base about."

"Right. I just... How long does it normally take to get medications we've been taking?"

That made him look at her, and he raised his eyebrows in interest. "Your forms say you don't have any disqualifying conditions. Do you have some kind of medical condition we need to know about?"

"What? No. No, I've just been taking something for a few years now. Helps calm me down, you know?"

"Uh-huh. What's it called?" The doctor flipped through the few papers in her file, his eyes skimming back and forth.

"It's... Well, my doctor calls it Anagracin."

"What's in it?"

"I'm pretty sure the main active ingredient is *Atropa belladonna*. Not really sure about the rest of it."

He blinked, looked back up at her, and slowly removed his glasses. "Nightshade."

"Yeah."

With a snort, the doctor scooted away from her on his wheeled stool and stood. "Very funny. Quit holding up the line. You can go."

Frowning, Idina hopped off the exam chair and headed

toward the *other* line standing around and waiting after the doctor saw them.

Yeah, okay. I know it's weird to be taking deadly nightshade daily, but come on. There have to be a few outliers for people the stuff doesn't poison. Like me. Dr. Kruchek said it was perfectly safe.

Finally, after waiting in the row of chairs with other recruits for who knew how long, the same NCOs stood in the doorway, and one of them called blandly, "Everybody up."

Confusion swirled in her head until she and the other recruits reached their next step in the process. None of them immediately realized that now, after answering numerous questions they'd already answered *before* taking the ASVAB and being poked and prodded by a doctor who only asked questions and said nothing else, it was time for their physical fitness exam.

Before they signed any real paperwork and were officially "in," everyone had to make sure they *could* withstand the physical rigors of Army basic training.

"Some people don't make it past this point," one NCO said. "If you can't handle this first test and flop out before you're a soldier, you can forget the whole thing. So you better hope you're ready."

The fitness test wasn't anywhere close to the level of physical difficulty Idina had expected. Two minutes of pushups, two minutes of sit-ups, and a timed two-mile run around the empty room.

Compared to Idina's training with Master Rocha, this kind of physical assessment was a joke. Still, it was the first time the NCOs leading them through this process livened up a little. As each recruit went through their testing, the NCOs watched, counted, took notes, and timed the run while counting laps around the room.

When Idina finally finished her test, she slowed to a jog and waited for the NCO with the timer to say something. He didn't.

She quickly caught her breath and swiped her hair away from her forehead before looking at the four other potential recruits. The skinny, redhead kid Brock looked like he might pass out. The other three young men grimaced and sweated profusely, but still, nobody said a thing.

Okay, fine. Maybe it's a little weird I've already had enough training at home to be able to handle this. But it's not that hard, right?

Then came more waiting and more silence in another corridor of the Springfield MEPS until one of the NCOs called her into a room. Idina grabbed her folder and went to sit with the female SNCO inside. The woman didn't bother to close the door—the recruits shuffled in and out too quickly to make it worthwhile.

Privacy isn't their top priority at this point.

"Have a seat, Moorfield." The woman scanned a few more papers, absently reached for Idina's folder, then looked it all over without an ounce of expression. "Okay. You've passed all the requirements for joining the United States Army. So now you sign here."

Idina stared at the pen in the woman's hand. "Signing this means I'm in?"

"Yep."

"What happens next?"

The SNCO tilted her head, but her deadpan expression remained the same. "You'll swear in and get your first official Army orders to basic training. Good news for you is Week Zero might last an actual week."

"That's reception, right? Before everything officially starts?"

Apparently, *that* was what the woman found worthy of a smile. "That's right. Easiest part of the whole thing. You'll blow right through it."

"Okay." Idina took the pen and pulled her Army contract toward her to sign all the marked spots where her signature was required. The whole time, she felt the SNCO's eyes on her. The woman was still smirking like she held some private joke and couldn't wait to reveal the punchline. But she didn't say a word.

When Idina finished with her contract, the woman extended a hand and nodded. "Welcome to the Army."

Idina was ushered back and forth through MEPS for the rest of the day, where she waited around with the rest of the recruits who'd signed on. Even more of them were shuttled back to the same hotel in Springfield for another night of waiting.

No one gave her more information than what the final NCO had stated when she'd signed her contract. The only new instructions she received from the shuttle's civilian driver were to be up, packed, and ready to get back on that shuttle at 4:00 a.m. the next morning.

After an entire day of testing and signing and waiting

around, she couldn't wait to get on the plane that would take her to Fort Leonard Wood so her new life could finally begin. As it turned out, a day of doing nothing *but* waiting made it all too easy to drift off to sleep.

The next morning, though, instead of getting shipped off first thing, she ended up back at the MEPS building with all the other recruits. Uniformed personnel ushered them into a new small room. This one was obviously for something important—mounted flags lined the side of the room, and there was a large plaque on the far wall of the U.S. Army seal.

Idina stood with her back straight beside the other new soldiers, none of whom looked any different than the civilians they'd been less than twenty-four hours ago. A few civilian witnesses were present for the occasion—the other recruits' family members, she imagined.

I can't believe this. A Moorfield standing in a room about to take the Oath of Enlistment and swear into the Army. The only thing that could make this any better is if my parents were here to watch. They'd never show up for this. I'm over trying to prove myself to them. I made it this far, and I'm leaving that whole world behind me.

A door at the far end of the room opened, and the officer in command stepped into the room. Every uniformed SNCO and NCO stood at attention until the OIC nodded and muttered, "At ease."

They didn't exactly relax. Idina recognized their position shifting briskly into standing at ease, but the air of formality in the room hadn't changed a bit.

At ease doesn't mean that, does it? At least not here.

She stood perfectly still with the other enlisted recruits,

all of them standing in their civilian clothes and looking like a raggedly assembled line of grown kids only playing at being soldiers.

This is the final step. This is it.

It was hard enough not to smile when the OIC nodded, smiled, and began the Oath of Enlistment to be repeated by everyone standing in front of him.

Maybe the green lights will fizzle away now that I'm not under my family's thumb anymore. Maybe all I needed was to do something on my own.

Idina's voice rose with the others' as they repeated the words that would change their lives forever in ways none of them could fully fathom that day. It was remarkably satisfying to move through the ceremony without a hint of an oncoming episode.

"I, Idina Moorfield, do solemnly swear that I will support and defend the Constitution of the United States against all enemies, foreign and domestic…"

CHAPTER SIXTEEN

The flight for the recruits entering basic training at Fort Leonard Wood didn't land in Missouri until 11:32 p.m. that night. It hadn't been that long a trip, but Idina still fell asleep for most of it. She stepped out of the plane with the other late-night passengers—most of whom were new soldiers like her—and two more NCOs in uniform greeted them.

They counted the heads, double-checked they had everyone, and turned to lead the new batch of incoming trainees out to the van waiting for them.

One of the NCOs with P. Mandel embroidered on a patch on his uniform smirked at Idina. "Have a nice flight?"

"It was okay, I guess."

"Uh-huh. Don't worry. We'll get you all into reception, and you'll finally have a chance to rest before you get into the real heavy stuff."

The other NCO snorted and shook his head. "Oh, yeah. You'll love it."

Idina rearranged the strap of her duffel bag over her

shoulder and couldn't decide if she should smile or keep a straight face and her head down.

More jokes. I guess reception isn't all that great, but it's another step, right? Fair enough. I can handle it.

The drive crammed into a large van with everyone else almost put her to sleep *again*, but she roused with renewed interest when they stopped at one of Fort Leonard Wood's security gates to be checked over and let in. The NCO at the gate this late at night didn't look particularly happy to be there, but he glanced inside the vehicle and snickered. "Look alive, fuzzies. You're in for a real treat, huh? Enjoy it while it lasts."

The NCOs shuttling them through the gates laughed and waved him off.

Once they rolled through the security gates and approached the reception barracks, though, it finally started to sink in that she *was* in a whole new world.

There were people *everywhere*. A lot of them looked like her and the other recruits shipped in to start the next cycle of basic training. Most of them stared around with wide eyes, taking in the dull gray concrete buildings, the vehicles, the uniformed soldiers hurrying back and forth.

Idina slung her duffel bag over her shoulder and followed the line of recruits into the barracks. *I'm here. For real. I never even thought about the Army until a month ago, and now this is where I ended up.*

Only now, under the bright lights illuminating the

barracks under the thick darkness in the middle of the night, did she realize how alone she was.

Nobody knows me. Nobody cares who I was before this or who my family is, or what I've done. I guess we're all alone in this at the very beginning, huh?

They moved through a narrow hallway toward what looked like a lobby, then one of the NCOs who led them in pointed at the NCO behind the desk. "This is it. You're here until Phase One begins, so make the most of it."

Then they were left there in the lobby without any other instructions. The recruits looked around with wide eyes as the minutes ticked on and the night stretched out into yet another unending period of nothingness. Then the soldier behind the desk looked up at them and cleared his throat.

"Processing starts over there. Get in line."

The lines, it seemed, were never-ending that night. They waited their turn to be processed, fingerprinted, issued their military ID and the Eagle Card that was good only for the small commissary in the reception barracks for toiletry items they'd need while they were there.

"Three hundred dollars on this," the woman told Idina blandly as she handed over the card. "It comes out of your first paycheck."

Idina tried to chuckle, but it was hard when she couldn't keep her eyes open the way she wanted. "Don't spend it all in one place, right?"

"Very funny. Keep moving."

Then the recruits shuffled in a tired, bewildered line toward another room where civilians stood behind tables stacked with crates of uniforms. The man Idina approached looked her up and down, pursed his lips, and shrugged. "Yeah, that should work."

"Work for—" She was about to ask for what, but the man grabbed a stack of four folded uniforms and practically shoved them into her arms.

"You're going that way." Then he waved her aside. She followed the line across the room to get her PT uniform—sized in the same way—Army-issued boots, a small collection of simple toiletries, bedsheets, an empty camelback backpack, and her paperback copy of the Army Blue Book.

With everything in their arms, the recruits filed back out of the room for more waiting in the reception area. Another NCO finally arrived to lead them through the barracks to a different area where more lines filled the hallways. They waited for anyone to tell them anything about what was happening next.

Most people sat on the floor against the walls, each of them too tired to talk much at all. Even if they had the energy, NCOs stalked up and down the lines every few minutes to tell anyone chatty enough at this hour to stop talking.

Idina glanced at the girl sitting next to her with her head propped against the wall and her eyes closed. "You have any idea what time it is?"

The other girl opened one eye and let out a soft groan. "Late."

Then she closed her eye again and said nothing else.

Idina raised her eyebrows and looked blearily around the hallway again. *Looks like the time doesn't matter to anyone. When are we supposed to sleep?*

Two NCOs stepped into the hall. "Get up. Men, come with me. Women, follow Sergeant O'Hare."

The female NCO nodded and waited for the women to separate from the men before taking off in a different direction. O'Hare didn't seem all that happy to be here in the middle of the night—or maybe early morning at this point—but she walked briskly through the barracks all the same with a dozen new female soldiers following wordlessly.

The next room they entered was massive and filled with bunks. "Women's bay," O'Hare called. "Find an empty bunk and put your stuff down. There's storage under the beds and a locker for anything extra. Anyone who didn't buy a lock when you got your things should seriously reconsider that."

Idina and the others staggered across the bay to find unclaimed beds. She found a bottom bunk and dropped her bedclothes on top of it before piling everything else into the empty drawer beneath it that didn't already have a lock.

Where's the girl who sleeps on the top? Shouldn't everyone else be asleep right now?

"Hey, don't bother making the beds," O'Hare said to another girl who exhaustedly tried to shake out her folded bedclothes. "You'll have time for that later. Right now, you have ten minutes to get into uniform and put your stuff away."

The girl turned in disbelief. "I thought we were going to bed."

"Ha. Nope." O'Hare glanced at her field watch and chuckled. "It's six o'clock. The docs are back in, so *you're*

169

getting in line for your med checks. Along with the rest of your unit."

Some of the other girls groaned, and Idina grabbed the frame of the bunk above hers with an exhausted sigh. *That's why the place is empty. Everyone else is already up.*

"What's that?" O'Hare raised her voice. "Did I hear somebody complain? This is the Army, not summer camp. Get moving. You can sleep later."

Once she'd stripped off her civilian clothes—which she assumed she'd be wearing for the last time until the end of basic—Idina fumbled to get her uniform on. After being awake for a solid thirty-eight hours, her limbs somehow didn't want to respond immediately, and she felt like an idiot for not being able to button her uniform shirt correctly until the third try.

Idina shuffled forward with everyone else, her arms now empty of all the gear she'd shoved into the drawer beneath her bunk and locked with the combination lock she'd bought from the commissary because the woman behind the counter had suggested it.

She looked up to see the brunette girl who'd been sitting beside her in the last hallway and managed a tired smile. "Great way to start, huh?"

The girl shook her head. "I can't tell if anyone's saying actual words right now."

They both at least attempted to laugh as the women filtered out of the bay.

"I'm Idina. Moorfield here, I guess."

"Petrie. Amber." The girl nodded and ran a hand through her hair.

That was as much as either of them could manage

under the staggering exhaustion as O'Hare led them back through the barracks to spend more time waiting in the lines that swelled with more recruits by the second.

If this is supposed to be the easiest part of basic, maybe I thought the rest was too easy.

The rest of that day stretched on like a waking dream—but not the restful, pleasant kind. Idina felt like she was moving through syrup as she and the others stood, sat, and stepped in line after line that moved with agonizing slowness. Before the first doctor could see them, another NCO arrived to announce they'd have to get in line again later because it was time for breakfast chow.

Once they went to the mess hall, Idina briefly wondered why the place was so incredibly silent before she realized how packed it was. The lines moved quickly as soldiers in reception got their food and took it to a table, shoveling it down as fast as they could because they only had ten minutes to eat. Nobody wanted to wait longer than they had to. Even if anyone wanted to have a conversation with the person sitting across from them, there wasn't time.

When Idina finally made it into a medical exam room sometime around mid-morning, the ridiculousness of being asked all the same physical questions she'd answered at MEPS made her want to scream. Then she was sent to more medical professionals to check her over in literally every category—dental, hearing, vision, reflexes, vitals, even the last time she'd had a bowel movement.

Idina considered herself lucky not to join the groups of young men getting their hair cut at 2:00 a.m. or that she didn't have a cavity that needed filling. A lot of recruits did. This helped her move through the first part of intake relatively quickly, but she still had to wait in line with the others for everything. There seemed to be a different process for each little thing, which required her to get into another line and wait with everyone else for hours.

Dinner chow seemed impossibly far away until the NCOs finally called them to it, and Idina shoveled food into her mouth like a zombie before cleaning up her tray and heading out of the mess hall with the others.

"You're free for the rest of the night," another NCO called from the mess hall doorway. "Lights out at twenty-three-hundred hours, but until then, your time's yours."

Idina stopped and stared at him, her eyelids drooping.

The NCO smirked as he met her gaze. "Looks like you just got in. Having fun yet?"

She didn't think about what she was saying before she mumbled, "Loads."

"Yeah, no shit." The NCO stepped away from her, snorted, and focused his attention on watching the other recruits cramming food into their mouths.

Idina blinked heavily and took off through the barracks, trying to remember where the women's bay was so she could flop down onto her bed. After she made it, of course. Two other NCOs pointed her in the right direction, chuckling as they watched severely sleep-deprived arrivals moving like the undead through the barracks.

Finally, she reached her bunk in the bay and must have taken twenty minutes to unfold the bedclothes and stretch them across the thin mat serving as a mattress. At that point, with a full belly and a complete inability to think anything at all, she rolled onto her bunk without bothering to remove her boots and groaned.

This is what I signed up for? This? Whatever. I'm here, and it'll be better in the morning.

CHAPTER SEVENTEEN

The days blended, and none of them were particularly "better in the morning." From 5:00 a.m. to 5:00 p.m., Idina went through the agonizing routine of dressing, waiting, eating, *maybe* being seen by one doctor for immunizations or blood tests, then waiting some more before eating again and waiting again and doing absolutely nothing else. It dawned on her that she was always with the same group of people.

The Army Blue Book was a frequent companion in most recruits' hands since they weren't allowed to talk in a crowded room with hundreds of other new soldiers sitting in the same miserable existence of reception. That Blue Book was the only source of entertainment anyone had during the day. From it, she learned that this was the beginning of her company.

Idina tried to focus on the fact that her paperback copy held everything she needed to know about what was waiting for her when she finally started the first phase of basic. It detailed the Soldier's Creed, what it meant to be an

Army soldier, and the types of training and drills waiting for her on the other side of this unending monotony. More often than not, it ended up putting her to sleep if she wasn't careful.

They weren't allowed to exercise, as evidenced by a sergeant stepping into the hallway outside another exam room and catching one of the newest trainees doing sit-ups against the wall.

"Shreider! Who told you to do PT?"

"Huh?" The guy stopped halfway through his rep and stared at the NCO.

"I asked you a question."

"Nobody. I was—"

"That's right. Nobody told you. Are you telling me you know better than the NCOs in these barracks?"

Shreider struggled to his feet and didn't say a word.

"I didn't think so. Don't let me see you pull that shit again. Sit down."

At the end of the first day, after once again cramming as much food as she could into her mouth before her ten minutes were up, Idina wasn't quite ready to sleep again when she returned to the women's bay. That was when she finally had a chance to talk to someone else who wasn't a doctor or a soldier stationed at reception to ask her questions or tell her what to do.

Amber walked into the bay not long after Idina had flopped down onto her bunk and lay there staring at the ceiling. "I'm pretty sure that shuttle took a wrong turn and ended up in hell instead of Fort Leonard Wood."

Idina chuckled and pushed herself up onto her elbows. "You think they know the difference?"

"Probably not. They're doing as instructed." The girl sat on her bed and huffed out a sigh before leaning forward to drop her head into her hands.

"Petrie, right?"

The girl looked up with a raised eyebrow. "Wow. *I* can barely remember my name right now. But yeah. And you're…"

"Idina Moorfield."

"Right. My brain fell out sometime yesterday." Amber smirked and jerked her chin up at Idina as more women filtered into the room, many of them sucking on their full camelbacks as they slapped their Blue Books and tossed them onto the bunks. "So. Moorfield. Why'd *you* join the Army?"

Idina snorted. "Honestly?"

"No, fucking lie to me."

They both laughed.

No surprise that talking to anyone in the Army feels a little like talking to Bryan. When he's stoned.

Idina shrugged. "I guess it started as me trying to give my family the finger. They gave it right back to me, so I enlisted."

"No shit." Amber snickered. "So you're one of *those*."

"One of what?"

Another girl with her dirty-blonde hair pulled sharply back in a ponytail paused at Idina's bunk. "Trying to prove a point with a 'fuck you' to the parents, huh?"

Amber burst out laughing. "See? *She* gets it."

"At least they didn't *make* you join the Army," the blonde added before climbing up onto the bunk above Idina's.

"Yours did?" she asked, craning her neck to look up at the other girl's face poking out over the mattress.

"I mean, it was either this or jail time. At least, that's the deal their lawyer came back with. Right now, I'm starting to think jail might've been better. Don't ask me what I did. My parents are shitheads who wanted to press charges on their kid, and that's all that matters."

Some of the other young women stared at her in confusion before quietly going to their bunks or private conversations with those they'd already had a chance to get to know.

Amber gave Idina an exaggerated grimace before picking some invisible lint off her uniform pants.

"What about you?" Idina asked her.

"Why am I here?"

"Yeah."

Amber shrugged. "My grandpa's a lieutenant general. Two of my brothers are Special Forces."

"So it's a thing your family does."

"No, I was sick of hearing all their awesome stories and tired of missing out."

Laughter came from some of the other women recruits who'd overheard, and the blonde girl on the bunk above Idina snorted. "Yeah, it's real awesome so far."

"Just wait 'til we get out of here." Amber unlaced her boots and tugged them off. "*If* we ever get out of here."

"When are you guys supposed to leave?" Idina asked.

"September first," Amber muttered. "Honestly, after the last few days, I don't know how they're gonna get us all processed before then. I haven't been able to sit with a doctor for more than two minutes before they call lunch break."

"I'm out the day after tomorrow," the blonde above Idina added. "Probably."

"To go where?"

The blonde stuck her head farther over the edge of the bunk to look Idina in the eye. "What's your name?"

"Moorfield," Amber answered for her as she lay down on her bed and closed her eyes with a sigh.

"Okay, Moorfield. I'm going wherever the hell they send me, and unless you're leaving reception in two days, it's not with you."

Idina raised an eyebrow at the other young soldier trying to bash her into submission with that kind of callousness. "So you screwed something up bad enough that you don't wanna talk about it, huh?"

A few other girls around them laughed, and Amber snorted. "She read you like an open fucking book, didn't she?"

The blonde grinned and shot Idina the middle finger before rolling back up on her bunk and falling silent.

I'll take that as a yes. She's right. It's none of my business. But it sounds like Amber and I might be heading in the same direction, so at least I'll know someone. Someone who comes from a military family and probably has an idea of what to expect when all this is finally over.

She thought about lying down like Amber and the blonde without a name above her, but she'd crammed too much food into her stomach to get comfortable enough for sleep. Some of the other recruits in the women's bay had formed smaller circles of conversation, but right now didn't feel like the time to start walking around trying to make friends.

I only have to hold out for another five days, and I'm in for real. There better be a hell of a lot more to do in basic. So far, it looks like all the boredom and exhaustion are better for my episodes than any meds. For now.

CHAPTER EIGHTEEN

Those five days dragged on with more physical exams, an unconscionable number of immunizations Idina didn't know existed, and wait in line after line with the others in her company. She read the Army Blue Book, ate and slept on command, and tried to remember a life that didn't consist of only those things. Idina figured out that when everyone had said reception was the easiest part of basic, they were full of shit.

She was ready to claw her eyes out by the time three NCOs entered the mess hall during lunch chow and barked out a list of names. "When you finish here, grab your gear and wait in the bay. You're heading out today, so hurry up. Ten minutes. Let's go."

Idina looked up to meet Amber's gaze from across the long mess table and smirked.

The other girl shrugged and shoveled the rest of her meal into her mouth as quickly as possible before chugging her water and standing. Idina was fast behind her, and those called to head out and finally start the first real phase of basic filtered out of the mess hall with renewed energy.

This is it.

The women's bay filled with female recruits hurrying to their bunks to pack everything they owned. That now only consisted of their Army-issue gear and the approved items they'd brought with them, minus cell phones and personal belongings marked as contraband for the duration of basic. Idina had everything strapped up tight and ready to go faster than most of the others, but she stood in a line and waited while Sergeant O'Hare kept a keen eye on the time and the recruits' movements.

Amber stepped in line behind her and leaned forward to whisper, "Now the real fun begins."

"Damn. And I was having so much fun here."

"That's it, recruits," O'Hare called. "Follow me."

The other women scrambled to finish packing and lugged their packs over their shoulders before O'Hare led them through the reception barracks again to a large room at the back of the building.

The men joined them shortly after, and Idina frowned at the display tables lining the empty room. One of them had a sign for a credit union. Another boasted signup forms for financial planning classes. Each table had something slightly different, but all of it was related to the handling of money and finances, offering opportunities for the recruits to learn about how to handle their Army paychecks and what was exclusively available to them now that they were soldiers.

Come on. This is the first step out of reception? I mean, at least they're not trying to sell us bad investment portfolios.

The thought made her snort, then the SNCOIC in the room—Staff Sergeant Remmington—shouted, "Take a look at everything here while we're waiting. You'll want to get a handle on this stuff if you pass your FTXs. So sign up for whatever you think you might need, and that'll be waiting for you on the other side."

Amber shrugged and stepped away from Idina to head toward the closest table, muttering, "At least we get to read something that isn't the damn Blue Book."

Idina muffled a laugh as the other girl headed across the room to join the other recruits milling around and checking out their options.

Yep, that's probably the only reading we have for a while. I should probably sign up for a few of these things now too. It's not like I still have an account with Moorfield & Associates after the way this turned out.

She headed across the room and stood in more lines to check out the station for the Army-affiliated credit union. This time, the line moved normally instead of feeling suspended in time for eternity.

The guy in front of her needed to decide how much he wanted to take out of his monthly check to put into a savings account. He seemed incapable of understanding the information the woman behind the table was giving him. Idina had seen the guy a lot over the last week and heard his name tossed around by the NCOs reminding him that they didn't have all the answers to his questions.

"But it's still *my* money, right?" he asked, his thick southern accent making his words sound fast even when he talked this slowly.

"Of course. You just wouldn't see it in your paycheck. It

would already be taken out and moved into a savings account if that's what you want to do."

"But...I mean, if it's not in my paycheck, where does it *go*?"

"I..." The woman behind the table looked up around the room, but no one was paying attention to how they could help *her*. "You know, all you have to do now is sign up right here. Just write your name down, and someone will contact you in a few months."

The soldier stared at the sign-up sheet and tilted his head. "If I sign that, you're not gonna take my paycheck, are you?"

"Well, we are a credit union, so technically, yes. We take your check. You get money in return."

"Man, why does this have to be so *complicated—*"

"Hey." Idina couldn't help herself and finally nudged the back of his shoulder. "McCoy, right?"

He turned to look her up and down. "Yeah, I'm workin' on it. Gimme a minute."

"Yeah, I know. Go ahead and put your name down. When I finish, I'll explain how it all works, if you want."

McCoy wrinkled his nose. "What do *you* know?"

"A lot. I grew up in finance. So go ahead."

With a hesitant shrug, the guy turned, picked up the pen, and jotted his name down on the signup list, muttering, "I didn't sign up for them taking all my money."

The woman looked up at Idina as he bent over the sheet, gratitude oozing from her wide eyes. Idina nodded and waited for McCoy to step aside. She didn't expect him to hang out there and wait around for her. However, the guy stood right at the end of the table, his arms folded and the hose of his camelback dangling from his mouth as he sucked water and squinted at her.

"So. Do you know what you're interested in?" the woman asked.

"Yeah." Idina tapped a printout on the table with a summary of the credit union's available service options. "Regular checking account and savings. Do you have a signup for a 401(k)?"

"Absolutely. That would be the Thrift Savings Plan. Put your name down on this sheet as well."

"Great." Idina bent over the table, trying to ignore McCoy's stare as she wrote her name down in two separate places. "What about IRAs?"

"I'm sorry?" The woman looked confused all over again.

"Individual retirement plans."

"Oh, I know what it is. I just... You're looking for both?"

"Yeah."

"Well, we do have some initial information on that as well." The woman pulled out a new sheet of paper and wrote IRA on the top. "But you're the first to ask. So I guess I'm starting a new list."

"Great. Thanks. I'll get all the information about the available investments included in that, right? I mean later."

"Yes..." Blinking quickly, the woman let out a surprised laugh and sat back in her chair. "I'm sure there will be someone who can answer your questions and guide you in the right direction."

Idina didn't bother to tell the woman that she'd rather get a list of the stocks and bonds in which the credit union invested funds on their clients' behalf. Instead, she nodded and stepped away from the table. "Thanks."

"You're welcome." The woman stared after her for a moment, then got sucked right back into helping the next recruit set up for their financial futures in the brief transitional time they had.

McCoy looked Idina up and down again. "Shit. I know I'm not the brightest crayon in the toolbox, but I know the alphabet. What the hell's with all the numbers and letters?"

Idina choked back a laugh. *I don't need my green lights to be able to explain financial options to a meathead.* "401(k)s are for retirement. Part of a pension plan, right? An IRA takes a certain amount of your money and invests it in... I lost you, didn't I?"

McCoy slowly shook his head. "I'm never gonna make it."

"Okay, listen. You don't need to worry about all that. You were asking about a savings account, right? And opting to put a certain amount from every paycheck into it when you get paid."

"Yeah, but that lady said she'd take my money and give it to someone else."

"Uh...nope. Both accounts are yours. You can use them whenever you want."

His eyes widened. "No shit?"

"No shit." Idina stepped out of the way as the recruit who'd stood behind her in line left the table to peruse the other reps around the room. "Listen, someone will probably tell you all this later, but a savings account is for *saving* your money, right? To use later if you need it for an emergency or something. So when they ask you how much, just go with something like ten percent. That's a good start."

"Of what?"

She finally couldn't help herself and let out a laugh halfway between a grunt and a full-blown bark in his face. "Your paycheck."

"Shit, how much is that?"

"Ten percent is… You know what? Start with a hundred bucks. That's easier."

"Damn. That's more than I've seen in… Huh." McCoy scratched his head, his beady eyes squinting so much they almost looked completely shut. "Thanks, I guess."

"Don't mention it."

He ambled away, pausing twice to look over his shoulder *toward* her but not really at her. Then he found a group of other young men he'd gotten to know at least a little, and Idina forced herself to ignore the way he botched trying to explain to them what had happened.

Not the brightest crayon in the toolbox. No kidding. That's what they said at MEPS, right? The Army takes everybody, just not liars.

Idina scanned the rest of the room to see what else she might have a use in signing up for and found Staff Sergeant Remmington standing halfway across the room, staring at her with his arms folded.

Great. I'm helping a crayon figure out what a savings account is, and it put me in the spotlight. And…now he's coming to talk to me about it.

Staff Sergeant Remmington nodded at a group of recruits heading toward the next table before he passed them, then called, "Giving out free advice, Moorfield?"

"Something like that, Staff Sergeant. Yeah."

The corners of his mouth turned down when he pursed them like he was trying to look impressed.

Then he's gonna watch how I act when he thinks I think he's impressed. That's what all this has been about from the beginning. Everybody's watching to see what we do.

"You know a lot about money?"

She nodded. "My family owns an investment firm."

"Sounds fun."

"Actually, it sucked." Idina flashed him a quick, closed-lipped smile that felt as tight and useless as her family's grip over her had been until a little over a week ago.

"So you enlisted in the Army instead, huh?" Remmington chuckled. "Listen, Moorfield. What you're about to head into isn't a cakewalk either, huh? It gets rough in there."

"I figured."

He searched her gaze and nodded. "Maybe. But it's good to go into this knowing from someone who's been there, yeah? You don't know what's gonna break you until it's happening. Everybody gets broken. Mentally. Physically. Emotionally."

Idina drew a deep breath. "I'm expecting it."

"Yeah. It's a little different when you're living it, but okay. You ever meditate?"

"What?"

"If you get to a point where you think you can't continue, focus on your breath. Remember none of this is impossible, even when it feels like it." Remmington glanced across the room and tilted his head. "Sergeant Hendricks is giving a little rundown over there of some breathing exercises. How to center yourself. You might wanna check it out while you've got the time now. Just in case."

"Okay. Thanks." Idina gave him another curt nod, and

the SNCO returned it before meandering around the room again, watching the other recruits scrambling to figure out what they wanted to learn about for their futures once basic was over and they entered active duty.

He thinks I need extra help with breathing exercises and centering myself? I figured that out when I was seven and training with a semi-renowned martial arts master, but okay.

When she turned to survey the rest of the room, though, she realized she wasn't the only recruit getting that kind of not-so-peppy pep talk. The SNCOs and NCOs around the room, including Staff Sergeant Remmington and Sergeant O'Hare, had joined other small groups of new soldiers to give them a similar rundown.

"Just remember everybody reaches their limits here. People cry. They puke. Fall on their asses during PT. They miss their families."

"You're gonna get to a point where you wanna call it quits. Throw in the towel. Even if you've never quit anything in your life, this is the hardest thing you'll ever do."

"Try to find that place in yourself where you knew this was what you wanted. Think about coming out on the other side of this. You will if you want it badly enough, but it won't be easy."

Wow. They're piling on the empathy here. I thought basic was supposed to be full of screaming drill sergeants and hardcore rules. I mean, I guess it technically hasn't officially started yet, but this is cool. My parents can't ship me off to the Army with anything remotely resembling an 'I love you,' but the SNCOs and NCOs are giving us a heart-to-heart about what it's like to break.

Frowning—and admittedly a little intrigued—Idina approached the group Sergeant Hendricks was talking to about breathing exercises during difficult situations and what those difficult situations might feel like without giving any real specifics. She listened to the step-by-step process of finding a breathing rhythm and a centering habit unique to each soldier. The recruits listened intently, their faces blank and their eyes wide as it started to hit them that they were in for the hell of a lifetime.

So reception either is or isn't the easiest part. Now I have no idea what to think.

After an hour at their last stop in the reception barracks, Remmington stepped through the door at the far side of the room and disappeared. Two minutes later, he came back inside and circled his finger above his head. "Bus is here, soldiers. Time to load up."

The conversation died down immediately, and the recruits headed toward the exit.

Sergeant O'Hare snorted. "Buckle up, kids. You're in for it now."

The trainees for the newest cycle of basic at Fort Leonard Wood filtered out of the barracks and followed the SNCOs and NCOs to a large bus parked behind the building. They readjusted packs, put on hats and pulled them tight, and boots scuffed across the asphalt. The six non-commissioned officers were all smiles and pats on the back, handing out encouragement like candy as the line moved quickly up into the bus.

"You got this, Jones."

"Get your ass up here and have fun, huh?"

"Best ride of your life. Trust me."

What is going on?

Despite her confusion, Idina couldn't help but smile when Sergeant Hendricks playfully punched a recruit in the arm and shouted, "Dude's arm is as hard as a rock!"

"Not for much longer," Remmington shouted back.

The seat beside Amber was open, so Idina peeled her pack off her shoulders and slid down with a sigh, *thumping* against the backrest. "Here we go."

"Yeah." Amber glanced at her sidelong and snickered. "Fucking finally."

"You think they're gonna tell us when it's time to start marching at attention?"

"Ha. Nope."

"Didn't think so." With a wry laugh, Idina watched the front of the bus until everybody had piled in.

Two non-commissioned officers each sat at the front, in the middle, and in back, joking and laughing with their recruits as the bus doors *hissed* closed, and the driver disengaged the brake to head down the road through Fort Leonard Wood. Idina caught the driver looking up into the rearview mirror at his passengers with a smirk.

This feels like a trap. I mean, fine. Maybe everything's a trap right now, but something's coming.

The bus filled with rowdy conversation, soldiers laughing and playfully punching each other, the energy high with excitement to get out of reception and into the basic barracks. Someone belted out a terrible song at the top of his lungs, and a wave of groans rose from the men.

"You've been singing that shit for a week, Tilborn. Shut the fuck up."

"My ears are already bleeding, man."

"Somebody put this dying animal out of his misery!"

They bumped down the road, loud and filled with energy, unaware of what lay in store for them at the bottom of the hill.

Idina watched it all with a small smile, gauging the staff sergeant's and NCOs' reactions to what sounded more like a party bus than their ride into basic training.

This is all about to change. It has to. Whatever happens next, I don't think anyone's ready.

CHAPTER NINETEEN

"Jesus, Donahue." Staff Sergeant Remmington chuckled and shook his head. "You're a real fucking standup comedian over here, aren't you?"

"But you laughed, didn't you?"

The bus finally reached the bottom of the massive hill and the front of the basic barracks on Fort Leonard Wood. The driver came to a quick stop, the *hiss* of the engaged brakes filled the vehicle, and as the door slid open, everything changed.

Idina had half a second to see the smile completely disappear from Remmington's and Hendricks' faces, then basic training began.

Remmington lurched to his feet, reached around the seat behind him, and grabbed the soldier's pack from the floor between his legs. "You think this is a fucking game, Donahue?" He tossed the pack through the open door of the bus and stepped into the soldier's face. "I'm not laughing. Do you see me laughing? Get your shit and move!"

At the same time, the NCOs broke into barked shouts

as they stood from their seats to grab loose packs and haul soldiers to their feet.

"On your feet, soldier! This isn't story time."

"When I say go, you *move*, motherfucker!"

"Nobody told you to sit on your ass all day. You don't sit until I *tell* you to sit."

"Let's go, maggots! Move, move, move!"

The confusion on the bus was as tense as the recruits trying to grab their gear before it was flung out into the parking lot and jostling into each other just to get out the door.

Idina strapped on her pack as quickly as possible and grunted when she tripped over someone's foot and stumbled into the soldier in front of her.

"Jesus Christ, Moorfield. Who the fuck taught you how to walk?"

One of the soldiers tumbled to his knees off the last step of the bus, and another NCO stood over him to shout, "You wanna spend time on your *knees*, soldier? I'll give you plenty of time on your knees. You have two seconds to get the fuck up and start moving!"

The soldiers streamed in a confused column away from the bus, ushered by the screaming drill sergeants pointing at them and the doors of the barracks as they walked sideways to shout in every face passing them.

"Don't look at *me*, Shreider. Eyes forward!"

"You want your mama now? Your mama isn't gonna do shit to help you!"

"You're mine for the next ninety days, Fuzzy, and you'll wish you weren't!"

The open doors of the barracks echoed with more

shouting as the soldiers streamed inside. They bumped against each other to get through the door and away from the NCOs shouting at them from what felt like literally everywhere.

"Are you an old fucking man, Kerrigan? Then stand up straight!"

"Look at me again, and I'll smoke your ass so hard, you'll fucking *go* blind!"

Any soldier with their cap still on when they entered the building got them snatched off their heads and tossed down the hall. "Where the fuck's your cap, Doolie? You better find it before I do!"

Any soldier who'd figured that part out quickly enough snatched their caps off their heads and shoved them into their side pockets. When those side pockets weren't buttoned again quickly enough, the NCOs pulled the recruit aside and threw everything out of those pockets before screaming at them to get their shit together and quit being a lazy slob.

Idina managed to avoid both obstacles and had her side pocket buttoned again. When the recruit in front of her bent to retrieve his cap from the floor, she sidestepped out of the way but turned enough to thump the side of her pack against Staff Sergeant Remmington's arm. "Don't fucking touch me, Moorfield! Am I too close in your personal space?"

She kept walking, trying to ignore him and following the line of other soldiers corralled into the barracks.

"I asked you a goddamn question, Moorfield. Is your bubble being fucking popped?"

He's trying to get me to screw up and answer without an order to answer. Now this is for real.

The line of shouting NCOs and scrambling recruits moved through the hallway of the barracks until O'Hare opened the door at the end of the hall and held it open with the heel of her boot. "Move it! You call that fast, Abernathe? My dead grandma moves faster than that!"

They were herded out into the yard and yelled at one more time for not having their caps on again as soon as they stepped outside.

"You're a fucking joke. Fall in, soldier! You're in *my* world now!"

"A line is straight! Do you know what straight is, Masterson? Doesn't look like it. Heel to heel!"

"Oh, are you scared? Go ahead, Stevens. Cry. That'll get you real far. Are those fucking tears?"

Idina hurried to stand in the line the drill sergeants wanted. She was fairly certain at this point *where* exactly to stand only because Staff Sergeant Remmington stood at the far right, barking orders and insults while he stabbed a finger at the asphalt in front of him. "If you can't form a goddamn line, you won't make it past day one!"

"Don't look at them! They're not gonna help you. Figure it out and get in line!"

Finally, the recruits figured out how to make a line with NCOs yelling in their faces and everyone shuffling around trying to make room for the entire company to do as ordered. Then the NCOs stopped yelling, and Staff Sergeant Remmington walked up and down the front of the line.

"Face forward. Look ahead. When your SNCO or NCO

gives you a command, you fucking *do* it. You'll do it wrong over and over until you get it right. Then you'll do it again. I don't care how many times it takes.

"When you're finished with Red Phase, you'll eat, sleep, and breathe how to stand in line like a soldier, how to work together, how to support your battle buddy, your team, your squad, your platoon, your entire company as a disciplined member of the U.S. Army. Not like a bunch of wide-eyed children shivering in your oversized boots. Right now, you look like fucking babies. I hope you don't run like babies."

The recruits were silent until Sergeant Hendricks shouted, "That means *run!*"

He circled his finger in the air to indicate their portion of the yard, and the line of recruits hesitantly started moving.

"The longer you take, the longer you'll run, Fuzzies!" another NCO shouted. "Get moving! Nobody told you to take off your gear, Nelson. Go!"

Idina followed the line running around and around the yard with the NCOs shouting at them to hurry, do better, keep going.

Here we go. First day of running laps on concrete.

Their gear weighed more than most recruits had carried on them at one time. Many of them slowed to a jog before a drill sergeant was up in their face yelling at them to keep going. Sweat dripped down every recruit's face and soaked their uniforms by the time Remmington shouted, "Bravo Company, fall in!"

Three NCOs echoed the command, one by one.

"First Platoon, fall in!"

"Second Platoon, fall in!"

"Third, fall in!"

The recruits jogged out of their running and tried to remember what that meant from what they'd read in the Blue Book. After running with their full gear on, they had a hard enough time remembering which platoon they'd been assigned to when they'd received their orders for Basic. Which also made it hard to figure out where they were supposed to stand, and no one gave them clear-cut instructions.

First. That's me. Idina broke away from the soldiers scattering around to figure out where to go and headed toward another NCO she didn't know who'd shouted for the First Platoon.

Soon, Bravo Company separated into its three platoons, and the drill sergeants started their instructions with those for whom they were responsible.

Staff Sergeant Remmington walked up and down the row of Idina's platoon, looking each soldier up and down. "This isn't a formation. This is a puddle. Sheldon!"

The soldier he stopped in front of widened his eyes and soundlessly opened his mouth before glancing at the staff sergeant with a croaking sound.

"Sir!" Remmington barked. "When I address you, soldier, I don't want you gaping at me like a dead fish. I want that response!"

"Sir."

"I can't hear you!"

"Sir!"

"Why are your boots an inch in front of Brock's? Do you not know what a straight line is?"

"Shit, sorry." Sheldon tried to shuffle back into line, but the other NCO who'd been standing slightly behind Remmington marched up and shouted in the soldier's face.

"Did you just say what I think you said?"

"I didn't—"

"Drop and give me twenty! That's *pushups*, asshole. If you say one more word, you'll give me another twenty. Think you can keep your mouth shut?"

Sheldon was already on his hands, pumping away at the pushups.

"I can't hear you!"

"Yes, sir!" he replied with a grunt.

While he continued his pushups, Remmington stayed where he was and addressed the platoon again. "The respect you show your commanders is the same respect you show the rest of your platoon. It's the same respect you'll learn to strengthen in yourself.

"That respect carries down to the tiniest detail of who you are inside and out. The way you think. The way you eat. The way you sleep. The way you put on your uniform. The way you take a shit. Corporal Watson is your PG. Anything she says might as well come from me as your platoon leader. Is that understood?"

"Yes, sir!" the platoon replied.

Sheldon finally stood from his pushups and hustled back into line, making sure this time that his boots didn't creep even a little forward past the boots of his fellow trainees on either side.

"Now, let's try this again." Remmington continued. "Ten-hut!"

Idina stood at attention like everyone else, her hands at

her sides and her elbows pulled back the way she'd seen and heard it described. *Of course, they're gonna find something they don't like. That's the point.*

She tried to stare straight ahead but couldn't help being distracted by the soldier beside her, and his fists pulled almost up to his waist.

Oh, come on. He's gonna get us—

"DeLafor!" Remmington stopped in front of the soldier beside Idina and leaned into the guy's face. "Where the hell are your hands?"

"My hands are at the end of my wrists, sir."

A few snickers rose from the platoon, and the staff sergeant turned to eye Corporal Watson standing off to the side. "You're a real funny shithead, DeLafor. Step forward. Turn around. Do you see the rest of your platoon?"

"Yes, sir."

"Do you see where their hands are? And no, not at the end of their wrists, smartass. At the proper position."

"Yes, sir."

"Where *are* they, DeLafor?"

"At their hips, sir."

"Fix it."

The soldier glanced down at his hips to try rearranging his hands to the proper position, and Idina had to force herself not to roll her eyes. *Does he seriously not know how to move his hands?*

"Right here." Remmington tapped the soldier's hips. "Weight forward. Back straight. You better figure out how to control your body, DeLafor. Your platoon's about to eat shit because you felt like being funny. And you get to stand here saying, 'I'm a funny shithead,' until they finish."

"Yes, sir."

"Run!" Corporal Watson shouted.

The sweaty, hot, tired recruits broke into another run to do laps again in the yard as Watson led them once to show them where they *could* run. The soldiers who groaned or looked even remotely tired were yelled at again and told to keep up.

Idina's pack bounced against her back as she jogged with everyone else in her sweaty uniform. It now chafed everywhere. *We have PT uniforms for a reason. But this is day one. We don't even get that much, do we?*

All the while, DeLafor repeatedly shouted, "I'm a real funny shithead!" while the rest of the platoon ran their punishment to the rhythm of his calls.

CHAPTER TWENTY

They must have drilled on standing at attention and nothing else for another three hours before Staff Sergeant Remmington ordered them to fall in again and Corporal Watson seconded the command. Then the recruits formed a line and were told to march to dinner chow. Most of them got reprimanded for walking the wrong way.

Then they had to learn how to grab their meal trays and their one plastic utensil, how to stand facing the wall, how to step sideways to get to their food and serve themselves no more than one scoop of anything laid out for dinner.

Two soldiers had to get down for thirty crunches when they sat before Remmington had given the command. Then the entire platoon practiced standing and sitting, standing and sitting again while their food went cold until they finally heard, "Soldiers, eat!"

Idina ate faster than she thought she could, shoveling bite after bite into her mouth and moving even quicker when Corporal Watson gave them a thirty-second deadline. Then it was time to stop and wait for the command to clean their trays. They ran through that drill for what felt like a million times before the way they'd stacked their trays and cups with the soldier sitting across from them was good enough.

After that, they went back to the yard and ran standing formation drills again for another two hours.

When the next recruit to mess up enough in those simple drills got the entire platoon smoked and ordered to run laps, several of them vomited their dinners and were yelled at to keep running and forget the mess. Matthews couldn't keep his stomach contents down anytime he came across one such mess left in the yard.

Remmington took him aside and told him to wait until the platoon had finished running. Then the soldier was handed a shovel and told to clean all the piles not trampled into sludge during the platoon's laps. Eventually, he didn't have anything left in his stomach, but he had to stop every few minutes under attacks of dry heaving before he finally shoveled every mess into a bucket and was ordered to go wash it out.

When they finished with drills, the orders continued for everything. Every step they took. Every line they formed. When the men and women split away from each other, Corporal Watson gave the women marching orders on their way to the women's bay. They also received orders for how to unpack their gear and store it beneath their beds, followed by commands to quickly change out of their fatigues and into their PT uniforms, which held a double purpose as their pajamas.

Finally, Watson looked over the women standing beside each of their bunks and nodded. "Lights out in ten."

Then she walked away and left the tired, breathless, weary female recruits to their own devices for their allotted ten minutes before lights out.

Idina climbed onto her bunk and stared at the lights set in metal cages hanging over the bay.

"This what you thought it would be, Moorfield?" Amber asked from a few bunks over as everyone else climbed into their beds with groans and heavy sighs.

"I'm not disappointed if that's what you're asking."

The other girl snorted and rolled over.

Idina sighed, closed her eyes, and went over her first day of basic training.

I can do everything I need to do all on my own to get every-thing right, but I'm not doing everything by myself anymore. Thirty-something people in this platoon, and there's always gonna be someone who doesn't get it right. That's what the drill sergeants are looking for, anyway. Any little thing to discipline. I guess I should start looking too. And hope like hell my green lights don't show up to get us all smoked double-time. Or get me kicked out.

That was what she did for the next week while First Platoon repeatedly drilled in formation, learning how to march, about-face, stand at attention and at ease, and form lines to move through the barracks. Idina watched both her fellow recruits *and* the platoon's non-commissioned officers as much as possible.

She watched who screwed up the most often, who looked the most pissed when they got their asses handed to them with twenty minutes of running or thirty pushups or jumping jacks until their legs turned to Jell-O. She observed the most likely times for Remmington and Watson to inspect their standing formation and which recruits repeatedly got their pockets emptied or were hounded especially hard for not picking up after themselves in the right way.

What frustrated her the most was when a male soldier went against regulation in the men's bay and got the entire platoon a massive round of disciplinary action without being able to see how the guy in question had seriously screwed up. Beyond that, she quickly formed a mental map of who was the most likely to get them smoked again and wipe them all out before they moved forward with a different kind of drill.

The platoon was assigned their battle buddies, meaning they had to stay in proximity with one of their own from when the platoon gathered after morning showers until their dismissal to the bays at night.

Somehow, Idina ended up with Collin DeLafor as her battle buddy. That made it harder for her to keep an eye on how the platoon as a whole operated and when and how the non-commissioned officers would come down on them for one person's screwups. Mostly DeLafor's. The guy wouldn't give up, constantly coming up with a smartass remark so the platoon spent most of their time running and getting in extra PT as punishment because he couldn't keep his mouth shut.

It came to a head at the end of the first week when they were standing in the chow line, moving a lot more quickly now that they understood the strict posture expected of them with a tray in their hands. Idina stood four recruits behind DeLafor, who bitterly snorted when he saw the cooked spinach among the food pans. The guy beside him slopped a giant pile of spinach onto his tray, and DeLafor groaned. "You know I have to sleep next to you, right?"

When the other soldier looked up at him in warning, he spilled a glob of spinach on the serving table, which of course didn't go unnoticed by Remmington.

"Pierce! Step out."

"Jesus Christ," Pierce muttered and glared at DeLafor. "You can't keep your mouth shut for one fucking minute?"

DeLafor rammed him in the shoulder when Pierce tried to turn with his tray, and the entire tray clattered to the floor, spilling his food everywhere. With a *hiss*, Pierce spun and socked the other soldier in the face. Two seconds later, they were grappling with each other on the floor and *in* the spilled chow before Remmington finally reached them.

"All right, that's enough. Hey!" The staff sergeant pried them apart and shoved the soldiers away from each other. "Pierce. Clean this up. Then go stand by the wall with your tray held out the right way to catch spills. If you move before chow's over, your battle buddy can join you. Maybe he can show you how to keep your food where it belongs. Do it."

"Yes, sir." Pierce grabbed his tray and went off to find a mop.

"DeLafor, where's your battle buddy?"

DeLafor searched the line of soldiers sidestepping toward the food and nodded. "In line, sir."

"Moorfield!" Remmington barked. "Get over here."

With her tray held out in the same position she'd been

holding it since they entered the mess hall—although her tray was no longer empty—Idina turned out of the line, marched toward him, and stopped. "Sir."

"DeLafor feels like throwing fists and making a mess. So give him your tray and go to the end of the line."

"Yes, sir." She shoved her tray as forcefully as she dared toward DeLafor, who took it and returned the glare.

"You're gonna join her," Remmington told him. "You don't find a seat until your battle buddy does, and now you get spinach. Move."

They both marched to the end of the line. Idina grabbed a new tray and a new plastic spoon, and they turned sideways toward the wall to bring up the sidestepping rear of the chow line.

She couldn't hold her silence for more than thirty seconds, which happened to be as much time as it took for the staff sergeant to move away across the mess hall while the tables filled with soldiers waiting for the command to sit and eat. "You're not gonna make it if you can't keep your mouth shut," she muttered.

"Wow. Someone wound you tight this morning."

"Yeah. You. Quit talking, huh? You're making it worse for everybody."

DeLafor snorted and looked straight ahead at the wall. "You're the one who's gonna start crying first. Not me. If you can't handle it, you should've stayed home."

"We're all in this together, asshole. And nobody's impressed."

"Bitch."

Idina clenched her teeth and gripped her tray tighter as

the line moved toward the chow she'd already served herself.

Yeah, I know how Pierce felt. This guy's gonna get himself in a lot more fights if he can't take this seriously like the rest of us. Or maybe he doesn't know how. Either way, I'm stuck with him for the next three months.

After that, Idina made it her mission to fall in line beside her battle buddy for every drill, every chow line, and every opportunity she had to ride him by always being right there in his face.

When he headed off to the bathroom during drills—and still wouldn't concede to the protocol for alerting their platoon commander or platoon guide that he had to go— she followed and declared DeLafor's needs to one of them. She made sure to say it loud enough for everyone to hear.

If he hadn't straightened out his posture when they fell in first thing in the morning, she'd quickly nudge his boot while staring straight ahead and kept doing it until he corrected himself. When he was on the verge of a smartass remark, she'd announce that *she* had to go to the bathroom instead and made her trips in the allotted two minutes they had.

It was a lot of extra work, but at least she could keep her battle buddy from making the same mistakes over and over and getting the entire platoon smoked a fourth, fifth, or sixth time in one morning as he had through their first week.

DeLafor hated her for it. He wouldn't talk to her and

gave her dirty looks whenever she showed up right beside him the whole time. The rest of the platoon took notice that their wannabe jester was starting to open his mouth less and pay attention more. They still got their asses handed to them when someone else screwed up, but the number of times they had to run laps and get down for unscheduled PT as a punishment decreased by half.

Idina had realized that he needed someone to give him constant reminders of how often and how badly he was screwing up. Not by saying it out loud but by reminding DeLafor that he was about to take the whole platoon down with him for something stupid they could've avoided.

By the middle of the second week, they'd practically mastered standing drills and simple commands and not screwing up the same monotonous routine repeating itself day in and day out. Then they started working with firearms.

No one was particularly excited to hear they wouldn't be firing the Army's standard M-9 pistol. Instead, they stood at tables and drilled over and over how to disassemble their weapons, clean them, and reassemble them in the provided timeframe.

Idina had her fair share of experience with firearms and took to the process in no time. She'd hardly noticed that her green lights had been practically nonexistent until they flickered to life again in her vision while she worked with her weapon.

The Moorfields didn't keep M-9s at the manor. That didn't mean her unexplained ability to *see* how the weapon's parts fit together was any more difficult than on the shooting range at home—courtesy of flashing green lights blinking around her M-9's next necessary component in perfect timing.

The skinny redhead Brock seemed to have a much harder time remembering which steps to take in which order, and he held the platoon up longer than anyone else.

Finally, while Idina moved through the motions for the twentieth time that day on full autopilot, she glanced at Brock's handling of his weapon and muttered, "Wrong piece."

"I got it," Brock snapped under his breath, his fingers fumbling with the disassembled parts.

Standing beside her, DeLafor shook his head and whispered, "Listen to her, man."

"Fuck." Brock grabbed the recoil spring instead of the recoil spring guide first and finally slid it correctly into the housing.

The second he got the slide back into place with a *click*, Watson called, "Time!"

Everyone set down their weapons and stepped away from the tables at attention.

Brock stared at his firearm, then flicked his gaze briefly up toward Idina and DeLafor as Remmington came to inspect the weapons.

Idina raised an eyebrow at him, then quickly returned her gaze straight ahead.

He won't forget now. *Just wait.*

Their platoon commander walked up and down both sides of the tables, studying the firearms until he paused behind Brock and looked over the redhead's shoulder. His eyes narrowed, Brock held his breath, then Remmington moved on to inspect the others.

When he was safely out of earshot, DeLafor snickered. "See? Moorfield's a real pain in the ass, but she knows what she's talking about."

Brock huffed out a surprised laugh, quickly swallowed it to compose himself, and kept staring at his reassembled and silently approved firearm.

Idina spared a glance at her battle buddy, who stared straight ahead and flipped her the middle finger while they all stood at attention.

He knows I can see that because I see everything else he does. Guess it was the right move to be a pain in his ass. As long as it sticks.

For no reason at all, the date flickered through her mind—September thirteenth.

She fought to keep a straight face.

Happy Birthday to me, I guess. I'm eighteen, off my inhibitors for two weeks, and in the fucking Army. We can call this my birthday present.

CHAPTER TWENTY-ONE

Idina kept up with watching everyone around her to see where she could silently be of service in nudging the First Platoon toward not sucking nearly as bad as they had at the start of basic. DeLafor finally started to fall in line, and they moved into the final stages of basic training's Red Phase and their first taste of what soldiering had in store for them.

They were assigned rotations to fireguard—nighttime patrols of the barracks that lasted an hour each and rotated through the recruits sleeping in the Bravo Company bay. Because the women in the company only made up a small fraction of the men, the fireguard rotation was a lot shorter for them, and Idina got her first taste of having to wake up on high alert in the middle of the night at least four times a week.

On her fourth rotation through the fireguard, she was nudged awake by Private Stevens.

"Here. You're on, Moorfield. Have fun." The other girl eagerly shoved the flashlight and clipboard for the women's fireguard into Idina's hands before marching back to her bunk.

Already prepared, Idina rolled out of bed fully clothed and staggered away from her bunk toward the bay entrance. Her job now was to walk around the barracks, flash the light, and document on the clipboard absolutely everything she saw. One seriously boring hour in the middle of the night.

Nothing ever happens, which is more likely to make us fall asleep while we're out here.

She clicked on the flashlight and started her patrol through the barracks. It always amused her to see whatever the fireguard before her had written on the clipboard, and Timbers' was as amusing tonight as ever.

0107: Carlton woke up for a piss.
0109: Carlton walked back from a piss.
0125: McCoy picked his nose in the stairwell. Flashed his light at me.
0137: Fireguard yawned.
0143: Someone had a nightmare in the men's bay.

Idina smirked. *What else are we supposed to write down when nothing's going on?*

That was their job, and they had to do it. The platoon had been run ragged during their first night on fireguard when the soldiers hadn't written anything down because they thought midnight bathroom breaks and nose-picking were too inconsequential. Now if someone so much as breathed funny, someone on duty that night would've written it down on their clipboard.

Eventually, she came to the hallway intersecting with the stairwell leading up to the men's bay. The sounds of echoing bootsteps were only too familiar. Usually, there were at least two other male soldiers on fireguard at the same time, and this was when they'd changed over their rotation too. Whoever it was would come down those stairs toward her at any minute, and they'd either see each other or not before continuing their patrol.

Then Idina heard something that *didn't* normally happen.

The bootsteps approaching down the stairwell stopped, replaced by the sound of a crinkling cellophane wrapper and heavy breathing.

Oh, come on. Who the hell thinks it's a good idea to eat contraband in the middle of the night?

She inched closer to the stairwell, moving quietly, then stepped around the corner and aimed her flashlight at the culprit halfway down the stairs.

Hughs froze where he was, his flashlight and clipboard tucked under one arm and an extra protein bar he'd snuck from chow half-eaten and still resting between his teeth.

"Hughs," Idina whispered. "What are you doing?"

"Shit." The guy tried to wrap up the rest of his protein bar, but he fumbled so much that his flashlight fell in the process and *clattered* down the rest of the stairs. "Damnit. Shit. Fuck my life."

She reached his flashlight first, glanced up the stairs,

then handed it back to him. The guy looked incredibly sheepish, probably because he was one of the larger recruits who'd come into basic, and it wasn't from a pre-established wealth of muscle. "Here."

Hughs took it back from her, but when she held on a little longer, his eyes widened. "Come on, Moorfield. I'm starving."

"I get it, but—" She glanced up the stairs again and lowered her voice. "You know what's gonna happen when they find *another* wrapper in the trash."

"Well, then what am I supposed to do with it, huh?"

"Don't sneak extra rations to start."

"Then you take it." He fumbled in his side pocket again, but Idina quickly stepped back and shook her head.

"That's on you to figure out. Don't throw it in the trash."

"Yeah. Fine. I'll just…" Only then did he seem to realize they were both on fireguard and that Idina had a patrol clipboard. "You're not… I mean, you're not gonna write this down, are you? Fuck, I don't wanna be *that guy,* but I already wake up starving even when I don't have to do this shit at night."

She glanced at her clipboard and sighed. "I have to say I saw you, but I'm not gonna rat you out in a report."

"For real?"

"Just make sure you write me down at—" She looked at her field watch. "Oh-two-one-four. Then get rid of the wrapper."

"Yeah. Got it. Thanks."

They exchanged a final nod, and Idina continued on her patrol around the first floor of the company barracks. She looked over her shoulder once when she heard Hughs' wrapper crinkling again and once more when he'd finally finished eating the stupid thing and had stuffed the wrapper into his pocket.

Shaking her head, she turned the corner and stopped to write down their quick passing interaction without mentioning anything about contraband that would get them all smoked to hell if he didn't figure something out.

We're all hungry. And tired. And done getting our asses beat by one person making stupid mistakes. I can't watch everybody in the whole platoon like I watched DeLafor.

Idina grimaced, stuck the pen through the top of the clipboard, and swung her flashlight left and right across the hallway to finish the rest of her hour.

———

She didn't think anything of it the next morning until Remmington and Watson commanded them to stand from the tables after their three minutes maximum of breakfast chow. They'd stacked all the trays across the table, and the recruits stood.

"Left face!" Remmington shouted.

The company turned. Then they were ordered to move, and half the soldiers who'd ended up with the stacked trays stayed behind for all of two seconds while the other half marched in a line toward the mess hall's exit. Then the dirty trays, stacked cups, and single utensils were returned to be washed, and the company headed out of the mess hall to begin their PT for the morning.

That was when Idina saw the silver glint of a protein

bar wrapper emerging from Hughs' unbuttoned side pocket.

Shit. Really? The NCOs are gonna find that too, and we're not gonna start PT with actual PT.

Someone tapped the small of her back from behind, and she knew it was DeLafor before he whispered, "You see that?"

"Yeah."

"What the fuck is he thinking?"

Idina shook her head as they marched out into the yard. Whether or not anyone else had a chance to see Hughs' indiscretion didn't matter. Watson had already spotted it.

The corporal waited until the company had split into its three platoons, then she stormed down First Platoon's line and snatched the wrapper from Hughs' unbuttoned side pocket. "Are you still hungry, Hughs?"

Forgetting himself, he turned to face her and took two seconds to notice the wrapper in Watson's hand before he went completely white.

"This is contraband. You know that. Stand fast. First Platoon, fall in!"

The recruits hurried to form their line. It was a lot easier now that they knew how to fall into formation after staying in a neat line the whole morning. Staff Sergeant Remmington passed Watson and Hughs with his hands clasped behind his back and glanced at the silver wrapper. He raised one eyebrow and kept walking toward the platoon standing at attention without a word.

Shit.

Idina tried not to grimace, and the other soldiers around her were trying to hold it together as they quickly figured out why Hughs was standing aside with the corporal before they'd really started their day.

Their area of the field behind the barracks grew incredibly silent.

"*Extra rations*," Remmington barked, "doesn't have a definition here. They don't exist."

Hughs swallowed thickly and clenched his eyes shut before remembering that could also get them all disciplined for his mistake.

"I don't want to see another wrapper, cigarette butt, or playing card from this platoon again, or you won't be able to close your fingers around them when I finish with you. Get down for thirty, then start running."

"Damnit, Hughs," DeLafor muttered.

Idina kicked his boot sideways before the platoon dropped and did as instructed.

"Hughs." Remmington returned to the culprit and pointed at the wrapper in Corporal Watson's hand. "The chow you get is the only chow in your mouth. Now you're gonna put *that* in your mouth and tell me you're not hungry until I say stop."

"Yes, sir." The color had returned to the soldier's face with full force and then some as he took the wrapper from Watson and did as commanded.

Idina and every other soldier getting smoked for the umpteenth time because someone else made bad choices ran around the yard. Only when they passed Hughs and the drill sergeants could they hear the recruit shouting a muffled, "I'm not hungry," over and over through the wrapper.

Yeah, that's totally the right way to get him to stop. Idina rolled her eyes and pushed herself to stay in line with the others. *We should be doing better by now.*

While the entire platoon was thinking the same thing and hoped Hughs would cut it out with his bad habit that got them all run ragged beyond their normal drills, none of them *expected* him to learn his lesson then and there. If they'd learned anything about their time so far in basic, it was that nobody stopped their bad choices "just like that."

So two days later on their third Sunday, Idina talked with DeLafor after their dismissal from breakfast chow. She found her battle buddy standing outside the laundry machines in the barracks, waiting for his uniforms to come out of the dryer while she lugged hers over her shoulder to do the same.

"Aw, come on, Moorfield. We have free time to do whatever we want for half a day, and you gotta ride my ass at the laundry?"

Idina snorted and leaned back against the wall beside him. They scanned the other soldiers milling down the hall to head to the barracks commissary or to check if they'd received mail sometime in the last week. She hadn't, but she wasn't worried about mail. "I'm not here to ride your ass. We need a plan."

"For what? Your big escape?"

"Very funny. I'm talking about Hughs."

DeLafor rolled his eyes. "Fucking Hughs. Four times this week. Dude couldn't *hide* a needle in a haystack."

"Well." She looked up at him and raised her eyebrows. "That's part of the plan."

Her battle buddy looked down at her with a sneer. "You're psycho sometimes. You know that, right?"

"I'd rather be psycho than smoked to shit four extra times because *one* soldier in our platoon can't stay away from the protein bars."

For a minute, DeLafor stared across the hall with his arms folded. Then he sniffed. "Fine. Let's hear it."

CHAPTER TWENTY-TWO

No one knew when or where Hughs would end up trying to hide the evidence of his late-night snacks in the side pockets of his uniform. The entire platoon expected it because he hadn't stopped by now, and they were as fed up with him collectively as they'd been with DeLafor at the start of basic.

Hughs kept himself out of trouble for the next three days, but then someone spotted another poorly hidden wrapper in the pockets of the one soldier who never remembered to button them. A whistle rang out through the mess hall as First Platoon filed out after breakfast chow.

The green flash in the corner of Idina's eye made her glance down at Hughs' side pocket. She spotted the wrapper—as did several other soldiers *without* green lights to alert them—and that was all it took.

They waited until they'd been marched back outside into the yard.

"First Platoon, fall in!" Remmington shouted.

As everyone moved into position, DeLafor kicked the back of Idina's boot during her next step. She made a huge show of stumbling over herself, conveniently in the direction of Hughs now that their line had split into two. "Shit, man. Watch it!"

Her shout was supposed to draw attention—and to mask the sound of her ripping Hughs' discipline-worthy rations wrapper from his pocket and crumpling it in her fist.

"My bad." DeLafor spread his arms and shrugged as he kept walking.

"Hughs," Corporal Watson barked. "Front and center."

The guy grimaced but did as commanded and stood at attention in front of the NCO as Remmington watched his platoon quickly assemble.

"Turn around." Watson looked Hughs up and down as he spun in a slow circle. Then she clicked her tongue and pointed at his pants. "Button up, soldier. How hard is that to remember?"

"Yes, sir." He quickly snapped the buttons and waited for her to dismiss him into the drill formation with everyone else. When Hughs stepped back toward the line, the confusion contorting his face made several platoon members press their lips together to force themselves into silence.

Idina watched the silent but still incredibly communicative look Watson shot Remmington and held her fists by her sides at attention. *Step one looks good. I can't hold onto this thing forever. Maybe Hughs will finally get the hint.*

The platoon ran through another marching drill, then the staff sergeant broke them up into squads and designated a squad leader for each to second their CO's commands the way Corporal Watson seconded the staff sergeant's. As the squads separated, Idina looked around at those broken off into Second Squad and made sure everyone else could see her and knew where she was.

While Watson gave them instructions and a rundown on the Physical Endurance Course across the yard, Idina felt Masterson eyeing her from across the formation. They didn't look at each other, but he nodded slightly, which was all she needed.

"Second Squad, about-face!" Watson shouted.

"About-face!" their squad leader echoed, and the soldiers turned on their heels to face the opposite direction.

"Forward march!"

Before the squad passed Watson, who stood right where she was with her arms folded while they headed for the course, Masterson reached out and quickly snatched the offending wrapper from Idina's hand.

One by one, the evidence of Hughs' contraband moved through the two lines of soldiers in Second Squad. Idina marched in time with the rest of them, daring only once to look in front of her and see the wrapper pass a final time to McCoy. The silver cellophane disappeared in his fist, and the squad leader called a halt when they reached the course.

Watson explained what they were doing today and the time they were trying to make. She detailed how every aspect of the PEC needed to be completed by every single soldier before they could not only pass through the course with a sufficient score but pass through Red Phase entirely and move on to the next. When she finished, she turned to face the squad. "Any—what are you doing, McCoy?"

The soldier who'd been as dumb as a box of rocks when it came to savings accounts was on one knee, his fingers flying through his undone laces. "Permission to tie my boots, sir?"

The corporal returned her attention to the rest of the squad and muttered, "Make it quick. You're doing a pushup for every second it takes you to do something you should've finished before morning chow."

"Yes, sir. One, Mississippi. Two, Mississippi. Three, Mississippi..."

Watson looked across the yard and nodded at Remmington and his squad leader escorting First Squad toward the course after them. "We're scoring you against First Squad, so make this count."

"Ten Mississippi." McCoy immediately hopped down to pump out ten pushups, which he also counted aloud for everyone to hear.

If Watson noticed the unusual amount of attention the rest of Second Squad paid to the one soldier who couldn't remember to tie his boots correctly, she didn't give any indication of it. Idina and every other soldier making up half the platoon watched the ground beneath McCoy's hands with a collectively held breath until he jumped to his feet and stood at attention.

The wrapper was gone.

Idina couldn't help a flickering smile across her face as

the corporal looked McCoy up and down with narrowed eyes.

"Fall in, McCoy. Next time you hold back your squad to lace up, they'll be pretty eager to show you how to tie a double knot."

"Yes, sir."

"All right. We're timing you. Second Squad leader, take it from here."

As it turned out, Amber was the most recent Second Squad leader in the rotation that switched out recruits with no apparent scheduled timing. She joined the rest of them and muttered, "Bring it in."

They crowded around, and Amber stared at McCoy for longer than the others. "Who needs help in the pit at the end of this?"

"I probably do," McCoy replied.

A few soldiers snickered.

"Yeah, like last time." Amber pointed at him. "Every soldier gets through this course as close together as possible. That means if McCoy here trips over his laces again and lands face-first in the mud, you drag him the hell out."

With that, they were ready to run the PEC in their squad, and Watson blew her whistle for them to start.

Second Squad surged over the course they'd run countless times already. It entailed rope climbs up a wall, swinging over two deep trenches, crossing horizontal bars, and helping each other across the swaying bridges that threatened to knock every soldier off each time a new boot came down on the wobbly wood. They gave it their best, stopping to help those who needed extra assistance to cross whatever obstacle lay ahead of them and encouraging each other with shouts to keep moving.

At the end of the course, McCoy sealed the deal by falling face-first in the mud pit—on purpose.

The rest of Second Squad jumped in to help him up, floundering for a total of five seconds in the thick, sludgy mud and grabbing McCoy's arms and legs to pull him out. With so much muck flying around, nobody saw the hand that grabbed Hughs' protein-bar wrapper from McCoy's left boot.

Nobody saw that hand submerge beneath the mud splashing in all directions. With so many different platoons in so many companies running this course for the duration of basic training, nobody would know who a single wrapper belonged to.

If they ever found it at the bottom of the pit.

Second Squad finished the course and streamed past Corporal Watson, breathing heavily and covered in mud and bits of straw and loose leaves. Their CO looked them over, then checked the time on her stopwatch without any expression whatsoever.

Idina clapped Masterson on the shoulder and gave him a breathless nod while the squad was permitted to take their time in recovering from their hustle. Then she met DeLafor's gaze, and though he looked as beat as the rest of them, he reached across his uniform to flick a lump of mud off his shoulder and jerked his chin up at her.

Ha. Yeah, he can flex. DeLafor got the word out so everyone would be ready to hide a stupid wrapper. I'm the one who came up with the plan.

Before Watson and Remmington ordered both squads

to re-run the PEC—again, and again, and again in an attempt to beat their last highest score—Idina couldn't help but notice them conferring privately about what she knew was their complete confusion.

The corporal had seen Hughs' contraband. Everyone had, and they'd all expected it to happen. It was a matter of when Hughs' stomach decided to get the better of him. Still, the evidence was gone. First Platoon got to focus on their actual objective for the day without having to run disciplinary laps or drop for pushups, sit-ups, and crunches. Both squads beat their best times at least twice, and neither non-commissioned officer brought it up again.

However, they held First Platoon back from their shower time after dinner chow that night to conduct a random barracks inspection focusing on both the women's and the men's bays.

Not so random. They know something happened, but they can't prove it. I swear, if anyone else is keeping contraband under their mattress, I'm gonna lose it.

They turned the bays upside down. Then told the mud-splattered soldiers to clean it all up in fifteen minutes before hitting the showers. They didn't find anything, at least in the women's bay. Only the next morning were they all sure that nothing surfaced in the men's bay either. No one got smoked before breakfast chow.

Hughs didn't have anything sticking out of his pockets that morning or the next. He never said a thing to Idina about it, but she was pretty sure she knew why he walked right past the table on the end where he'd normally pilfered his extra rations without grabbing anything at all.

After that, First Platoon worked a lot more smoothly together. They'd collectively handled one of their biggest obstacles in the first month that wasn't an endurance course, a sharp formation, the rigors of constant physical exercise, or making their beds on time in the morning without having the bedclothes stripped off and thrown on the floor. Plus, DeLafor had gotten his chance to run his mouth outside of drills. The men in First Platoon knew what everyone expected to avoid getting their asses handed to them on another concrete platter if Hughs messed up again.

He didn't.

Everyone else finally figured out how to button their side pockets and *keep* them buttoned.

It was just in time, too, because as they neared the end of Red Phase, no soldier wanted to be the one to get the entire platoon in trouble for something stupid they'd already figured out how to do. Then the moment came when every platoon came together for a final exercise none of the company NCOs felt like explaining in any real detail.

The entire Bravo Company marched across the yard toward a large, squat building in the middle of nowhere, each soldier carrying their previously distributed gas mask. They'd drilled on how to put them on and take them off, and now, apparently, they were being drilled on how to use them effectively.

The company commander, whom Idina had only seen a few times in passing during training exercises, stood in front of the door with his gas mask in hand and a tight smile. "Think of this as a final test. You're not getting out of here 'til you complete it. So you'll complete it, one way or the other. Masks on."

Every soldier swiftly strapped on their gas mask, some of them chuckling at the way it contorted their faces and made their breath echo especially loud.

The company commander then nodded toward another platoon sergeant, who opened the door and held it open for the company to step inside. "Everybody in."

When slightly fewer than one hundred recruits and sixteen non-commissioned officers had stepped into the building, the door closed behind them. The soldiers looked around, waiting for their next instructions.

So they're gonna gas us. Hence the masks. How is this a test?

Loud, heavy breathing filled the room. Then there were a series of deep *clicks* and a hiss as thick, yellow-brown smoke flooded all around them from various points in the floor and ceiling.

Idina didn't know which of the NCOs standing at ease in the gas chamber with them was Staff Sergeant Remmington until he shouted the requirements of their final test. "This is one more step in showing your dedication to the solid foundations of becoming an Army soldier. You've done this plenty of times already, so it should be a piece of cake. Company, remove masks!"

Every soldier did as commanded, and Remmington immediately followed it with, "Recite the Soldier's Creed!"

Voices rose together in a combined shout. "I am an American soldier."

Idina drew a breath to continue, and the noxious gas

burned down her throat into her lungs. The first burst of wracking coughs and retching filled the gas chamber. Still, the soldiers carried out their command to the best of their ability, quickly picking up speed as they gasped and choked.

"I am a warrior and a...member of a team. I serve the..."

Idina clenched her eyes shut and shouted as quickly and loudly as she possibly could while all around her, her fellow soldiers groaned through their words. Some of them could barely get the syllables out in the first place, and the non-commissioned officers inside with them watched the whole thing without reacting.

"Louder!" one of them shouted.

"...American way of life. I am an American soldier!"

The NCO standing at the back door of the gas chamber threw it open, and the recruits surged forward to get out of the burning, nauseating smoke that felt like it was climbing into every pore to stay there. Muffled laughter came from behind the NCOs' gas masks. The trainees fought to get through the smoky haze as quickly as possible, only to find more NCOs on the other side of the gas chamber standing there to block their way jokingly.

Idina couldn't see a thing, but she heard retching from several soldiers on her right amid all the coughing. She staggered into another body, looked up to see tears streaming down Matthews' face, and shoved him away from her and the sound of puking on her right.

It wasn't that she didn't want others to touch her after being gassed almost to the point of losing all her senses to the sting and the nauseating fumes.

He's gonna puke all over me if he sees someone else getting sick. Everyone else. Including me, I think...

Sergeant Hendricks appeared and pulled out the cell phone only the SNCOs and NCOs were allowed to keep on them before drawing several recruits together and wrapping his arms around their shoulders. "Hey, let's take a fucking selfie, huh?"

He held the camera out in front of him as the other NCOs laughed and stood in the way of more desperate recruits trying to leave the gas chamber.

Idina got a glimpse of the posed shot—Hendricks grinning like a lunatic beside three soldiers from the Second and Third Platoons, all of whom were red-faced, squinting through their tears, and grimacing through the torture.

So this is how the Army celebrates. Put us through hell, make fun of us for it, and we move on.

Idina's family had raised her to value manners and etiquette and to carry herself with respect, but she felt the last of their teachings fade away beneath the undeniable urge to spit. She tried to hock up the rest of the gas still floating around in the back of her throat and her lungs and had no idea how long she spat out the taste over and over.

This finally feels like being in the Army. No one gives a shit if I'm over here spraying slime all over the bushes. They're all doing it with me. That was insane.

The thought made her chuckle, but her laughter quickly died under a renewed burning of her eyes and the uncontrollable tears through which she could hardly see.

Then she noticed Amber standing beside her. The other young woman stayed doubled over, her hands propped on her thighs and her mouth hanging open somewhere between vomiting and pulling herself back together.

"Having fun yet, Petrie?" Idina muttered.

"Fucking blast." They looked at each other's tear-streaked faces and laughed as best they could as the rest of the company jostled each other and started to recover from their final big test of Red Phase.

One down, two more to go. We're still here.

CHAPTER TWENTY-THREE

The next month had a lot more in store for them than drilling and cleaning weapons and running the endurance course. That was all still included, of course, but now the company added weapons firing to their training.

First Platoon marched out to the shooting range with their long-range weapons and full combat gear. As light sapper combat engineers, their job would be to travel everywhere on foot because that was what they'd signed up for when they chose their occupational specialty. Idina couldn't hold back a grin despite the rigorous march.

I've been shooting at targets since I could hold a firearm on my own. This'll be easy.

Of course, a Moorfield's armory and the weapons provided by the United States Army were two very different things. The weapons the Army issued them in basic training weren't anything close to the newest models Idina had been firing most of her life.

Staff Sergeant Remmington stood in front of the

platoon and gave them a rundown of their next stage in training.

"Your firearm is an extension of you," he shouted. "It stays on you at all times. Would you take off your arm and toss it aside at the end of a long day?"

"No, sir!" they replied in unison.

"No. You wouldn't. You won't do that shit with your firearm. To make it through White Phase, you have to qualify not only with the carry of your firearm but zeroing your weapons. And hitting what you're aiming at, obviously."

Some of the soldiers snickered.

"Targets are out there. No one pulls a trigger until everyone's zeroed their weapon and you can calibrate the firearm you have in your sleep. As an extension of yourself, these weapons need to become as easy to clean, load, zero, and fire as it is for you to clench your fist or pick up a fork. So pay attention."

Remmington walked them through the steps of zeroing their issued M16 rifle then zeroing it again and again and again. The weapons came standard with the iron sights that didn't exactly make aiming as easy as it looked when the staff sergeant raised his gun and fired shots across the range. A puff of dust burst into the air when he hit his target dead-center.

The excitement among the platoon was contagious, and the soldiers ran drills on calibrating their weapons over and over, lifting their firearms, aiming, and that was it. They spent the entire day making those weapons an extension of themselves and didn't fire a single shot beyond the demonstrations their platoon leader offered.

Spending all day at the firing range also gave them their first opportunity to experience MREs firsthand.

When Remmington commanded them to sit, pull out their MREs, and serve themselves lunch, Idina was almost glad they hadn't permitted anyone to fire their weapons. Because a surprising number of her fellow trainees apparently couldn't read directions.

"How does this damn thing work?" McCoy snarled and shook the pouch of cold, gelatinous food substance in one hand and the heater in the other.

"It says on the box." She poured water from her canteen into the heater.

"Yeah, but they don't say what's what. How am I supposed to know where to put one thing in the other thing?"

Pierce snickered as he shoved his heater and food pouch back into the Meal, Ready-to-Eat box that held all the assembled components. "Go ahead and open 'em up, McCoy. Whichever one tastes like shit is the one you don't wanna eat."

The corners of McCoy's mouth turned down in thought, then he shrugged and grabbed the wrong pouch to try opening it.

"Are you serious right now?" Idina said through a laugh. "That's not—"

"McCoy!" Remmington barked. "What the hell are you doing?"

"Trying to figure out which is which, sir."

"Jesus." The platoon leader stalked toward him and ripped both items out of the soldier's hands. "This is the only packet not completely sealed, McCoy. This is your heater. Come on. They even put pictures on the back. What's wrong with you?"

"I'm hungry, sir."

"Well, being hungry makes you stupid. Hurry up."

As Remmington stalked away, the other recruits snickered at McCoy's baffled scowl.

"Hell, I can't figure it out."

"These are food. That's the heater." Idina pointed at her heater and the packet of "pasta with garden vegetables" shoved into the box standing upright in front of her. "Water goes in there. Don't try to open it up and figure it out."

"Why not?"

Pierce burst out laughing. "MacGyver over here wants to know how it works. Bet you could even drink that hot water afterward and get a little extra warmth out of it."

McCoy's eyes widened in excitement, but the wrong lightbulb had gone off. "For real?"

"Fuck no!"

The soldiers laughed and bemoaned having to open so many packets at once to get one thing cooking, not to mention the ten minutes of waiting for the stuff to heat up into something marginally palatable.

Idina wolfed hers down with the rest of them and couldn't help imagining the looks on her parents' faces if they saw her out here eating hot mush from a bag.

They wouldn't even recognize me. Good.

After chow, they lined up again and zeroed the metal sights on their weapons over and over, taking aim, repeating the motions until most of them were itching to pull the triggers and test the efficacy of all their work.

Instead, they rucked back to the barracks to call it a day and start all over again in the morning.

———

By the time they finally received authorization to *use* those weapons, Idina had hers calibrated and her sight tuned in to the way the gun rested against her body when she aimed. Firing the M16 for the first time felt like second nature.

The firing range filled with the staccato *clack* of rifles being fired at will once Remmington gave them the go-ahead to test their skills.

Idina was fairly satisfied with her first shooting round at eighty-eight percent accuracy and her target peppered with holes. She hadn't expected to be the best with the metal sights and the M16s, even with the occasional green burst of light directing her to correct her aim by a fraction of an inch. She also didn't expect the biggest idiot among them to be the soldier who *did* have the highest score starting.

Nobody did.

When McCoy started shooting, though, it was hard not to pause in her firing and turn to watch him squeezing that trigger over and over. He didn't stop until the thirty-round magazine was empty, which happened *after* the empty oil drum he'd been shooting let out a massive, echoing crack across the range and buckled. It looked like someone had taken a giant can opener to the thing and cut it raggedly through the center.

"Hold," Remmington barked. Most of the soldiers had

already stopped firing at this point, so it wasn't particularly necessary. The platoon leader stalked toward the one recruit everyone was staring at and looked him up and down. "What the hell was that, McCoy?"

"I was firing my weapon, sir." The tall, lanky southern kid who'd believed he could drink used MRE heater water turned toward the staff sergeant with wide eyes. "You did say fire—"

"Damn right I did. Now you're telling me you can't figure out how to put an MRE together, but you know how to shoot like that?"

McCoy shrugged. "I go huntin' sometimes."

"Not with that weapon, you don't. Reload and fire at will."

The guy's hands moved with incredible speed as he grabbed another magazine from his gear, shoved it into the weapon, took three seconds to aim, and fired with equally quick bursts as the last time. When he finished, the oil drum lay in two separate pieces across the range.

The rest of the platoon cheered, laughing and shouting at the First Platoon's resident idiot who could shoot better than any of them.

Remmington smirked and nodded at McCoy before turning to address the others. "Pay attention to McCoy. You have questions, don't come to me about it. Go to him. I want everyone shooting half as good as that by the time we finish."

Idina smiled through pursed lips as she checked over her weapon.

Everybody has a skill. It's about putting them in the right place with the right tools. Not like he needs to be able to read cooking instructions or understand how a savings account works to shoot an oil drum in half.

McCoy, true to form, looked entirely confused as to why the other soldiers were patting him on the back and ribbing him for his skills that had remained hidden until this point.

Over the next few weeks, First Platoon excelled at making their firearms extensions of themselves. Then they started using the CTO red-dot sight and learning how to zero with that. Aiming and efficiently firing was a hell of a lot easier when there was a little red dot on their target. They spent days honing their skills with firearms and got even more excited when introduced to the M240B machine gun.

Some of them, including Idina, had difficulty steadying the weapon as it fired through round after round in quick succession even McCoy couldn't rival in speed. Timbers was smaller than Idina. She was also a lot scrappier with her constant willingness to throw punches if someone else in the platoon got on her bad side—usually out in the yard during PT—but she couldn't hold the thing steady long enough to hit her target more than twice. Even with the weapon mounted on the ground for stability.

Idina could only watch the other girl for so long before she finally had to step in and offer some advice. The slight error in the way Timbers had positioned the machine gun kept flashing green whenever Idina glanced at the other soldier, and she couldn't keep ignoring it.

"Here." She hunkered down beside Timbers and

gestured at the weapon. "Support the stock closer to your chest, not only on your shoulder."

"Are you fucking kidding me, Moorfield? The recoil's gonna blow me apart."

"You'll get used to the recoil. But if you can't hit what you're trying to hit…"

Timbers clicked her tongue and made a slight adjustment to the way she handled the machine gun. The next time she fired from her station on the ground, her shots were a lot more efficient, though she had to step back into a half-crouch to give her small frame more support. But she unloaded the machine gun completely, and a few shouts of encouragement rose from the other soldiers.

"Fuck." Timbers set down the weapon and grimaced as she rubbed her chest muscles beside her shoulder. "I'm gonna be rucking around like a tenderized piece of meat. Thanks a lot."

Idina grinned and shook her head. "You're still in one piece, and you hit the target. You're welcome."

When she turned to watch the other recruits testing their abilities with the machine gun, she caught Remmington looking at her from the other side of their station on the firing range. He raised his eyebrows and tilted his head.

Not quite a nod of approval, but okay. If we weren't supposed to help each other, he'd tell me to cut it out and make me do pushups until we head back. I guess that's as much encouragement as I'm gonna get. I'll take it.

There was a lot to be said for understanding the military weapons First Platoon used day in and day out. The real kicker came when Staff Sergeant Remmington and Corporal Staffhouse—who'd replaced Watson once she'd received her orders to move on somewhere else—told them they'd be negotiating the hand grenade assault course.

No one looked particularly excited to be running around another obstacle course with live explosives, but they didn't start there.

"You'll know the assault course like the back of your hand before that hand even touches an M67," Remmington called. "Lucky for you, you already know how to hold a grenade."

DeLafor grimaced and whispered, "He's insane."

"You've been doing it since day one," the platoon leader continued before reaching into a box on the ground beside him and pulling out an actual grenade.

The recruits blinked and cast each other wary glances as they stood at attention.

Idina stared at the explosive. *Live grenades. I mean, I'd be an idiot to think becoming a combat engineer didn't involve explosives, sure. But* here? *Right now?*

Remmington smirked and wiggled the explosive clenched in his fingers. "Inert hand grenade. They don't deploy fully. At least, they're not supposed to."

Behind him, Corporal Staffhouse grinned.

The platoon leader gripped the grenade with both hands and his finger looped through the pin as if he meant to pull. Then he stopped and looked over the recruits to gauge their reactions. Fortunately, no one ducked for cover, which Idina had fully expected from at least a handful of them.

Moving slowly, Remmington went through the motions of miming out the activation of the grenade, pulling away with his left hand, lowering it again, and holding a demonstration of what otherwise would've been a live and activated grenade ready to be thrown.

Idina narrowed her eyes. *Wait a minute. He wasn't screwing around when he said we already know how to hold a grenade.*

Surveying the platoon, Remmington smirked again and lowered the inert grenade at his side. "Look familiar?"

The platoon remained silent.

Seriously? No one has an answer for this?

"That's permission to speak freely if you have an idea you'd like to toss around," Remmington added. "Anyone?"

She let another five seconds pass before shouting, "Sir."

"Let's hear it, Moorfield."

"It's the same motion and positioning for drinking our two cups of water at chow, sir."

He looked over his shoulder at Corporal Staffhouse, who shrugged and nodded. "Good eye, Moorfield. If you haven't already figured it out, there's a reason for everything we do here. First Platoon spent the first weeks of training learning the basics for some of the most important commands, movements, and mindsets now ingrained in you as second nature.

"That second nature becomes your last line of defense and will save your life. You won't always have time to think. Especially once you've pulled the pin on a live grenade. First Platoon, right-face!"

The soldiers turned smartly in unison, and Corporal Staffhouse continued, "First Platoon, forward march!"

They were led to the hand grenade assault course and allowed to see it being run through by both of their commanders so they could assess the rigors of completing it *without* a live explosive. It included a bunker, a trench, and multiple enemy targets each trainee would have to neutralize with live grenades once the time came. First, they ran through the entire thing over and over, practicing the motions they'd already cemented in their minds from carrying and drinking their two cups of water three times a day during the strict drills before chow.

Remmington wasn't kidding about knowing the course like the back of their hands. By the time they were ready to start using inert hand grenades, Idina was sure she could've run it in the dark without any night-vision gear and probably with her eyes closed.

Being handed dud grenades and hearing the safety brief took it to a whole different level. The weight of the explosive in her hand drove home how powerful such a weapon could be—and how deadly.

Pulling the pin didn't prime the grenade. Instead, it allowed the spoon—the part that resembled a handle—to release. The released spoon primed the grenade for throwing. The typical fuse was roughly five or six seconds, but there was always a chance of a short fuse that would set off the grenade early. They also learned that if the spoon never released after they pulled the pin, they could reinsert it to make the grenade "safe" again.

Now the recruits had to hit their targets with the inert grenades, lobbing the explosives over the low wall and the high wall with complete accuracy before they could run the assault course with weapons that did explode.

Throwing a grenade and *not* hearing the ensuing explosion she could only imagine up to this point was incredibly anticlimactic. With the drill sergeants shouting at them to keep moving, always stay low, find their targets, and hit them either with grenades or with their firearm strapped across their chest, there wasn't much time to be disappointed.

Finally, the day arrived when every platoon member had received the all-clear with their practice runs on the assault course. That meant it was time to trek out to the live grenade bay to finally experience what arming and throwing a live grenade felt and sounded like.

Before they headed out, each soldier was given two live grenades and immediately strapped them to their combat gear the way they'd practiced. Then Remmington led them across the base, past the assault course, and toward the live grenade bay. It was nothing more than an open field pockmarked with craters, where so many soldiers who'd gone before them had been through the same harrowing experience of carrying live explosives to be deployed.

As the platoon marched toward the grenade bay, Idina glanced to her right and found Hughs huffing and puffing up the hill beside her. The guy had lost at least thirty pounds since their first days of basic, and while the trek wasn't nearly the most vigorous trek they'd made, the guy sweated profusely.

"Shit, shit, shit," he muttered through clenched teeth.

"Hughs," she whispered.

"Fuck. I'm gonna blow myself up."

"Hughs."

He flinched away from her, holding his firearm farther away than necessary from the two grenades strapped to his gear. "I can't do this."

"Yeah, you can. Nobody's taking those grenades off you. Nobody's shooting at you. You passed the assault course. You're good."

"I can't fucking do this. I'll drop it. Or throw it in the wrong direction. Or—"

"Shut the fuck up, Hughs," Sheldon hissed behind them. "If you're gonna piss your pants, do it where the rest of us can't smell it, huh?"

Hughs pressed his lips together and flashed Idina a worried look.

"Look, I'm not exactly a fan of this either," she muttered. "We're gonna do this like we do everything else. You're good."

The guy muttered something unintelligible but forced himself to draw deep breaths as they climbed the last of the hills on base and finally reached the grenade bay.

There were high walls, low walls, and trenches out here too, but shrapnel had splintered them and halfway crumbled them to dust. Remmington ran them through the steps they had to take before it was time to launch their grenades. Second Squad and First Squad broke apart to tackle different areas of the grenade bay. Then it was time.

Idina had no idea who pulled the first grenade and tossed it over the low wall in front of her. The ensuing explosion that made Second Squad duck together and her ears start ringing was a *lot* different than she'd expected.

Dirt and rocks flew in all directions, peppering the wall.

Idina found Hughs cowering behind the rest of the squad and doubled back to grab him as grenades exploded on the other side and First Squad shouted at each other to keep moving.

"Keep moving!" she shouted over another explosion. "It's only practice."

The platoon leaders shouted firm, barking encouragement while squad leaders echoed the sentiment.

Hughs was as white as a ghost, but he nodded and scrambled after her to join the rest of Second Squad.

Explosions rocked through the bay. The grinding roar made it impossible to hear anything else. As the current leader of Second Squad, Amber turned back to survey everyone she was leading and barked, "Hughs! Toss 'em!"

He pulled his first grenade and held it at the perfect position like everyone else. Another explosion made him flinch, and that small movement pried his hands apart with the telltale *click* of the spoon falling.

Then he stared at the live grenade in his hands that definitely wouldn't wait any longer until *he* was ready.

"Fucking throw it!" someone shouted. The rest of Second Squad screamed at him, and that was what it took to yank the guy out of his fear. He stood, drew back his arm, and screamed before lobbing the grenade over the wall. It detonated before it hit the ground, and Hughs kept screaming through the explosion.

He probably wouldn't have stopped if DeLafor hadn't charged toward him and socked him in the jaw. The startled soldier reeled backward, stumbled toward the ground, then righted himself again.

"What the hell, man?"

"You almost blew us all to shit, you fucking moron!"

"I didn't."

DeLafor snarled and shook his head as more explosions wracked the grenade bay. "I should've punched you harder."

Second Squad moved on to the next target, and Idina turned her focus to activating and throwing her live grenades with everyone else. When she saw Hughs draw his second explosive and pull the pin, she was glad and more than a little relieved to see the guy chuck it immediately before barking out another shout of effort and victory that the detonations all around them drowned out.

Nothing like throwing grenades outside *of live combat to get you ready for the real thing. That was way too close. He figured it out.*

CHAPTER TWENTY-FOUR

First Platoon continued their practice at the shooting range as they moved closer and closer to the day they'd officially have to qualify with their handling of weapons and both types of sights.

They didn't run the grenade assault course again but instead were led to a massive tower rising thirty-five feet into the air. It looked more like wooden scaffolding than anything else, with a wide, steeply slanting wooden ladder on one side and a wall of wooden slats on the other. Those slats were held together by rope weaving in and out of them, instantly reminding Idina of the thin bamboo blinds installed in the dojo windows at Moorfield Manor.

That's not a solid surface at all.

"This is the Warrior's Tower," Remmington told them. "Pretty straightforward. You climb up, tie in, and rappel down. You're responsible for tying yourself off up top and getting yourselves down again. It's all on you. So before any of you head up, we're gonna be damn sure you know how to tie a knot."

They went through the proper way to tie their lead ropes to an anchor, then how to fashion their harness with the other end of the rope to keep them securely fastened while they let rope through that makeshift harness to rappel down.

Idina struggled with the initial makeup of the harness she had to strap around herself. Interestingly enough, the green lights flashing around her vision to show her the next steps were muddled and confused by the lines of rope coiling and twisting around each other.

That only meant it took her two minutes longer than it normally would've to get the process down correctly. When she figured it out, the rope rested securely around her waist and hips with the slipknot loose enough to feed herself more rope when the time came.

They practiced on much lower walls first to get comfortable with the necessary actions of stepping down backward off a ledge and sitting back in their harnesses before letting themselves down to the ground. In teams of two, the soldiers tied their knots at the top of the shorter walls serving as practice runs for the thirty-five-foot Warrior Tower. When Idina was up beside Brock, she found the guy still fumbling with his harness before their order to descend.

"Shit. How does this—"

"Down, Brock!" Remmington shouted. "Let's go!"

The skinny redhead hissed and leaned back into his harness. He and Idina kicked off at the same time, and the first descent was a jerky process of trying to balance the footwork with feeding more slack into the rappelling rope. At least for Idina.

Brock yelped in surprise and tilted sideways in his self-made harness, then dangled against the short wall at almost ninety degrees.

The other recruits laughed and shouted for him to right himself, but he couldn't quite manage it. So the platoon surged toward the base of the small practice tower to help him down, everyone putting in their two cents about how to correctly tie the harness. Then the next pair were up, and the platoon kept running the practice rappel.

Idina quickly got the hang of it, so when she wasn't up top getting ready to descend, she stood at the bottom to shout occasional instructions up to the other soldiers who weren't as quick to figure out the process. And she watched Brock.

Even with another round of personal instructions from Corporal Staffhouse on how exactly to fasten the rope around himself and create the harness, Brock couldn't seem to get it right. Every time he descended, he ended up tilting to the left and sliding out of his rig. One time he almost flipped upside down, and the other recruits rushed to the base of the tower to catch him if he slid out completely.

No one could figure out why the guy couldn't complete the practice rappel with any measure of success, and the next time Brock reached the ground, he stormed away from the rest of the platoon with an angry growl.

Idina pursed her lips. *He's trying to sit back in a harness made the same way as everyone else's. But he doesn't sit like everyone else.*

The next time she climbed the smaller tower and sat at the top with the other recruits getting ready to try again and prepare for the Warrior Tower, Idina waited for Brock to finish having a silent fit in the corner. Eventually, he climbed back up, ready to do this one more time and expecting to fail one more time.

"Hey."

"Yeah, we all know you can handle it, Moorfield." Brock grabbed the rope at the top and started tying a harness around his mid-section and legs. "I'm not making it down from the big tower. Not if I wanna walk away from it afterward."

Idina smirked. "Hold on a sec. Can I give you some advice?"

"Can you tell me how the hell it's different from everyone else's?"

"Yeah. Because you don't sit like everyone else."

He snorted. "What are you talking about?"

She leaned toward him and lowered her voice as the next two soldiers tied off and stepped backward off the ledge. "Listen, I was watching you. I know it's a weird question, but did you have any issues with your hips or something before you got here? Like, I don't know, maybe when you were a kid?"

Brock's eyes widened. "What the fuck?"

Idina shrugged. "I told you it was a weird question."

"You're freaking me out, Moorfield. That's some creepy mind-reading shit right there."

"I'll take that as a yes. Look, you're doing everything right. For everyone else, that works, but your center of gravity is way off. Tying your harness the way everyone else does won't help you."

He frowned at her. "So, what? I'm supposed to fail this thing?"

"No. Here." She grabbed his rope and looped it three extra times around his left side before adding a second securing loop around his thighs to serve as additional support for the sling. With the green lights glittering and flickering in her vision, her hands moved swiftly and efficiently. She tugged a little too hard at the end with a little too much focus.

A puff of glowing green mist and glittering specks rose from her hands right beside Brock's left hip.

He sucked in a sharp breath and stepped away from her. "What the fuck?"

"What?" Idina tried to look completely clueless, shaking out her hand as if she'd gotten a rope burn instead of unleashing the precursor to another one of her episodes at the wrong fucking time.

"That...green shit." He stared at her hands. "Christ, Moorfield. Are you trying to fuck with me right now?"

Deny it. That's all you have to do.

She smirked at him. "I don't know what you're talking about, man. I get it. You're pissed and stressed."

"I'm not fucking hallucinating."

"Okay, well, whatever you saw, forget about it. I don't know what to tell you other than I fixed your harness. Look." She tapped her knuckles against his rope. "You're always falling to the left. And your feed's on the left, which works, but not if your hips aren't square enough. So doing it like this with more support on the left should tighten things up and keep you straight."

Brock studied the reinforced lines of his harness, and

his frown morphed into wide-eyed surprise before he huffed out a laugh. "What are you? Some kinda rock-climbing expert?"

"Nope. Just observant, maybe. Give it a shot."

"Right." He turned and backed up toward the ledge. "If this doesn't work, I'm never listening to a fucking thing out of your mouth."

"Deal."

Holy shit, that was close. Doesn't look like anyone else saw anything. Which is good for me and probably not that great for Brock if he thinks he's starting to see things. We'll chalk it all up to the pressures of basic. Sure. And never bring it up again.

Idina looked down at those in her platoon standing at the base of the tower, getting ready to catch Brock yet again because he couldn't descend straight.

Staff Sergeant Remmington folded his arms and briefly rubbed his lips as he prepared to see the same result from Brock as every other time.

"Hey, Brock!" someone shouted from the ground. "Lean right this time!"

Even when more recruits laughed at that, they meant it as a helpful suggestion. The same suggestion Brock had been getting all day that hadn't helped him at all.

Idina stepped toward him and shook her head. "Don't lean right."

"I hate this," he muttered before jumping down off the ledge and releasing the slack from his makeshift harness inches at a time.

Crouching at the edge, Idina caught a brief glimpse of the redhead's eyes widening as he descended straight down the practice tower and didn't tilt in any direction. His boots landed squarely in the dirt for the first time, and the platoon erupted in raucous cheers as they rushed him to jostle the guy around and celebrate his successful rappel.

"We didn't even have to catch you!"

"Jesus, Brock. Took you long enough."

"So you don't always swing that way after all, huh?"

Idina grinned and waited for Brock to unfasten himself before she could haul the rope up and create her harness. He looked up at her with a confused frown and a disbelieving grin. She held up three fingers to remind him about doubling up on his left-side support, then hauled up the rope. A small group of other recruits swept Brock away, thumped him on the back, and cheered for him finally finding success in his biggest hurdle before the real test with the giant Warrior's Tower began.

Idina ran one more rappel herself before she heard her name called across the yard.

"Moorfield!" Remmington shouted. "Come here."

"Yes, sir." She jogged toward her platoon leader, fighting back a smile and wondering why he'd called *her* out when she didn't have an issue with descending the practice tower.

He looked her up and down, then nodded toward Brock. "What was that?"

Fuck. He saw my lights. How the hell am I supposed to explain that when my own family couldn't?

She steeled herself and firmly replied, "That was Brock rappelling, sir."

"Uh-huh. It also looked like someone gave him extra instructions in how to fasten that harness against the regulations taught for this FTX."

Relief flooded through her. *I helped a soldier figure out how not to topple off a rope from thirty-five feet, and it doesn't matter because it's against regulation. At least he's not asking about floating green glitter and a bunch of weird smoke that shouldn't have popped out when I was tying a rope.*

"Yes, sir." Idina nodded. "That was me."

"Why?"

Her eyes widened at the surprising question, and it took her a moment to form an answer. "It's hard to see it when he's walking or standing, but Brock sits heavy on his left side, sir. Really heavy."

"You thought changing up the way he tied his harness would alleviate the issue."

"It did alleviate the issue, sir."

Remmington drew a deep breath. "No one authorized that, Moorfield."

"No, sir." She stood at ease in front of him and spared a glance at her commander. *If I keep talking, he'll smoke me up and down this tower 'til I can't hold a rope.*

"Why didn't you bring this to my attention before you let your fellow soldier rappel that tower with an unapproved modification to his harness?"

"Brock and I were already at the top of the tower, and I thought it was more important to help him succeed than to bother you with a suggestion for those modifications, sir."

Remmington stared at her for what felt like an eternity before he chuckled. "Good. You won't always have time to run every little change through your CO for approval when you're in the field. That was a good suggestion, Moorfield. Don't let it go to your head."

"Never, sir."

"You're dismissed."

Idina turned smartly around and hurried back to join her platoon, all of whom could now rappel down the practice tower with little to no difficulty. With her back to Remmington, she let herself smile and broke into a jog.

Clear on the weird green lights. Now I have to be careful, 'cause I have no meds and no one around to explain for me that this shit just happens. First time someone's commended *me for thinking outside the box, though. That was always my biggest downfall at home. I wonder if Remmington would feel the same way if he knew who'd planned getting rid of Hughs' contraband evidence in the PEC.*

Between firearms training, rappelling practice, and field exercises to give them a working knowledge of the terrain on base that stretched farther than it was possible to guess, morning PT had changed significantly. Over the last few weeks, it had morphed from running, pushups, pull-ups, sit-ups, and weight training into something altogether different.

Something else for which Idina Moorfield was particularly qualified—combatants classes.

Close hand-to-hand combat became her favorite part of the day as the platoon broke up into squads and received their instructions. Once Remmington and Corporal Staffhouse demonstrated the various maneuvers they wanted the soldiers to practice with partners, Idina almost laughed out loud.

Jiu-jitsu in the Army. I don't even have to try.

She didn't.

The other pairs of soldiers ran through the moves and grappled with each other across the floor. Most of the men paired with men since the women were fewer in number. Idina sparred with whoever her leaders paired her with and had to show a good deal of physical restraint while her partner learned the moves she'd known for years.

The training arena where they first learned to grapple filled with the grunts and groans of recruits tackling each other to the mats with precise moves. The stink of sweat on the mats became a new daily part of their routine, as were the odd exclamations from the men.

They could handle getting smoked whenever the COs thought it necessary—it now involved more rigorous punishments like miles of running with their weapons held in both hands above their heads. Grappling with another sweaty man in PT uniforms was a particular hurdle.

The first time Remmington called up one sparring team to show the platoon what they'd learned, the staff sergeant dove into his shouted encouragement and the proper terms for what they were supposed to accomplish. "That's it, Kerrigan. Hook your leg over his—yes! Now mount him!"

DeLafor grunted as his opponent grappled with him for a good hold and craned his neck toward the platoon leader with wide eyes. "Do *what* to me? This—"

Kerrigan cut him off when he rolled them both across the mat before he got his legs wrapped around DeLafor's middle from behind, hooked his ankles, and squeezed with arms and legs.

"Fuck! Fucking—dude!" DeLafor tapped the mat, and his partner immediately released him.

"Rear mount, DeLafor," Remmington said flatly. "That's what it's called."

"Yeah, but do you have to say it like that?"

"I'll keep saying it like that, and you'll keep running laps around this arena with the rest of your platoon until I think you're able to handle this combatants class like a soldier. Now!"

The platoon gave DeLafor dirty looks as they quickly got in line to run again and again and again. "Thought you finished opening your mouth, DeLafor."

"What did you *think* he was telling Kerrigan to do?"

"We should be done with this shit."

The admonishments were all delivered in barely more than a whisper as the recruits passed DeLafor in their laps, and he kept his eyes straight ahead with a scowl as he ran, trying to ignore them all.

Idina didn't feel the need to talk to him or warn him against speaking out like that again.

He knows. He's pissed that he did it anyway after he's gone so long without *being a smartass.*

When Remmington finally decided they'd had enough running, he ordered them down for twenty pushups and quickly got them back into grappling. No one else talked back to the platoon leader, but the training arena filled with the kinds of comments from young men completing their focused moves that made Idina roll her eyes.

"Dude, get your fucking nuts out of my mouth."

"Oh, yeah. Nice mount, but I'm tired of staring up your ass."

"Hey, wanna grab a little higher? I got an itch that needs scratching."

Idina didn't have nearly as much difficulty learning the moves and practicing them during PT. She ended up inadvertently teaching whoever she partnered with to help them better understand the mechanics. When she paired up with Amber, the girl kept laughing every time Idina got her in a front or rear mount or in an armlock she couldn't get out of.

"Jesus, Moorfield. Were you a fucking ninja before enlisting?"

"Nope. Just trained in martial arts." Idina released her partner and offered Amber a hand up to her feet.

"I'm gonna get you on your ass one of these days."

"Ha. You might need a bō staff to do that, so good luck."

Then came the day when their COs led First Platoon to the Warrior's Tower to qualify their rappelling abilities. Remmington gave them a quick pep talk that was mostly a reminder of the potential for falling and breaking bones and having to take recovery or even medical discharge if they screwed up their harnesses and didn't pay attention.

"If that happens, you get the care you need, recover, and you cycle through with the next group of recruits for the rest of basic. Or you might have to start over. So don't screw this up, and don't fall."

"Well, *now* I feel great about this," McCoy muttered as the platoon headed toward the tower's base.

Second Squad climbed up the thirty-five-foot ladder

first, while First Squad stationed themselves at the base of the Warrior's Tower to watch, encourage, and help mitigate any potential disasters should someone lose their heads at a height none of them had reached before now.

Idina climbed up with her squad, and they lined up at the top of the tower to look down at the drop.

"Squad Leader." McCoy turned toward Amber. "Your call for the lineup."

She didn't answer.

"Petrie!"

"Shit." The woman stood a foot from the side of the tower's edge, staring at the drop and swallowing thickly. "I'm gonna puke."

"Squad Leader's out," DeLafor muttered. "So just... whoever's closest to the edge."

While the first two soldiers tied on their harnesses and double-checked that they'd securely fastened the top lead, Idina sidled toward Amber. "You got this, Petrie."

"The fuck I do. That's like...high enough to kill me."

"It's only a bigger version. You had the other ones in the bag."

"Yeah, and I'm gonna end up in a *body bag* after this. Shit."

"Hey." Idina nudged the girl in the arm and smirked. "At the Olympics, the divers jump from something twice this high."

"Bullshit."

"Look it up. You know, once we're out of here and the outside world exists again."

Masterson snickered. "Come on, Petrie. You're not

gonna let a bunch of dickheads in speedos show up a uniformed soldier, are you?"

Amber looked up to flip him off, and he laughed before returning his attention to the first two recruits getting ready to descend.

"I mean, he has a point," Idina muttered.

"Fuck you too, Moorfield. Your pep talks suck as much as Remmington's." Despite Amber's harsh tone, she smirked as she stepped toward the edge of the platform and watched the rest of her squad tackle the Warrior's Tower.

Idina sat to wait her turn and offer encouragement to the others. She couldn't help but watch the change in Amber's demeanor—her back straightening, her arms unfolding, her fists finally unclenching. *So Private Petrie needs a little comparison to kick her into gear. It would suck to have a fear of heights up here, but she'll make it.*

When it was Brock's turn to head down the wall, both squads of First Platoon belted out their cheering support while he tied his harness with extra strength on his left side the way Idina had shown him. His freckled and usually pink face had gone ghostly white, and he gritted his teeth before stepping backward toward the ledge. "If this doesn't work, Moorfield, I'll fuck you up."

"Yeah, I bet you will." She laughed at his grimace flickering between rage and apprehension.

Then Brock leapt backward, and the *thump* of his boots against the *clacking*, jiggling wall of wooden planks followed him down. The soldiers on the ground erupted into cheers again when he reached the ground—just like they had for every other First Platoon recruit who'd completed the rappelling wall.

Then Idina and Amber were the only two left.

"Squad Leader's last," Amber muttered.

"Yes, sir." Idina tied her harness and held the other girl's gaze. "You're coming down."

"Shit, Moorfield. Olympic speedos jumping off the high-dive is one thing. If the flipping fucking ginger down there can do this without cracking his head open, what excuse do *I* have?"

"None." Idina launched herself off the edge of the tower and let the slack out on her rope as quickly as she dared. The descent lasted less than ten seconds, then she was on the ground and surrounded by everyone cheering her on like each of the other successful recruits.

She looked up at the top of the tower to see Amber standing there with her harness fastened. The other girl squinted down the thirty-five-foot drop, her lips grimly set.

"Oh, shit," someone muttered. "Petrie's gonna hurl."

"No way, man."

"Look at her. Her eyes are all dead and glassed-over."

"Shut the hell up, Shreider. You can't *see* her eyes from down here."

Idina raised her fist in the air so Amber could see, then clapped her hands above her head and mimed diving. For a minute, Amber just stood there.

"Matthews."

"Yes, sir." Matthews turned toward Remmington and waited for instructions. "Get up there and see what Petrie's—"

He stopped when Amber spun and leapt daringly off the edge of the tower. She flew out wide and swung back toward the wall of dangling wooden panels. The platoon let out a communal groan and a few shouts of surprise before Amber's boots hit the wall. She scuffed them across the wood for as fast a drop as she could manage, which was pretty damn fast.

She hit the ground, staggered sideways, then looked up at the top of the tower and thrust a fist in the air. "Fuck you!"

Laughing and echoing her cry at the Warrior's Tower, the soldiers rushed toward her to give Second Squad's designated squad leader rough thumps on the back and a few shakes in congratulations. Idina was among them, glad to see her first friend from reception had overcome a fear of heights Idina never would've guessed existed.

"That enough of a dive for you, Moorfield?" Amber shouted through a grin as the color quickly returned to her cheeks.

"You didn't do that for me. Now you have a few stories to tell your brothers."

"Shut up." The other girl still looked a little woozy but let the rest of the platoon accost her with good-natured ribbing and jokes and slaps on the back.

Idina studied the top of the tower. *Not as high as the high dive. High enough to be a hell of a fall. And to help someone push through their fear. That's why we're here, right?*

CHAPTER TWENTY-FIVE

Now they were officially two-thirds of the way through Army Basic Training at Ft. Leonard Wood, and the end seemed more in sight with each passing day. First Platoon tackled combatants classes until every soldier had paired up with every other soldier at least once and the competition came out evenly matched no matter who they sparred.

Staff Sergeant Remmington thought it was time to switch up the designated squad and team leaders again on the next rotation. Every soldier was given a chance in at least one leadership role during basic. Idina had caught her platoon leader's attention, but she hadn't really considered the fact that she'd be placed in one of those leadership positions until it happened.

"First Platoon, fall in!" Remmington shouted.

The soldiers converged in the yard, fitted with full combat gear as instructed that morning.

"First Platoon, ten-hut!" Corporal Staffhouse shouted. Every recruit tightened their muscles and adopted a near-perfect stance at attention. At least, it was perfect enough at this point in their training.

"Petrie. Bristol. You're off squad command. I want Reardon to take a stab at First Squad leader and Moorfield at Second Squad."

"Yes, sir!" all four of them replied in unison.

"We're heading out for a hell of a day," Remmington added. "So look alive."

Corporal Staffhouse gave the command to move out, each squad leader echoed the commands, and the recruits marched dutifully behind their platoon leader and platoon guide to wherever they were supposed to be. All they knew was it had to be somewhere far enough from the barracks for them to have not one MRE pack but two.

As it turned out, the nearly two-and-a-half-mile road march through the semi-charted terrain sprawling away from the barracks and the quickly thickening woods was only the start of their training that day.

When they reached the land navigation site and Staff Sergeant Remmington called a halt, no one had any idea what to expect. "Squad leaders, front and center."

Idina and Reardon hurried forward to stand at attention in front of their CO.

"At ease." Remmington nodded at them as they adopted the halfway-relaxed position, then he pulled his pack off his shoulders, opened it, and produced two maps and two compasses. He handed one of each to the squad leaders before shouldering his ruck again.

"Five checkpoints out here, with their relative locations designated on those maps. You have three hours to get your squad to at least three of those five checkpoints. That ends at twelve hundred hours. Then wherever you are, you hoof it back here to regroup."

"Yes, sir."

"Clock's ticking."

Idina hurried back to her squad and relayed the information for their latest field exercise.

"Three hours?" McCoy asked, gazing with wide eyes at the valley stretching out below them before the woods resumed and covered the landscape. "How big is this place?"

"A lot bigger than your brain, McCoy." Amber snorted.

"Shut the fuck up."

"Okay, who knows how to use a compass?" Idina asked. No one said a thing. "Seriously? All right, Matthews. Look. Wherever the red needle points means we're facing that direction. Easy."

"Yeah, I got it."

"You'll keep us on track. Timbers, you're in charge of the map."

"Right." Timbers reached out to take the map with a determined frown.

"You know how to read a map, right?"

The other young woman shot Idina a sarcastic glare and nodded. "Yes, sir."

"Good. So find us the farthest checkpoint that'll be the hardest to negotiate."

The entire squad stared blankly at Idina, and Timbers didn't bother to start looking at the map.

"Hey, you heard me. Farthest checkpoint—"

"I don't get it," McCoy drawled. "Don't we wanna hit the easiest first?"

"Look, it saves us time and energy to go for the hardest first," Idina muttered quickly. "Then everything after that will feel like a cakewalk in comparison. Plus, we won't have to trek however many miles it is back from the farthest checkpoint when we've already been moving for three hours and might be running out of steam."

"Four," Timbers said.

"What?"

"Looks like four miles. I think."

Idina nodded. "Great. So we hit that first. Get with Matthews to point us in the right direction, and we'll head out."

The soldiers stared at her for a moment longer before the team members Idina had designated as the holders of map and compass got together to map out their route to the farthest checkpoint as their squad leader had instructed.

Okay, fine. Maybe they're confused why there's a squad leader all of a sudden who can think for herself. It's not rocket science. It makes sense. I don't even need green lights to figure that out.

"This way." Matthews pointed ahead. "North-northwest."

"Then let's go." Idina glanced over her shoulder, but First Squad had already taken off in the opposite direction. After the quick look she'd taken of the map before handing it over to Timbers, she was fairly certain First Squad had gone off in the direction of the closest, most easily reachable checkpoint. Assuming both maps were the same.

They'll think they're ahead of us for most of the three hours. If we do this right, we can grab all five checkpoints by then.

Second Squad marched down the heavy slope into the valley. Matthews held the compass out in front of him like it was another hand grenade about to detonate if he steered them off course. He set a sustainable pace across the terrain that didn't need to slow once they reached the tree line and entered the forest.

He and Timbers decided on their own to check in with their progress on the map every twenty minutes, and Idina didn't tell them to stop. *They're working together. That's the point.*

Even after an hour and a half of trekking through the woods, the squad was still working together. That was especially important when Timbers alerted them they should be coming up to a river any minute now. Because when they did, they were all surprised to find the current incredibly fast and violent with the heavy rush of falls somewhere close by.

"Damnit." DeLafor clapped a hand to his combat helmet and readjusted it around his sweaty head. "We've already spent ninety minutes trying to get this far, no checkpoint, and now what? We gotta build a bridge?"

"Not a bad idea." Idina thumped him on the shoulder and stalked forward, scanning the trees. "Alpha Team, look for fallen logs. Bravo Team finds the shallowest part of the river within half a mile. We won't need a bridge if it's shallow enough, but we *do* need to hurry."

The team split up to do that, and Idina scanned the river to find a good place to build said bridge. However past squads had crossed this river to reach that farthest checkpoint, there was no sign of it where Second Squad came to the riverbank, but it didn't matter.

As soon as we cross, we'll hit the checkpoint, cross back to this side, and book it toward the others. They're closer together anyway, so we should have enough time to make it to all five.

"Moorfield!" Amber shouted. "This looks like the best spot."

Idina marched toward her and studied the swirling eddies of the raging river. "You're probably right. Still too fast to walk across without getting swept up or losing more time."

"Good thing we found trees," McCoy hollered over the crunch of snapping branches and leaves beneath multiple pairs of boots. "Didn't even have to cut 'em down."

The rest of the Bravo Team emerged from the woods with two long, thick logs carried between two soldiers each.

"Awesome. Right here." Idina pointed at the shallowest part of the river where they stood, and the squad worked together to lift and carefully lay the logs across the water from bank to bank.

DeLafor stepped into the water on his own—without opening his mouth for a smartass remark or the usual complaint when NCOs were around—and carefully helped steady the heavy wood at the right angle until he couldn't hold it up any longer. The ends of each fallen tree crashed against the opposite side of the bank, and the squad rolled them together as close as they could get.

"Who wants to test it?" Idina asked.

Someone barked out a laugh.

"It's cool. I'll do it." She stepped up onto the logs, bounced a little to test how well they held, then shuffled across the rough bark. Enough river water hadn't sprayed it yet to be dangerously slippery. The rest of her squad held the base of both logs, and Idina jumped onto the other riverbank. She turned to face them with a grin and waved them forward. "Let's move."

All fourteen soldiers in Second Squad worked together to stabilize the logs while they crossed one by one. It wasn't a long or especially dangerous crossing, but it was time-consuming enough to keep them all intently focused. Pierce muttered something about having chosen Bravo Company and not Charlie Company for a reason when he'd enlisted. "We're not fucking bridge-builders. This isn't our job."

"It is today, Pierce. Come on."

When the last soldier crossed the river, Timbers and Matthews took thirty seconds to reorient themselves toward the checkpoint, and they took off again.

Ten minutes later, they reached a small, squat bunker in the mountainside. Before the entire squad even made it out of the tree line, a shout rose from the bunker. "Soldiers, identify yourselves."

"Second Squad, First Platoon, Bravo Company, sir!" Idina shouted.

The buzzing static of a radio echoed toward them before whichever NCO manning the checkpoint bunker muttered into a radio, "Second Squad at Point Five."

He didn't say anything else, so Idina figured it was safe for them to move on. "Next checkpoint, Timbers. Where's the closest to this one?"

Timbers and Matthews convened again to discuss it and double-check their navigation. Then they headed southeast toward the next checkpoint.

Idina looked over her shoulder at the bunker and squinted. *He checked us in without even seeing the entire squad. So technically, if we don't all have to be there, we can split up and cover twice as much ground. As long as that's not how only that NCO handles it and everyone else just needs a shouted identification from behind the trees.*

She couldn't help but smile as her new plan formed and Second Squad's designated navigators led them back across the river and down through the woods toward their next checkpoint.

An hour later, they'd made it to two more checkpoints and had officially qualified with the field exercise. The squad was sweaty, breathing heavily, and trying hard to pick up their feet as they all took turns shouting encouragement to each other to keep moving and keep up the pace.

Idina called a quick halt to check in with Matthews and Timbers. "How much farther would you say we have 'til we reach the center point between the last two checkpoints?"

"Um…we're basically there right now." Timbers pointed her spot on the map. "Why?"

"Okay, here's what we're gonna do. Alpha Team goes to the checkpoint farther north. I'll take Bravo Team to the southern checkpoint."

"We can't split up," Brock muttered. "Can we?"

"Remmington didn't tell us we couldn't."

DeLafor sighed. "Come on, Moorfield. We already hit three checkpoints. We can call it."

"Sure, we could. Then we'd be mediocre soldiers at

basic training doing the bare minimum to get by." Idina raised an eyebrow at him. "I didn't think that was your jam, DeLafor."

He snorted and rolled his eyes. "Asshole."

"Why would we wanna do all five?" Amber asked.

Idina grinned and looked at each face in her squad. "Because I'm pretty sure it doesn't happen all that much. Look, they have five checkpoints here to keep us flustered about not being able to hit all five, and we only need three. We're good. But we still have..." She glanced at her field watch. "Twenty-six minutes. If we split up, we can hit the last two in that amount of time and regroup here after twelve hundred hours."

"They'll know we cheated."

"It's not cheating if the people operating the checkpoints don't bother to count how many soldiers show up. They haven't. Trust me. All you need is to call out Second Squad, and we're in." She looked around the squad again, finding wide eyes, squinting eyes, and a very confused-looking McCoy.

Finally, DeLafor punched his palm and nodded. "Fuck it. Why not?"

No one else objected, and Idina's smile widened. "Great. Alpha Team has the compass. Bravo takes the map. We'll note landmarks on the way in and get ourselves back that way. If Alpha Team gets lost with a compass, that's not my fault."

The recruits chuckled, then the teams broke away to head for the last two checkpoints as only half a squad each.

Idina oriented herself with their location on the map after pinpointing the angle between both checkpoints and the direction Alpha Team was going, then led Bravo Team toward their final checkpoint. In twenty-one minutes, they reached the other bunker and the soldier handling it for this particular exercise.

"Second Squad, First Platoon, Bravo Company," Matthews shouted.

The static of their check-in being radioed back to Staff Sergeant Remmington filtered toward them through the trees, and DeLafor pumped a fist at his side. "Fucking nailed it."

"With five minutes to spare," Idina muttered. "Time to regroup with Alpha."

Then hopefully not have to explain to Remmington how Second Squad hit two checkpoints at once.

Just before thirteen hundred hours, Second Squad marched up the hill in the valley toward their starting location. First Squad was already there with Staff Sergeant Remmington and Corporal Staffhouse, who'd ordered the squad to sit and pull out their MREs for lunch.

With nothing else to do but wait ten minutes for their MREs to heat, the soldiers in First Squad chuckled as they watched the other half of their platoon sweat and huff as they trekked up the rest of the hill. Idina took up the rear of her squad, then Remmington shouted, "Get comfy and whip out that five-star meal, Second Squad. You earned it."

"All that just for lunch?" DeLafor let out a low whistle. "Now I'm afraid what we have to do just to—"

Amber elbow jabbed his ribs to shut him up before the

whole platoon got smoked again at the top of the hill for his smart mouth.

Everyone pulled out their canteens and MREs to make their lunches. Opening no less than eight packages for a single meal—sometimes more—had gotten easier the more they ate out during field exercises. Idina poured water into the heater and slid the food pouch inside before stuffing it all in the box and standing it upright. Today's main course was beef stew.

Nice. That'll look like sloppy joes paste and taste like dog food. Can't wait.

The second she sat back to wait for the MRE to cook, Remmington called her away from the rest of the platoon.

Here it comes. He's gonna ask. I'll have to tell. The squad leader's responsible for the decisions, so it's all on me.

She leapt to her feet and approached the platoon leader. Corporal Staffhouse stood beside Remmington with his arms folded but didn't say a word.

"Sir?" Idina sat flatly.

"I'm a little confused here, Moorfield," Remmington began, making a show of stroking his chin. "That doesn't usually happen. So maybe you can clear up a few things for me."

"I'll do my best, sir."

"I received two radio check-ins within one minute of each other from two different checkpoints. Both of them awarded to Second Squad. What do you think happened there? Speak freely on this one, soldier. I'm honestly intrigued."

Idina cleared her throat and looked back and forth

between her commanders. "Second Squad hit two check-points within one minute of each other, sir."

"That goes without saying." Remmington fixed her with a curious smile. She didn't expect the sudden wave of relief that washed over her. "That happened how?"

"Because we were in two places at once, sir. I made the call to separate Alpha and Bravo Teams to attempt hitting all five checkpoints within the three hours."

"You made the call." Remmington turned toward Staffhouse, who raised his eyebrows and had nothing important to add to the conversation. "That doesn't happen very often, Moorfield. Five checkpoints in three hours. I'm guessing there was more to your strategy than splitting Second Squad up for the last two."

"Yes, sir. We located the most difficult checkpoint to reach, geographically and by distance, and went there first."

"Huh." Remmington nodded. "You made it work. Impressive from an execution standpoint. You put a lot of faith in your teams' ability to find each other again when one of them had only a map or only a compass or both."

"I had no reason not to have faith in my teams, sir."

"Obviously." He grunted out a subdued laugh and folded his arms. "Next time you lead Second Squad back to the rendezvous point half an hour later than everyone else, you're not getting time to eat."

"Yes, sir."

"You're dismissed."

"Thank you, sir." Idina spun and marched back toward her gear and the rest of her platoon sprawled out for lunch.

Amber met her gaze and nodded behind Idina toward the platoon leader. "What was that about?"

"Impressive from an execution standpoint." Idina shrugged. "No big deal."

"I knew it." Brock slopped his spoon back down into his MRE packet. "We're fucked."

"Only if we have to hit five checkpoints again and make it back at the same time as First Squad." Idina grinned and snatched her food packet out of the box to dig into a well-earned meal.

Remmington looked surprised. So did Staffhouse. Splitting up my teams doesn't go against any rules. No, each team didn't have a complete set of navigation tools, but we all had what we needed to meet up again. Thinking outside the box finally got me somewhere.

———

They stayed out at the land navigation site for the rest of the day. Once Remmington led them to a completely different rendezvous point, they ran more drills, cleaned their firearms, and broke for their second round of MREs, all while they waited for nightfall.

Once it was dark, the squads were handed new maps to replace the old ones and told they had three hours to find two out of the three checkpoints set up for the night phase. After Idina's decision to split up Second Squad for the day phase, she was content enough to take opinions from her squad and go with the most popular option among them.

We don't need to risk getting turned around at night to hit all three checkpoints. Nobody likes a greedy winner.

Beyond that, most of her squad were a lot more unfamiliar with navigating the woods at night. Many of them hadn't spent so much as a single night camping. Even with night gear illuminating everything in thick shades of greenish-gray, they stumbled and made way more noise than would've passed in the field during active duty.

The thick forest around them didn't help. Moonlight and starlight enhanced the night-vision goggles, and there was very little of that beneath the heavy tree cover. Idina handed the map and the compass to two different squad members this time. She took a page from her platoon leader's book to see that her fellow soldiers had the responsibility and the chance to pick up new navigational skills if they didn't already possess them.

This time, they beat First Squad back to the rendezvous point by eight minutes, and both squads had reached their objectives with two out of three checkpoints during the night phase.

After that, the entire platoon stayed outside at the navigation site for their first night of Army basic camping. With nothing more to support them on the ground but their issued sleeping bags, it was a long, cold night at the end of October. They still had to run their shifts of sentry duty around the encampment. One soldier stayed up for an hour as lookout before they woke the next and continued the rotation.

When they woke the following morning, sore, stiff, and sweaty from the sleeping bags designed to keep them warm in negative-degree temperatures, Remmington led them through more exercises on-site. They learned how to erect a field-expedient shelter, the basics of occupying an assembly area and preparing a hasty fighting position, and how to move with proper technique as a member of a cohesive squad.

"I heard you out there the whole time last night," Remington barked. "You were too loud, and you talked too much. Because nobody knew what they were doing."

So they ran through those drills over and over until the platoon leader finally called it quits and commanded the platoon to march back toward the barracks for lunch chow.

Despite not having gotten any real sleep and not having eaten since dinner chow the day before, none of the soldiers complained. They'd made it through their first truly arduous Field Training Exercise. It left them with a whole new appreciation for handling working in the field during the day or night, no matter the weather, the temperature, or how much food they didn't have.

Idina was especially proud of her squad for pulling together and handling things the way they did, even with Timbers' constant groaning and cursing when she couldn't find "a comfortable spot" for her sleeping bag.

If anyone had told First Platoon that the final phase of basic training would start like a cyclical nightmare, not a single soldier would've believed the claim.

CHAPTER TWENTY-SIX

It was supposed to be the start of Blue Phase, the third and final phase of basic training that would combine everything they'd learned from the previous two and add additional skillsets and maneuvers. It started like any other day —morning PT in the training arena with more combatants classes and learning more advanced techniques for hand-to-hand combat.

Then breakfast chow.

Then they went out to the shooting range again in full gear and practiced as a squad with hitting moving targets and stationary targets while *they* were moving.

The day progressed like any other day, with a new skill added to their combatants classes—proper fighting techniques with pugil sticks.

Idina caught Amber's gaze as Remmington explained to them the basic forms with this kind of padded tournament weapon, and the other girl smirked.

Okay, not exactly a bō staff, but I told her I know what I'm doing. And that she could only take me with something like this.

The soldiers were excited to get into the fighting technique and learned there would be a tournament against the other platoons toward the end of Blue Phase.

No one expected what was waiting for them after lights out. Including Idina.

At 11:00 p.m., both bays for men and women fell silent. Every soldier wore their PT uniforms to be ready for the physical training they expected early in the morning. An hour and a half later at 12:30 a.m., the lights clicked on, and Sergeant O'Hare's voice echoed around the room.

"Off your asses, soldiers! Make your bunks! Move, move, move!"

Startled out of the sleep they'd slipped into, the women rolled out of bed and did as ordered.

Another female sergeant for Second Platoon joined O'Hare in the screaming. "You think this is a game? You think you made it this far so you don't have to worry about straight lines in those bedclothes anymore?" She whisked the sheets off one soldier's mattress and threw them on the floor. "Do it right, Stevens. Now!"

Stevens scrambled to make her bed again, which hadn't fallen below Army standards the first time, but she didn't say a word.

The women lined up in front of Sergeant O'Hare, who looked them over with narrowed eyes as they waited for Stevens to finish and hurry to the back of the line and stand at attention.

"Let's go, recruits." She spun and headed through the hallway of the barracks' ground floor. The other female sergeant scrutinized every one of them as they passed, then she brought up the rear of the escort taking the women who knew where.

Idina blinked wearily and tried to focus on the rhythmic *clomps* of boots rising from the women in line around her. More sounded from the intersecting corridor where the men were being led down from the men's barracks to join them.

The male drill sergeants' voices crashed down the stairwell as they barked at the soldiers just like they had on the very first day of basic from the second the bus had rolled to a stop in front of the barracks.

A knot of dread tightened in Idina's gut. *What did we do? We went back to the bay for lights out. Now they're screaming at us like we haven't been through months of this already? Who screwed up this badly?*

Drill sergeants screamed and shuffled sideways as they ushered the tired soldiers into another bay. This one was empty, and it sounded incredibly strange at first until Idina realized it was the *lack* of sound.

They'd turned off all the fans.

When the recruits fell into formation at the center of the bay, and all ten drill sergeants for Bravo Company's current basic training cycle joined them, the doors at both ends of the bay were closed and stayed closed. The room was so silent that the recruits were afraid to breathe at that point—in case it pissed off a drill sergeant enough to punish them even further for whatever they'd done.

Staff Sergeant Remmington paced in front of the entire company's formation with a scowl. "In case you were wondering why you're not all cozy in your bunks tonight, here's your answer. Start running."

The newly transitioned Blue Phase soldiers didn't talk back or scoff or react in any way other than what the Army expected of Blue Phase soldiers. Even when their COs treated them like they'd arrived on base for the first time. The drill sergeants screamed at them as the company ran midnight laps in the bay large enough to hold them all. They shoved their faces at any recruit who looked like they were slowing down and even those recruits who didn't show any sign of being bothered by this surprise smoking.

It was the smoking of a lifetime, Idina quickly discovered.

After Remmington finished barking orders for the company to run, drop for pushups, and perform jumping jacks in place for a full three minutes, Idina didn't dare hope they'd finished.

"Bravo Company, fall in!"

The soldiers lined up again instantly in the center of the empty bay.

They wouldn't wake us up in the night for ten minutes of extra physical strain. What is *this?*

Remmington turned to look at the other drill sergeants and nodded. "Sergeant O'Hare. Wanna have a go?"

"Yes, sir."

O'Hare stepped up with her hands behind her back and stood at ease with the entire company facing her. "Drop and give me sit-ups! You have three minutes, soldiers! If I see anyone pausing, the whole company starts over from the beginning. Hansen, check your damn boots! You call that flat on the floor?"

For fifteen minutes, the company hustled to complete every rigorous physical task Sergeant O'Hare commanded of them. When she finished, she handed the reins over to the next drill sergeant. Who handed it to the next. And the next.

All ten drill sergeants had their chance to smoke the living hell out of Bravo Company for ten to fifteen minutes at a time. When Remmington finally ordered them to fall in again, it was 2:30 a.m. The soldiers wheezed, coughed, and doubled over as they fought for breath. Massive puddles of sweat coated the bay floor. With the fans off and the doors shut tight, the bay felt like an oven.

This is worse than the gas chamber. Somehow, somebody screwed up so badly that the entire company's getting smoked. They won't even tell us why.

"Get back to bed, soldiers," Remmington shouted. "You still have three and a half hours. Sweet dreams."

Without a word, the heavily breathing soldiers marched back to their respective bays to attempt what little sleep their COs afforded them. It was impossible. Idina was sweating so badly that she couldn't get comfortable in her hot, sticky PT uniform.

The other women in the bay tossed and turned, getting up with much more frequency than they had since day one to drink from their camelbacks, go to the bathroom, try to cool down, and warm up when the rigors of being smoked for two hours straight in the middle of the night wouldn't let them get comfortable.

"Petrie," Idina whispered.

From three bunks down, Amber rolled over with a groan. "What?"

"Did you hear anything about what happened?"

"Like they'd tell us shit. Stop talking."

Idina flopped onto her back again beneath her standard-issue Army bedclothes and stared at the bay's dark ceiling.

There has to be a reason they're doing this. They do everything for a reason. What the hell could be such a huge mistake that they're making the entire company pay for it in the middle of the night? With all ten drill sergeants. I don't get it.

Then the worst possibility imaginable entered her mind.

They know. They know about my episodes and the green lights. Somebody saw it when I helped Brock with his rope harness, and they were holding it in their back pocket for when we least expected it. Or he told someone Fuck.

The more she lay there thinking about it, though, the less likely that seemed.

A soldier with green specks and mist bursting from her hands once would still only get kicked out of basic. Or herded to the doctors on base and studied like a science experiment gone wrong. So it had to be someone else.

The fact that this was one puzzle Idina couldn't figure out by watching her commanders and other soldiers of her platoon like she had been for the last two months kept her awake much longer than she could afford. By the time 5:30 a.m. rolled around and it was time to get up, make her bed, and head out to morning PT, she'd only gotten a total of two hours' sleep.

The next day wasn't any better. Instead of heading to the firing range or spending more time in combatants classes or rucking across difficult terrain, the entirety of Bravo Company found themselves out in the yard like the beginning of White Phase.

"Bravo Company, fall in!" Remmington shouted.

Each platoon leader echoed the command. Then the differing orders began for individual platoons. The company split apart, and Corporal Staffhouse called for First Platoon to turn and march toward the east end of the yard and an unknown destination.

When they finally stopped, they found nothing but a massive pile in front of them. It consisted of tiny shreds of tire rubber as if five hundred decommissioned vehicle tires had been thrown into a giant blender and dumped out onto the yard.

"First Platoon, halt!"

The soldiers stood at attention, not daring to look at the pit or their platoon leader in case that was what Staff Sergeant Remmington was waiting for them to do. "Today, you're moving this rubber heap. You're not stopping until every single piece makes it into that crawl pit over there."

He pointed across the yard at the pit the recruits had jumped into and crawled through during their exercises. It had helped prepare them for the endurance course. "One piece at a time."

The platoon's shock was immediately apparent by the complete silence alone.

Every single piece of rubber by hand. One at a time? Oh, come on. They're still smoking us. Why?

"If I see anyone picking up more than *one* piece at a time, you're running laps in full gear until lunch chow. If I hear a single word out of any soldier's mouth, a laugh, a groan, a fart I don't like the sound of, you're running laps in full gear until lunch chow. Get it?"

"Yes, sir!" the platoon replied together with the kind of precision they'd honed over the last two months.

"Go." Remmington stepped aside with his hands clasped behind his back to watch his platoon carry out his orders.

It wasn't exactly back-breaking work. Just dull, monotonous, and pointless. Every soldier knew it, and every soldier did as instructed without making a sound.

Idina felt like she was about to explode.

This doesn't make sense. We're supposed to be in Blue Phase. What happened to advancing through basic?

A rippling tremor of electric energy raced across her back and shoulders, and she sucked in a sharp breath.

No. Pull it together, Moorfield. You are not having an episode now while the entire company's getting smoked for someone else's fuckup. Shove it down and obey your orders.

Fortunately, that was all it took to snuff out the warning tingle that had heralded her biggest episodes at home—the kind that had gotten Dr. Kruchek to double her dose of inhibitors slightly under a year ago now. The fact that she'd somehow found a way to dampen her weird abilities through sheer willpower alone gave her the confidence she needed to grit her teeth and bear down with the rest of her platoon to do as ordered.

For three hours, First Platoon moved the shredded rubber from the pile to the pit one piece at a time. If someone stooped to retrieve another chunk and it was too slow for either Remmington's or Staffhouse's liking, the drill sergeants kicked the base of the pile and scattered it across the yard before barking at them to clean up the mess.

The task was impossible to accomplish in three hours before lunch chow. When the platoon finished eating, they were marched right back to the rubber pile in the yard and told to keep at it.

At the end of the day, sore from bending and walking back and forth for no reason other than the company must've done something major to piss off the drill sergeants, Idina joined the other women in the women's showers to try washing off the end of the worst day since entering basic.

No one said a word. They shuffled around the showers during their allotted ten minutes, eyes closed, thoughts contained. No one looked happy.

No one was.

Idina couldn't find it in her to ask the other female recruits one more time if anyone knew why they'd reverted to the stupidly, agonizingly mundane drills and disciplinary tasks they'd carried out during the very first stages of basic.

It doesn't make sense. Apparently, things that don't make sense piss me off.

Finally, when she settled down into her bunk in her PT uniform, and 11:00 p.m. arrived for lights out, she found it a lot easier to close her eyes and let exhaustion overtake her.

Until the lights clicked on at 12:30 a.m. again, and

Sergeant O'Hare appeared in the bay's doorway with another female drill sergeant.

No. No, no, no. Not again.

The women lined up and prepared to march toward whatever midnight punishment awaited them this time. As it turned out, it was the same punishment as the night before—two hours of being run ragged by every Bravo Company drill sergeant sounding more and more pissed that they were up in the middle of the night with their recruits.

That might've made them even *more* dedicated to smoking the shit out of Bravo Company until several soldiers crumpled to the floor, vomited under the strain, or cried because that was the only thing they *could* do. The punishment kept going.

First Platoon missed lunch chow the day after that because Staff Sergeant Remmington didn't like the way they'd scrubbed the exterior walls of the barracks with old toothbrushes and water handed to them in buckets without any soap. So he made them do it all over again.

Then they were lined up inside the mess hall and instructed to inspect every plastic tray, cup, and utensil. Every soldier had to get a good look at the company's dinnerware before passing it on to the next soldier behind them to do the very same thing.

For what purpose? None of them knew. Each of them secretly hoped that if they kept their heads down and did as told, this unexpected hell in the middle of basic training would finally come to an end.

They barely managed to restock the dinnerware in the mess hall before it was time for dinner chow. Remmington made them wait until Second and Third Platoons had scooped their single helping of whatever dishes they wanted onto their plate before First Platoon was allowed to join them.

Everyone looked pissed.

This is the opposite of happy. This is miserable. Idina stood in front of her seat at the long chow table, waiting for the company command to sit and eat as much as possible in three minutes. It was hard enough to keep her eyes from crossing in exhaustion, let alone hold her tray in its upright position until she could place it on the table.

This is the opposite of taking pride in being a soldier. They're jerking us around for no reason at all. If this is Blue Phase, fuck Blue Phase.

The feeling stayed with her when Staffhouse dismissed the company. Normally, that would've meant they could return to the bay and have some downtime before lights out. Not today.

Remmington had First Platoon step out into the yard again. The entire collection of rappelling ropes from the Warrior's Tower and all the practice towers sat piled in front of them. He commanded the recruits to inspect every single rope and snip off any tiny fibers that stuck out from the rope's body.

Pointless. Useless. Busy work with absolutely no purpose, but they finished the task half an hour before lights out. Which meant every soldier returned to the bay *past* lights out and had to change out of their OCPs and into their PT uniforms in the dark.

When Idina finally crawled under her bedclothes—feeling like a dying animal—she heard two different women in the bay trying to muffle their sobs in their pillows.

This shit would make anyone cry. Even the guys. Even DeLafor. Fuck, what are they trying to do to us?

She almost screamed when she was ripped out of sleep for the third night in a row by the bay lights blasting on hours before their regular time and Sergeant O'Hare barking orders at them again. The march through the barracks wasn't much of a march at all.

The exhausted women staggered against the walls, groaning, cussing, sometimes whimpering. The men weren't any better. The whole time, the drill sergeants screamed in their faces to move faster, stand straighter, keep their eyes forward, be silent.

When they returned to the empty bay with the fans off and the doors closed for the third time, Idina stumbled sideways and shook her head to try ridding herself of the violent nausea overwhelming her. It was less from such a late hour and getting no more than six hours of sleep over the past three nights and more from the horror of what lay ahead.

This is what we have to go through for the final three weeks? I can barely stand. How are we supposed to deal with this every night until we reach the end? None of us will reach the end if this keeps up.

The company fell into formation at Remmington's command. They tried their best to stand at attention. Still, they couldn't keep themselves from swaying or dropping their chins to their chests in a brief moment of falling asleep on their feet. Several couldn't hold back the tears threatening to spill from their eyes as they waited to be smoked by all ten drill sergeants again.

They were.

The drill sergeants picked up the ferocity of their barked orders, the strenuousness of their commands for each physical task that none of the recruits thought they could accomplish this time.

After the fourth drill sergeant finished making them do pushups for five minutes straight—and those who couldn't manage it had to run laps around the bay, which was most of the soldiers—they were called in to be handed off to Corporal Staffhouse.

"Bravo Company," he shouted. "Drop and give me fifty!"

Idina's eyes rolled in her head as if they had a mind of their own. Half the company had thrown up already. Most of them made it to the trashcans, but there were the unlucky few who couldn't control their bodies the way they thought they'd trained them.

The hot, cloying, stagnant bay filled with the stench of vomit and acrid sweat. Soldiers broke down in their way. Idina still got down on her hands and knees to set up for doing even more pushups.

She got to ten—which might've been her hundredth for the night with no sleep, for all she knew—and her arms shook.

"I said fifty, Moorfield!" Staffhouse roared. "What's wrong with you? You can't handle fifty pushups?"

A boiling rage that felt like fire flashed through Idina's entire body. For a moment, she thought she would pass out right there. Another ripple of intense heat and icy cold joined the rage, this one stronger than any of the others she'd experienced in the last three days.

Green mist flickered around her vision, growing brighter and pulsing as it converged to cover the floor of the bay she'd been glaring at during her pushups.

Nobody sees this. It's only in my head still. If they did see it, I'd be up and running laps 'til I passed out. Keep going.

Her muscles burned with fatigue and the strain of holding herself up.

"Where's your discipline, Moorfield?" Staffhouse barked. "This is pathetic!"

He didn't keep riding her after that and walked down the line of recruits who were still trying to do as instructed for a punishment none of them understood. After his harsh barking to continue with fifty pushups, knowing what she and every soldier in Bravo Company had been through in the last three days—Idina Moorfield finally reached her limits.

She dropped out of her pushup position and onto her knees, let out a sharp, clipped scream, and slammed both hands down on the bay floor. Her cry barely rose above the noise of other soldiers breaking down and losing their shit all around her. No one was paying attention to her—one soldier among so many who were failing.

So no one saw the burst of green light that flickered brightly between Idina's palms and the bay floor when she screamed, and the boiling surge of rage and physical pain and the urgency to *keep going* despite her body betraying her rushed through her body.

She froze and stared at her hands pressed into the floor.

The old concrete beneath her palms felt like it had cracked beneath her. Small, thin tendrils of green mist rose across the floor to curl up around her wrists.

No. No, no, no. Not now. I've gone through all this bullshit in basic without a real episode. Not now!

Her entire body tingled, fueled by the familiar rush that was impossible to stop once it started. The rush she hadn't felt in years because her parents and grandfather had decided that pumping her full of meds was the best way to keep her from unleashing what had only been freed from Idina Moorfield twice in her life.

Fuck, fuck, fuck. I can't do this. Shit, it won't go away. Just go away!

The green light beneath her hands pulsed, letting out a thicker surge of mist.

I'm broken. They broke me, I broke the damn floor, and now everyone can see fucking lights coming out of my hands!

She leapt to her feet and stormed across the bay, stumbling every few steps because her mind and body were at war with each other.

"Moorfield," Remmington called after her.

"I need a minute." Idina reached the far wall of the bay and propped herself up against it with both hands. An instant surge of horror flooded through her, and she stared at her palms.

Pull it back down. Pull it together. Just breathe. If you let this out right now, you're fucked. No Army, no Dartmouth, nothing. Your family won't take you back. Don't let this out!

She turned, *thumped* her back against the wall, and slid down until she sat there with her knees bent in front of her, still trying to catch her breath. Her heart felt like it would explode.

Staff Sergeant Remmington calmly approached her and squatted two feet away. "What happened?"

"What happened?" A bitter laugh escaped her. "I don't think I can do this, sir."

"All right, drop the formalities for now. Tell me what's going on."

"I just...I'm psyching myself. I don't know what happened, but this is making me insane. I'm insane—"

"Listen, Moorfield." He nudged her knee with the back of a hand. "Remember when I told you everybody breaks? If you're only reaching this point tonight, I'll go ahead and say this is your break."

"That doesn't make me feel any better."

"Not right now, it doesn't. But it happens to everyone. We all go through it."

Idina clenched her eyes shut and tried to breathe slowly through her nose. Her hands were shaking. Everything was shaking. She thought she might've at least bruised a rib at some point, and every limb and joint in her body burned.

That wasn't the worst of it. The worst was trying to look ahead into the future and seeing only an endless string of sleepless nights and pointless tasks.

And my fucking episodes finally kicking into high gear because I don't have my meds. I don't know which is worse. The possibility that happened or that I'll go insane trying to force it all back down so nobody notices.

She finally opened her eyes, looked at her palms, and muttered, "I don't think what's happening to me happens to everyone."

"Hey, hey. I know what you're going through, Moorfield." Remmington lowered his head to catch her gaze and nodded. "We've all been through it. This shit is *hard*. I get it. Harder than anything you've ever done. But it's not impossible."

She swallowed. "I really don't think you understand..."

"I took an oath for this too, you know." He bounced a little in his crouch. "'I will lead by example, never requiring a soldier to attempt any task I would not do myself.' That's the Drill Sergeant's Creed.

"All this? It's not bigger than you. You can handle it. All you have to do is follow me, okay? Do everything I say. Don't worry about what it means or how it's gonna turn out, or why we tell you to do whatever we order you to do. That's *my* job."

Something between a laugh and a sob burst from her lips, and Idina wiped the massive beads of sweat trickling down her forehead and the sides of her face. "That might be the part I can't handle."

Remmington chuckled. "Well, you're gonna handle it, Moorfield. You *will* graduate. Just follow me and keep going. Hey, true to form with you, you'll be leading by example, huh?" He nudged her in the shoulder. "Right?"

"I guess." *Not if my example is unleashing holy green hell in the middle of the basic barracks. I almost seriously hurt a maid three years ago. What'll it say about me if I hurt another soldier with this shit I can't explain?*

"Okay." Remmington nodded. "Sit tight for another five minutes until Corporal Staffhouse is done up there. After that, I want you to fall in with your company and finish what you started. Can you do that?"

She scanned the floor in front of his boots as he stood and muttered, "Yes, sir."

"That's right, soldier. You can." The platoon leader turned away and rejoined the other drill sergeants who weren't smoking the rest of the company. Some of them had broken off to have conversations with other soldiers who'd reached their breaking point during all this, and Idina watched those private conversations with a frown.

Sure. It gets this bad, and now *they start acting like they care about who we are and what we're going through and how much this fucking sucks. Maybe he cares, but he doesn't understand. Not what I'm dealing with right now.*

Sergeant O'Hare crouched beside Brock, who full-on sobbed into his hands and shook his head while the drill sergeant muttered encouraging words to him. Another sergeant from Third Platoon stood in front of Amber, who paced back and forth in a wide-eyed panic and wouldn't say a thing. But she was listening.

The entire ordeal of the last sixty hours finally started to make sense, and a massive shift in Idina's perspective made her sit up a little straighter against the wall.

This isn't a punishment. This is a test. Holy shit. They want us to break completely. We've built our confidence up to this point, and now they're testing it. Making sure we have what it takes to keep going and keep following them even after they pull shit like this. We didn't do anything wrong. No one did. This is all part of it.

Somehow, the realization made it possible for Idina to push herself off the floor while Corporal Staffhouse finished shouting commands at the ragged, weary, sweat- and tear-stained company. When he switched out with another drill sergeant to keep going for their two hours of nightly hell, Idina did as Remmington had instructed and rejoined the company in the center of the bay. She didn't feel strong, but she felt different. Better.

There's a reason for this, which makes it worth it. So I'll fall in and finish what I started. That's what a Moorfield does, right? Fuck the episodes. That's not who I am. I'm a soldier in the U.S. Army.

CHAPTER TWENTY-SEVEN

They didn't get any more sleep that night than they did the two previous nights after the drill sergeants dismissed them to return to the bays. Idina dropped into a deep, dreamless, undisturbed sleep for slightly less than three hours until it was time to get up and keep moving forward. To follow her platoon leader and platoon guide because that was *her* job.

Somehow, she did it.

So did every other woman in Bravo Company but one. She'd collapsed while running during their midnight session and had to be evacuated to the med bay with a concussion. That was part of this.

Some soldiers would get hurt. They'd have to heal, recover, and make up for lost time if that recovery lasted too long. Everyone else had to keep moving forward through the last few weeks of basic training because this was what they'd signed up for, and this was who they were now.

First Platoon was asleep on their feet during morning

PT, but they made it through. Shoveling as much food into their mouths as possible during the three minutes of breakfast chow was a mindless act that could be easily accomplished and completed on time because they'd been doing it for months.

Although she was numb, exhausted, and completely drained in every way imaginable, Idina grew used to the sensation. She might have even enjoyed it. *Just follow them through whatever they send our way. That's all I have to do. That's it.*

Through the numbness, she realized the burning tingle of energy that had surged through her at an ungodly hour of the early morning while the company got their asses handed to them on a silver platter was gone. It didn't come back.

After chow, Idina marched in formation with the rest of her platoon out to the yard, where Staff Sergeant Remmington and Corporal Staffhouse looked almost as exhausted as their recruits. When the platoon stood at attention to receive their next orders for the day, fully expecting it to be another useless round of menial tasks that got them nowhere fast, it took a moment for Remmington's next orders to sink in fully.

"I hope you're ready this morning, soldiers. If you're not, tough shit. We have a little ruck ahead of us."

The entire platoon marched out in full combat gear, with heavy packs and firearms in hand, not knowing what the hell "a little ruck" meant. No one knew, and it was hard enough to figure out anything other than the fact that Remmington had been screwing with them when he'd called it *little*.

It wasn't little at all. After two and a half days and three nights of constant hell without the chance to give their bodies what they needed, First Platoon followed their drill sergeants for a twelve-mile ruck across the open land nav sites stretching out beyond the barracks. They didn't stop to rest. They didn't break for lunch chow, and Idina quickly realized they wouldn't have even if they'd been given MREs for the trek.

The platoon moved at a constant speed in a massive circle, looping wide around the open wilderness surrounding Fort Leonard Wood. Whenever a recruit stumbled or looked like they were about to call it quits, their fellow soldiers hauled them back to their feet, righted them, and silently urged them forward in miserable solidarity.

No one wanted to fail out of this. No one wanted to get smoked again like they'd been because one of their own didn't think they could make it. They were all in this together, and it sucked for everyone.

Then they finally arrived at the shooting range. Seventy-two hours without any real sleep, with half the food they'd grown accustomed to and nothing since breakfast, and their COs expected them to set up at the shooting range and *qualify* with their weapons in that state.

Staff Sergeant Remmington and Corporal Staffhouse didn't seem to notice how exhausted, dejected, and flat-out done their soldiers were.

They notice, all right. Idina grabbed her automatic rifle and prepared to aim with the rest of her platoon as the first wave fired shots and attempted to hit their targets. *They don't care. Because they know we can do this. I can't even see straight, but I—*

The ringing *ping* of McCoy's shots hitting every single target in quick succession made her pause.

Fuck, if McCoy can do it, we all can.

She zeroed her sights with the next wave of soldiers and unleashed hell on the firing range. The air filled with the deafening roar of weapons fire pelting the targets with bullets. Maybe the platoon hit their targets. Maybe they didn't. Each soldier focused on their task, putting one foot in front of the other to get through the rest of this nightmare.

When that was over, First Platoon immediately marched back to the barracks and fell into formation in the yard.

Remmington stopped in front of them and looked over the haggard, broken faces of his platoon. "That was your stress shoot, soldiers. You're combat engineers. There *will* come a time when the rigors of active duty put you in the same stressful, debilitating situations. No sleep. No food. No obvious way out.

"Your duty as an Army soldier is to keep moving no matter what. To continue your mission with your team, your squad, your platoon the way we expect of you. To stay sharp and alert even under the worst physical and mental strain. This is your job. This is who you are."

He scanned the formation one more time and nodded. "Congratulations, First Platoon. You're still alive. You're dismissed for the rest of the day."

The soldiers fell out of attention in a daze, not daring to

believe their dismissal for the rest of the *entire* day without it being some kind of trick.

"First Platoon, dismissed!" Staffhouse echoed. "The rest of the day is yours, soldiers. Are you gonna waste it by standing around in the yard?"

That got them moving again. The platoon fell out of formation and shuffled like zombies into the barracks.

They'd missed lunch chow, but as hungry as they were, they were even more exhausted. Idina went straight to the women's bay and didn't last long enough to unlace her boots before passing out on her bunk and falling into the heavy, blissful weight of sleep. Even her aching muscles and the burning behind her eyes weren't enough to keep her awake.

We did it. Doesn't matter what it is. We're still here. And we still have another two and a half weeks to go.

Idina slept fifteen hours straight through, and even that length of time didn't make it easy to crawl out of her bunk at 5:30 a.m. the next morning to head to PT. She was sore, stiff, still exhausted, and ravenous, but combatants classes and sparring for PT that morning seemed a hell of a lot easier.

Every First Platoon soldier piled their plates extra high during breakfast chow, and they managed to wolf it all down in their allotted three minutes anyway.

Then they were told their final PT test was coming their way. "One hundred fifty points minimum required to pass basic training," Remmington barked. "If you didn't receive those points during your initial PT test, you sure as hell better receive that minimum now. The only way to move forward through Blue Phase into your final FTX is to pass PT."

Some of the recruits snickered. They'd been doing so many pushups, sit-ups, and untimed runs over the last two months that repeating the same physical fitness test to complete basic seemed like a joke. Especially after everything they'd been through in the previous four days.

The soldiers who'd made it this far passed the PT test with far more than one hundred and fifty points per recruit. They were ready. Being ready meant they were now prepared enough to handle field problems—AKA camping.

After the time they'd spent rucking through the woods, drilling how to erect emergency shelters, and moving together much more efficiently as a platoon and individual squads, Idina and her fellow soldiers had no issue solving these field problems. The worst of it at that point was that it was now November. The nights were incredibly cold.

They had their sleeping bags to keep them warm, but that gear was for much colder weather. So the nights were also spent alternating between sweating puddles in their sleeping bags and unzipping the things to get fresh air, only to be freezing minutes later and have to bundle up again.

Then came more field training exercises in the form of nighttime combat operations, in which the drill sergeants also participated. Just not to the recruits' benefit.

The individual squads planned out their attack routes for each exercise—in the woods, in open fields, in urban settings erected on base, and around the barracks during enhanced fireguard patrols. Those required the soldiers to be in uniform, full combat gear, fully armed, and juggling a flashlight on top of it all.

Meanwhile, the drill sergeants did everything possible to sabotage the plans First and Second Squads worked diligently to form.

The soldiers drilled flanking maneuvers, this time during their FTXs. They learned through trial and error what it meant to execute an ambush on the enemy—their drill sergeants—as well as what it meant to *be* ambushed.

During nighttime combat operations, their issued night-vision gear helped them only when the moon was out, and the darkness of the woods didn't enshroud them. Each squad learned to work together in combat situations, to operate as one entity, to wordlessly and soundlessly give and receive commands and carry them out effectively.

Even in the cold. Even in the dark. Even when they'd been up for twenty-four hours straight because they didn't have the time to sleep during nighttime exercises.

Idina excelled at these, especially at night. That was because her green lights had come back, but they were different.

Her mind moved faster than it ever had. She managed to run through five different scenarios at a time in seconds and discern the one most likely to be successful. At first, she thought it was merely due to all the time she'd spent watching her drill sergeants. She'd gotten to know them and the way *they* reacted to certain situations, as she'd accomplished with her fellow soldiers. She'd learned how to play the game, so to speak, the way she'd learned how to play it with her entire family at Moorfield Manor.

There wasn't much of a difference between the two when she looked at it the right way. The Army didn't care about Idina Moorfield as a person—about who she was, what she wanted, where she came from, whatever baggage she carried. All they wanted to know was that she could do her job and carry out her orders.

Her family had been very much the same all her life.

First Platoon engaged in another FTX at night and received their objective against "enemy" drill sergeants she *hadn't* had the last nine weeks to study and understand. That's when Idina's ability to find strategic solutions to her squad's obstacles became something entirely different.

It was the first time her green lights showed up again after her close call with a full-blown episode.

For as long as she could remember, those green lights illuminating the next step—the right answer, the missing piece, the additional line in one of her art projects—had been contained to what was directly in front of her. She could see the answers others couldn't, just like they couldn't see her green lights when it wasn't a full-blown episode. As far as she knew, that had only ever worked when the problem and the solution were literally at hand.

Now, Idina's green lights appeared in ways much bigger than only her and her immediate individual surroundings. They started mapping out how she saw her entire squad's obstacles and the startling solutions she couldn't help but trust.

"Okay, here's what we're gonna do," Masterson whispered as Second Platoon huddled beneath tree cover with their objective in sight—a large, plain concrete tower in the middle of nowhere, Fort Leonard Wood. "Alpha Team flanks left. There's a junk pile on the west side of the tower to use for cover. You won't move in until Bravo Team flanks from the right to storm the door. When we're there…"

Idina stopped listening because the lights she saw in the dark sky around the tower captured her attention.

Not regular lights. Nothing that should've existed at all in a normal setting—FTX or otherwise.

Green, shimmering threads raced through the air from the junkpile Masterson had indicated and up at a sharp angle toward the tower's side. They were so much thicker than the shimmering strands like spider silk that had appeared on her art projects or when she'd worked through a numerical solution—before her family had fired her.

These were threads she hadn't seen before.

Idina studied the tower and the glowing strands of green and knew without a doubt what they meant.

There's a window there. We can't see it, but that's how the drill sergeants will know we've moved in. How the hell do I know this?

"That won't work," she interrupted.

Masterson stopped going over his strategy as their current squad leader, and everyone stared at her. "Why not, Moorfield?"

"There's a window in the tower's west side. Direct line of sight to the junk pile. They'll see Alpha Team the second we reach that perceived cover, and Bravo Team won't get halfway to the door before they're on us."

Amber scoffed. "How the hell do you know there's a window?"

Idina shook her head. "I must've seen it during another exercise a while back. Trust me. It's there."

Now I sound insane. This whole thing is insane. I see green lights again. Only they're not coming from my hands or lighting up the right answer. Just a giant spider who started spinning a web in the air or some dumb shit my mind's cooking up, and I'm the only one who can see it because I'm either insane or possibly cheating.

"Well shit." Masterson shrugged. "Not like Moorfield's ever been wrong."

"That's not true." She stared at him in the darkness. "I'm not always right. I just am about this."

"Good enough for me. Scratch the junkpile." Masterson glanced over his shoulder at the tower. "We'll wait for the sentry to make his rounds. The second he disappears around the north side of the tower, Alpha Team—"

Idina tuned him out because actual *images* had started flashing through her mind in blurred, green-hued colors. The "enemy" sentry they'd seen making rounds along the tower's base. The time between each round. The numbers that didn't add up.

"It's not a timed round," she muttered.

"Christ, Moorfield," DeLafor whispered through a smirk. "We get you're acting leader for Bravo Team, but are you gonna let the squad leader finish a fucking thought, or what?"

"Yeah. It's just—" The images appeared again, numbers and timed seconds and the count of enemy combatants in and around that tower flashing through her head in quick succession, all of them floating through a haze of green light. Idina clenched her eyes shut and shook her head.

"Whoa. Moorfield, you didn't skip chow, did you?"

"No, I'm good."

"You look like shit."

Idina steadied herself, opened her eyes, and gave her squad the information bursting into her mind without explaining how or why it was there. Even *she* didn't have one. "The sentry doesn't have a consistent round. He's been changing it up for the last fifteen minutes. Sixty seconds then a turn. A full rotation with a five-second pause. Thirty seconds out of sight on the other side of the tower with no pattern as to whether he's circling left or right around the rest of it."

Pierce snorted. "Moorfield's going idiot savant on us."

She ignored him. "We can't come at the tower from the ground."

"What the fuck, Moorfield? We don't have aircraft—"

"No, I mean not *ground-level*." Idina looked up behind the tower and found a rocky wall of the mountain face blasted away who knew when to create room for that particular tower. Even without her night-vision gear, the top of that cliff glowed with a shimmering green light in the darkness only she could see.

I have no idea why my lights went full-on superpowered, but I do know that's gonna work.

"See the ridge on the north side? About a kilometer behind the tower."

Her squad turned to peer through the darkness.

"What about it?"

"The cliff's a huge logistical obstacle. They won't expect

anyone coming in from the north. Who would go all the way around to the top to climb back down when there's tree cover here, a junkpile on the west side, and a sentry who can't see all sides of the tower at one time?"

Her squad stared at her in bafflement, then Masterson leaned away from her. "Fuck. You're right. Okay, new plan, because Moorfield's tripping her balls off on something, but it makes sense."

As their squad leader laid out the new plan, Idina forced herself to look like she was listening. Her attention was on the weirdness of what had happened—the images in her mind, the green threads as thick as cabled wire, the knowledge she suddenly seemed to have that didn't come from anything she'd intentionally done.

I can't tell anyone about this. They'll call me insane. Even if they did believe me, seeing lights in the sky and somehow knowing what they mean feels like cheating. I can handle tiny flashing lights right in front of me and the occasional mist bullshit, but I have no idea what this is.

Second Squad didn't execute their plan to complete success, but they *did* take the "enemy" drill sergeants by surprise. That alone seemed to be a massive win before their opponents captured them and the current exercise was over.

Idina couldn't help but smile at the pride on her fellow soldiers' faces when they received commendations for getting as far as they had. No one mentioned a thing about

Idina's odd ability to come up with a much different plan in a fraction of the time because no one asked.

Her moment of dizziness during the unexpected bombardment of all the images in her mind and the information she had no idea how to justify also went unmentioned. They'd gotten the job done. Pitting a bunch of trainee soldiers against experienced drill sergeants didn't start them out with high chances of successfully executing an ambush and capturing enemy combatants.

The surprise was more than enough reward, even when Idina and her squad were captured, roughly handled, and ordered to camp out again beside the tower before returning to the barracks in the morning.

CHAPTER TWENTY-EIGHT

As the recruits neared the end of basic training and all they'd known of life as a U.S. soldier, word circled about Bravo Company running the night infiltration course— otherwise known as NIC at night and the final FTX for non-infantry recruits.

The only thing they knew about this specific field exercise was when it would be and that it was the last step in their training. It wasn't enough to assuage any doubt or nervous expectation in the new soldiers, but it was a lot more information than they'd received about anything before this point.

When the day came at the end of their final week, tension was high among the recruits. They'd made it this far. They were almost finished. Once they graduated, they'd move on to AIT to receive the necessary training for the operational specialty they'd chosen before ever reaching basic at Fort Leonard Wood.

At 9:30 p.m., the recruits were summoned out of the bay and into formation in the yard, once more in full combat gear, including night-vision gear and their firearms. Staff Sergeant Remmington marched them across the Army base toward the NIC course in silence, as always. Then the recruits got a glimpse of what they were dealing with for their final training exercise.

"Bravo Company, ten-hut!"

The company stood at attention at the start of the course, and Remmington walked in front of them. "This is your mission. Breach the wall under enemy fire. Two hundred yards out beyond the berm is a village. That's your infiltration target."

In the darkness, Idina saw dozens of witnesses to their final exercise. Drill sergeants, combat veterans, the company, battalion, and brigade commanders—all were here to watch the next batch of newly minted Army soldiers run through their final test at the end of their training.

They all came to watch. I guess this is a big deal.

"This is it, soldiers," Remmington continued. "Bravo Company, move out!"

The first lines of soldiers acted immediately, running full-tilt toward the wall. The assembled watchers lining the course started shouting, encouraging the recruits to move, to get up over the wall, to storm the enemy territory the way their mission dictated.

Idina had no problem jumping up the thick stone wall. When she reached the top, she paused only to lend a hand down to Brock, who'd slowed down as he briefly struggled against the wall to get to the top.

"Go, go, go," he shouted at her, then they both dropped

to the ground behind the soldiers in front of them and got on their bellies.

The soldiers belly-crawled through thick mud, intending to stay out of sight of the target village at the end of the course. Once the front lines of crawling soldiers made it ten paces out from the wall, the air exploded with the quick, terrifying roar of machine gun fire.

Filled with live rounds.

The ammo peppered the ground on every side of the trampled, splattering mud, bright muzzle flashes seemingly coming from every direction until Idina recognized the difference between them.

Only one machine gun on either side and the rest are blank rifle rounds. Doesn't mean they're not still shooting blanks at *us.*

The NCOs and veterans walked down the line of soldiers scrambling madly on their bellies through the mud, shouting encouragement and orders to keep moving. To finish the job.

Then the first grenade went off.

A spray of dirt, mud, and plant matter spattered across Idina's back, but she kept moving with everyone else. On her right, the brilliant blaze of an honest-to-God fireball lit up the sky and whizzed overhead across the course. The machine guns fired nonstop, peppering the ground. Muzzle flashes nearly blinded her. Grenades detonated near, far, ahead, and behind.

They're pulling out all the stops for this—

Another simulated grenade explosion detonated a yard away from her at the edge of the course, splattering her gear, helmet, and face with mud. Idina jerked sideways on her belly to get away from the blast, part of her expecting shrapnel that never came. The other part of her wanted to laugh at how real this whole thing felt.

That was the point.

With soldiers crawling all around her and everyone screaming from the sidelines, Idina moved through the muck with her firearm strapped to her back and finally reached the coils of barbed wire intended to thwart them.

So we're simulating D-Day. Fun.

She maneuvered through the first layer of looped barbed wire as explosions racked the air and the heat of the fireballs launching overhead felt incredibly close. Her heart pounded in her chest, and her breathing was heavy and sporadic despite knowing in the back of her mind that this was all for show. Only a test.

Still, one wrong move from a terrified recruit toward the lines of live machine gun fire or an addle-brained decision to stand and run before a fireball whizzed overhead could be seriously life-threatening. Idina didn't plan to do any of these things, but it sure as hell felt like she was crawling through an imminent threat toward her mission objective.

Before she could extract herself from that first layer of barbed wire—and entirely without warning—Idina's senses sharpened. Time seemed to slow in those fractions of a second. She heard the *clack-clack-clack* of machine gun fire before the sharper *crack* that signaled a pause in rounds fired.

She made out the triggers being pulled back in long-range rifles, the sparks igniting, the rounds slicing through barrels. She listened to the roar and *thump* of another fireball launched overhead, and the sharp *click* before another simulated grenade explosion threw more clumps of dirt and mud and shredded grass into the air.

It all made sense.

There was a rhythm, a pattern, each part of it moving on its own like clockwork. Part of the larger whole.

A terrified shout from someone beside her ripped her out of the odd new suspension in time. Everything roared back to life. The sky blazed with muzzle flashes and fireballs. The watchers eagerly shouted. Mud sprayed across the side of her helmet, and she looked over her shoulder to see DeLafor tangled up in the barbed wire two yards behind her.

"Fuck, fuck, fuck," he muttered, scrambling around to free his boots from the coil around his ankle and only making it worse.

Out of everybody, I wouldn't have pegged my battle buddy as the first one to panic tonight.

Idina doubled back toward him, staying low. "DeLafor!"

"Fuck! I'm stuck! I can't—" Another grenade detonated in front of them beside the course, and he flinched away, further tangling himself. "Jesus Christ. They're insane!"

"DeLafor. Hey. Look at me."

Short, choppy whines burst from his mouth as he struggled with the barbed wire, his eyes wide and his head jerking in every direction under the assault of so many live and blank rounds firing all around them.

"Collin!" Idina shouted.

He paused long enough to stare at her with wide eyes.

"It's not real. You know that." She finally crawled close enough to untangle the worst of the barbed wire from around his ankle. One of the sharp steel barbs slashed across her right palm, but she hardly felt it. Then his boot was free.

He might've kept scrambling forward if another grenade hadn't gone off and made him topple onto his side into the mud. "Hey, hey. Listen. It's all planned out. Watch. Fireball in two seconds..."

"What the hell are you—"

As she'd predicted, another blaze of churning flames soared directly overhead and disappeared into the darkness beyond the course.

"Christ, Moorfield."

Idina punched him in the shoulder, nodded, and got back on her belly in the mud. "Come on."

They crawled together as other soldiers writhed past them to reach their objective.

"Grenade on the left," she shouted a second before another explosion erupted from beneath the ground.

"Five seconds of machine guns." The machine gun nest on their left sprayed ammo across the open ground beside the course, and she silently counted until she heard the heavy *click* of the mechanism stopping. *Exactly five seconds.*

"Two more fireballs. Two seconds apart."

Again, her prediction was one hundred percent accurate as the roaring balls of flame lit up the air and the mud-splattered soldiers crawled around them.

"What the fuck, Moorfield?" DeLafor shouted. "How'd you—"

"Machine guns!" she shouted. "Grenade left. Grenade right. Machine guns." Everything played out exactly as she'd called it, and when she glanced at DeLafor beside her, he fixed her with a mud-splattered grin.

"Fucking idiot savant."

Whether one of the combat veterans had heard her shouting her impossible predictions or had come up with the fun idea on his own, she heard him shout up to the machine gun nest on the left. "Mix it up a little, Sergeant!"

"What the fuck is he saying?" DeLafor shouted.

"Something about—" The left nest machine gun aimed the live rounds closer to the edge of the course and directly into the mud. Of course, he stopped in time to *not* hit any of the soldiers, but those closest to the live rounds shouted in surprise and threw themselves sideways into the mud.

Idina barked out a laugh and pushed herself to the edge of the barbed wire and the trampled mud.

"You're a fucking psycho," DeLafor muttered.

"They switched it up!" Somehow, catching on to the rhythm of the simulated attacks and being caught *by* an Army veteran who wanted to keep the NIC unpredictable was hilarious.

Fuck, this is fun.

Two hundred yards past the wall, they reached the end of the mud and came to the berm of decaying trees, branches, and plant matter in front of them. The soldiers scrambled up the incline, darted down again, and drew their weapons on the makeshift village that of course was uninhabited.

Idina screamed in triumph with the rest of her company as they surged toward the buildings, opened fire on the squat stone walls, kicked in doors, and generally ransacked their mission objective.

All the pent-up energy from moving with agonizing slowness on their bellies while the sky lit up with weapons fire and simulated attacks...all the rage and frustration and aggression held at bay by nine weeks of intensive, rigorous, stressful training keeping them in line like so many cinched straitjackets around their uniforms... It all exploded from within every soldier as they reached that village.

The drill sergeants and Army commanders let them unleash hell. They'd earned it.

The whole thing couldn't have lasted more than five minutes tops, but in the heat of the moment, five minutes felt like an eternity.

Finally, the urge to strike down anything in their path and demolish the village waned. The massive bonfire on the other side of the buildings where the others now waited for them drew the soldiers' attention.

Whooping and jumping and jostling each other, Bravo Company headed around the village toward the bonfire.

Idina grunted under a rough hand clapping down on her shoulder, and Amber gave her a vigorous shake.

"That's fucking *right*, Moorfield!" The other girl grinned, her eyes wide and flickering in the glowing firelight as the company reached the bonfire. "Goddamn, we're done."

"Thank fuck," Idina muttered, and they both laughed breathlessly.

Now, the soldiers had the opportunity to celebrate in a way they hadn't been able to for the last nine weeks. They gathered in groups, shouting at each other and laughing about what they'd been through.

"Dude, I thought you were gonna knock me out with your fucking rifle."

"We fucking made it, bud. That was it!"

"Yeah! *Yeah!* Fuck that mud."

"At least it's not shit."

"He'd still be grinning even if it was."

Idina huffed out a laugh and watched the celebration, too overwhelmed with her excitement and relief to think about the strange moment in the mud and barbed wire when time had slowed, and she'd heard *everything* around her. Enough to count the seconds between simulated attacks and prove to DeLafor that their instructor had staged every aspect of it.

It all came racing back when the noise of the entire company commemorating their success in true soldier fashion filtered out of her hearing. The bonfire seemed dimmer. The silhouettes of trainees, drill sergeants, and commanders shimmered around the edges.

A crackling roar seemed to rise from the very earth itself, which trembled beneath Idina's mud-splattered boots and made her vision tilt.

Then she heard a voice.

It sounded like stones crashing against each other, like detonated grenades, like the world caving in on itself despite nothing around her happening.

"It's been so long, Warrior. I can feel *you..."*

Then, just like that, Idina's hearing returned to her, and the suspended moment of seeing and hearing things that weren't there ended.

She looked down at her hands and caught the last faint shimmer of green light illuminating in the slash on her palm from the barbed wire. The wound burned now, caked with mud as it was, but the green light was a lot more terrifying. Especially because for the first time in her life, it did more than glow.

The burn in her slashed palm flared with a split-second of agonizing heat, the green light pulsed, and the cut vanished.

With her heart racing, Idina scrubbed furiously at her palm, swiping away blood and mud and bits of plant debris, but what she'd seen was real. Her green light had *healed* her. In seconds.

"What the fuck?" She spun to see if anyone else had heard the voice or felt the tremor through the ground or had seen one Private Moorfield inadvertently healing herself with creepy green light.

Instead of finding her fellow soldiers, she found the battalion commander, Lieutenant Colonel Elmscomb, standing in front of her. She'd only seen the man twice before but most definitely knew how to recognize a commanding officer, including this one.

"Lieutenant Colonel." Idina instantly drew herself to attention and saluted the man.

He returned her salute and chuckled. "You can relax, Private. This is a party, not a parade."

"Yes, sir."

His eyes glittered in the light of the bonfire, and he extended his hand toward her. "Impressive work out there. Congratulations."

Idina took his hand and felt something there between their palms that wasn't her cut opening back up. "Thank you, sir."

"I'm looking forward to seeing how far you take your career in the U.S. Army, Private Moorfield."

Before she could say anything else, Elmscomb released her hand and walked away to congratulate the other soldiers.

Idina looked down at her healed palm and the patch the battalion commander had given her. It marked her as no longer a recruit in basic training but as a United States Army soldier.

I did it. I fucking did it. This is it!

She clenched her hand around the patch and surveyed the rest of her company celebrating with each other and their commanders. Pride bubbled up inside her, although it was dampened by what had happened before she'd stood face-to-face with Lieutenant Colonel Elmscomb.

Or at least what she'd *thought* had happened.

Is this what happened to Uncle Richard? He ran away from the family after having his episodes, lost his mind when they turned into hallucinations, and everyone called it not having the family talent? Whatever signs my family saw in me... Did they know this would happen? The green lights I can deal with. Those have been around forever. There's no way that voice I heard was real...

"Moorfield!" Hughs shouted as he waved her toward him and the soldiers she'd gotten to know the best. The guy had lost at least sixty pounds during basic, but his smile and wide eyes were exactly the same. "What are you doing standing there? Get the hell over here!"

The rest of the group echoed the shout, and Idina grinned.

Fuck it. It's probably some kind of stress response. No big deal.

She looked down at her hands again, searching for the

green light she'd first seen during the worst of her basic training, and the moment she'd thought she couldn't keep going. Her palm was still healed, without a trace of the gash that had been there. Not even a thin scar remained.

Maybe it was a fluke—the data flashing through her mind in green, the images, the growling voice, the trembling world around her. Perhaps it had only been a product of the heaviest pressure she'd experienced in her life. Her mind playing tricks on her. Hell, her lights playing tricks on her.

It doesn't matter. Voices in my head or not, I'm an Army soldier now. We all are.

Get sneak peeks, exclusive giveaways, behind the scenes content, and more. PLUS you'll be notified of special **one day only fan pricing** on new releases.

Sign up today to get free stories.

Visit: https://marthacarr.com/read-free-stories/

AUTHOR NOTES - MARTHA CARR
WRITTEN NOVEMBER 28, 2021

I'm not immune to traveling down the social media rabbit hole. Maybe I've been writing for a while and just need a five minute break, or when I was on chemo there was a good chance I was up in the middle of the night. Let's just check and see who else is up.

I know, I know. There are better things to do with even those five minutes. Like use the Calm app and meditate. Or go stand in the garden for five minutes. Yeah, yeah. Sometimes I want to see a picture of a large cat in a tiny box or someone's magnificent garden. Facebook algorithms are so accurate, until they're not and throw some weird curveball about Icelandic men. I have no idea why I got that one.

Anyway, there I was noodling down some pathway when I saw a picture of a very sad grey pit bull sitting on a dog bed in the middle of pavement. I have a very soft spot for pitties. I lost my sweet pittie, Leela in August to cancer after twelve years and I know firsthand they're the biggest snugglers out there. What happened to this dog?

Turns out someone abandoned her in the middle of a

parking lot downtown and a good Samaritan called animal control. But the county was already beyond maximum capacity, and they needed a medical foster immediately to help save this little girl.

No one was raising their hand so I stepped up.

After a meet and greet with the good dog, Lois Lane, and setting up my wide hallway with gates and a crate, I went and picked up Bluebell and her meds and found out a little more about her background.

Apparently, Bluebell lived with the homeless, for maybe all of her life, but definitely most. Her joints are thick and weathered from concrete living and she had an old knee injury that healed wonky. Signs of a lack of medical care.

But, before we condemn whoever left her – one big thing I noticed right away is how gentle and sweet Bluebell is, no matter the circumstances. Even with Lois giving her plenty of side eye once Lois realized Bluebell wasn't here for just a visit. Bluebell was still trying to get her to play.

Someone loved Bluebell very much and was kind to her. And based on the laundry list of ailments she had – mange, ear infections, worms and more delights – they were probably trying to do right by her and left her where she was most likely to be seen and rescued.

My heart actually goes out to them too. I wish there was a way to let them know Bluebell got all the love and care she needs and even rode home in style on the back seat of a Mercedes.

It took a solid week, but I know a gift out of nowhere when I see one. I foster failed and let them know, Bluebell was already home. Her blue foster collar was replaced with a new, pretty pink collar and the gentle pittie quickly found out a couch is a wonderous place to take a nap.

Some may wonder about my timing – just off of chemo and still recovering. But that's life. It marches on whether or not we decide to join in and we get up and go try and push the boundaries and delight in how our world expands to include more love and friendship. All of it makes up a life in the end that's a marvel to behold.

If you want to see pictures of Bluebell and the wild child, Lois Lane, join me in the Facebook group. Until then, more adventures to follow.

AUTHOR NOTES - MICHAEL ANDERLE
WRITTEN NOVEMBER 30, 2021

Thank you for not only reading this story but these author notes as well.

If you have never read anything by me or one of my collaborations with another author, I'll drop an "About Me" at the very end. For the rest of you, welcome back!

Dammit, Carr!

This is my third set of author notes for the day (I hadn't expected to write three. I thought I would get ahead of myself and surprise Steve with being a day early with a set!)

Now, I have stinging eyeballs and tears to wipe off my face as she related her story of foster failing.

Now, I've heard the story straight from Martha (a part, anyway. She didn't go into as much detail on the phone) but her words stabbed me in the heart and opened the tear ducts.

I suppose it proves I have a heart to be touched, so that's a good thing—right?

While I give Martha grief over author-note blocking*
me (ALL.THE.DAMNED.TIME), I have to say this:

Anytime you do such good for a dog that deserves this?
Author Note block me all you want.

I'm blessed to know Martha, and the woman you read
in these author notes is the woman she is. There is no bullshit in her.

Perhaps there is a little too much *nice* in her, but that's a
discussion for another set of author notes ;-)

Have a good week or weekend. Talk to you in the next
story!

Ad Aeternitatem,

Michael Anderle

*Author Note Blocking was a term I coined with
Martha a LONG time ago as **a little** dark humor to make
her laugh.

Martha has so many stories of just CRAP situations
that happen to her that aren't fair, and she shares them
poignantly in our author notes. That said, she makes damn
near ANYTHING I say after her author notes at the end of
the book...pointless.

So, I told her "You author-note blocked me with your
cancer story. Who wants to read anything I have to say
after that?"

She got a good laugh out of it, which was all I wanted.

Ok, now a little about me if you haven't met me.

I wrote my first book *Death Becomes Her* (*The Kurtherian Gambit*) in September/October of 2015 and released it November 2, 2015. I wrote and released the next two books that same month and had three released by the end of November 2015.

So, just under six years ago.

Since then, I've written, collaborated, concepted, and/or created hundreds more in all sorts of genres.

My most successful genre is still my first, Paranormal Sci-Fi, followed quickly by Urban Fantasy. I have multiple pen names I produce under.

Some because I can be a bit crude in my humor at times or raw in my cynicism (Michael Todd). I have one I share with Martha Carr (Judith Berens, and another (not disclosed) that we use as a marketing test pen name.

In general, I just love to tell stories, and with success comes the opportunity to mix two things I love in my life.

Business and stories.

I've wanted to be an entrepreneur since I was a teenager. I was a very *unsuccessful* entrepreneur (I tried many times) until my publishing company LMBPN signed one author in 2015.

Me.

I was the president of the company, and I was the first author published. Funny how it worked out that way.

It was late 2016 before we had additional authors join me for publishing. Now we have a few dozen authors, a few hundred audiobooks by LMBPN published, a few hundred more licensed by six audio companies, and about a thousand titles in our company.

It's been a busy six years.

Solve a murder, save her mother, and stop the apocalypse?

What would you do when elves ask you to investigate a prince's murder and you didn't even know elves, or magic, was real?

Meet Leira Berens, Austin homicide detective who's good at what she does – track down the bad guys and lock them away.

Which is why the elves want her to solve this murder – fast. It's not just about tracking down the killer and bringing them to justice. It's about saving the world!

If you're looking for a heroine who prefers fighting to flirting, check out The Leira Chronicles today!

<u>AVAILABLE ON AMAZON AND IN KINDLE UNLIMITED!</u>

JOIN THE ORICERAN UNIVERSE FAN GROUP ON FACEBOOK!

CONNECT WITH THE AUTHORS

Martha Carr Social
Website:
http://www.marthacarr.com
Facebook:
https://www.facebook.com/groups/MarthaCarrFans/

Michael Anderle

Website: http://lmbpn.com

Email List: http://lmbpn.com/email/

https://www.facebook.com/LMBPNPublishing

https://twitter.com/MichaelAnderle

https://www.instagram.com/lmbpn_publishing/

https://www.bookbub.com/authors/michael-anderle